1/24

KU-733-681

SL10001779948 0

WITHDRAWN

COLD COMFORT

Solihull
LIBRARIES & ARTS

www.**booksattransworld**.co.uk

Also by Susannah Waters

Long Gone Anybody

SOLIHULL MBC LIBRARIES	
CE	
SL1OOO1779948 O	
Askews	
AF	£12.99
	L8034

COLD COMFORT

LOVE IN A CHANGING CLIMATE

SUSANNAH WATERS

Doubleday

LONDON · TORONTO · SYDNEY · AUCKLAND · JOHANNESBURG

TRANSWORLD PUBLISHERS
61-63 Uxbridge Road, London W5 5SA
a division of The Random House Group Ltd

RANDOM HOUSE AUSTRALIA (PTY) LTD
20 Alfred Street, Milsons Point, Sydney,
New South Wales 2061, Australia

RANDOM HOUSE NEW ZEALAND LTD
18 Poland Road, Glenfield, Auckland 10, New Zealand

RANDOM HOUSE SOUTH AFRICA (PTY) LTD
Isle of Houghton, Corner of Boundary Road and Carse O'Gowrie,
Houghton 2198, South Africa

Published 2006 by Doubleday
a division of Transworld Publishers

Copyright © Susannah Waters 2006

The right of Susannah Waters to be identified
as the author of this work has been asserted in accordance
with sections 77 and 78 of the Copyright, Designs and
Patents Act 1988.

All the characters in this book are fictitious,
and any resemblance to actual persons, living or dead,
is purely coincidental.

A catalogue record for this book is available
from the British Library.
ISBN 978 0385 607476 (from Jan 2007)
ISBN 0385 607474

All rights reserved. No part of this publication may
be reproduced, stored in a retrieval system, or
transmitted in any form or by any means,
electronic, mechanical, photocopying, recording,
or otherwise, without the prior permission of
the publishers.

Typeset in 11.5/15pt Sabon by
Falcon Oast Graphic Art Ltd.

Printed and bound in Great Britain
by Clays Ltd, Bungay, Suffolk

1 3 5 7 9 10 8 6 4 2

Papers used by Transworld Publishers are natural, recyclable products
made from wood grown in sustainable forests. The manufacturing processes conform to
the environmental regulations of the country of origin.

'. . . It has been said from generation to generation that when a person starts to get frozen and is beginning to get unconscious, he feels that he is putting on a nice new jack rabbit parka, and is starting to get warm. But that is really the end of him.'

—James Wells, *Ipani Eskimos*

PART ONE

There was a fall through the ice. A man seated at a picnic table on the river bank saw the girl go through. She raised her arms above her head, he tells the police, as if she were getting ready. He babbles: It's this weather we've been having, one day it's forty degrees, the next twenty below, it makes no sense, nothing's making sense, you know? The policeman taking the statement from the witness is a patient person. He stops writing down anything the man is saying after filling two pages of his small notebook. Glancing over at the stretcher being lifted into the back of the ambulance, he thinks to himself he's got to remember to bring home the groceries his wife said she needed.

The river is chunky with ice, clotted. The spot where she had been standing is now a clear pool of pale blue water. Occasional breezes send its outer edges lapping over the perimeter, running across the hard white surface of the ice like a water spill across a tablecloth. On the opposite bank, near to where she must have stepped out, stands a municipal waste bin stuffed to overflowing. During the afternoon, other people pass by this spot, back and forth. No sign remains of what has happened. In a few hours, the ice will re-form.

THE ICE

Tammy does her experiments early in the morning when everyone else is asleep. A pencil takes eight seconds. Spilt milk is much faster. An orange is hard to measure; it's difficult to control a spherical object, and if she uses force to ensure it crosses the full diameter of the table, then the timings are meaningless. Taken in all, the pencil provides the clearest results, and there is no doubt – the journey times are getting faster, about a second a month.

She finds it difficult to sleep. In the slant of her bed, all the blood in her body rushes towards the top of her head, but if she lies the other way round she is in a mattressed toboggan out of control and she dreams all night that she is falling down the side of a glacier into what should be an icy sea, but on steep approach turns out be a volcano, white-hot. In the bath-tub, she runs the water until it is full and, no matter how she bends and twists in an effort to submerge her entire body, one side, one thin hipbone, protrudes above the waterline, a singular outcropping. The schoolbooks on her shelves want to tip the same way. A fried egg slips through butter to one side of the pan. This house – every room in it – is like the *Titanic*, tipped up and heading under. And it's not the only one. Everywhere she sees evidence of a blighted world. Craters appear overnight in the tarmac of parking lots, on the bike paths, in the playgrounds. Front porches are falling away from front doors, spruce trees and telephone poles leaning drunkenly, criss-crossed. Things don't freeze the way they used to; in December, she places a jar of rubbing alcohol on the outside sill of her bedroom window. In February, the liquid moves when she shakes the jar. In March, the ice on the river, it fails her.

Since that day, she's stopped going to school – something her parents don't know about. She's got a job at Kroger's supermarket on Driveway Street. At first, she just hangs out there. Mr Asawa, the manager, is nervous of her. From the end of an aisle he watches her – a small girl for her age, walking around in her khaki-green parka with the artificial husky-dog trim – but she never causes any trouble, never steals anything, and after a while he asks her if she wants a job bagging groceries. Mr Asawa is short and stocky and always wears striped shirts under his apron. He jokes with her, in his heavily accented English, when he sees her hanging around near the refrigerator cases: 'You tryin' to keep cool, Tammy?' He says this to her often, like he's forgotten he's ever said it before. 'You wanna ice cream?' Tammy wonders if he likes her, if he wants her. He's one of the only people who talks to her.

Sometimes, when nobody's around, she slips into the refrigerated lock-up at the back of the store. She likes to see how long she can stay in before she starts to shiver. Cold is stronger than warm, she thinks. When something is frozen, its molecules are closer together. Place a bowl of frozen water in a microwave and it will not boil; the radiation can't get between the molecules. Cold wins out, every time. Standing between the ten-foot-high shelves piled with frozen turkeys, boxes of pizzas, oven fries, Black Forest gateaux, popsicles, Eskimo Pies, she finds she can see things more clearly.

Eskimo Pies used to be a favourite. In their matt silver wrapper with the polar-bear silhouette on the front, they were guaranteed to please. They were *her* pies, *Eskimo* pies: their

12

square shape made them different from other ice-cream novelties, and the polar bear on the label told her if she ate enough Eskimo Pies she might be rewarded by seeing a real polar bear some day. She must have eaten nearly three a day the summer she was nine years old, 1999, buying them with any spare change she could find. Until one day a group of kids in the Bentley mall, hanging their meaningless limbs over the railings of the upper level, spotted Tammy walking along below, on her own, eating an Eskimo Pie. They tumbled down the escalators en masse to fall into step behind her, chanting in voices too low for any passing adult to hear: 'Eskimo . . . Eskimo . . . Eskimo Pie! Eskimo . . . Eskimo . . . Eskimo Pie!' She tried not to eat them so much after that.

Tammy is fourteen. She is brown-skinned and wide-cheeked, with a scar above one eye inflicted in a car accident when she was three years old. Everybody said the scar would disappear as she grew older, but it never has. She has thick, black hair, and pale blue eyes she's inherited from her maternal grandfather, a white US sergeant stationed in Fairbanks who'd used his free time to get a few Native girls pregnant. Growing up in Fairbanks, surrounded by American girls, American people, she's never felt inconspicuous. The most she hopes for from other people is indifference. When other children look in the mirror the face they see tells them something about their future, about who they might become in time. For Tammy, there has never been more than one future in her face.

Alison Vanderesse, a college student with smooth blonde hair and tiny cupid lips who works the checkouts at weekends, approaches Tammy one afternoon outside the refrigerated lock-up. 'Why aren't you in *school*?' she asks in a loud voice.

Tammy examines the collar of Alison's white button-down shirt where it is being squashed under the neck strap of her green apron, and shrugs.

Alison is frowning. She nods towards the refrigerator. 'Don't you get *cold* in there?'

Tammy says no, but Alison is still standing in her way.

'Is that a Native thing?' she asks. 'Do you build up stamina or something?'

Another employee standing near by, lifting orange crates onto a stainless-steel trolley, sniggers.

Alison turns towards him and tells him to shut up, though she's looking pleased. 'I'm *serious*, Josh.'

Tammy makes a move to go but Alison spots it, spins round and takes one step to the left.

Tammy looks up. 'Are you asking me if Eskimos are genetically programmed to better withstand cold temperatures?'

There's a pause and then Alison tips back her head and starts to laugh. '*What?*' She turns back to the guy loading oranges. 'How *old* is she, anyway?'

Tammy manages to get past Alison this time.

'I thought they didn't *like* being called Eskimos,' she hears her say in the same penetrating tone before the double doors swing shut.

Tammy's able to get home most evenings by five-thirty or six, so her mom can get to the hospital where she works evenings as a cleaner, leaving Tammy to look after her eighteen-month-old sister, Jess. Her mother is tired all the time. Her eyes are blank, like she's being asked too many questions. It's easy for Tammy to intercept the letters coming from the Public School Board, because her mom is still asleep at eight in the morning when the mail arrives. With both parents working, things are good, better than they've ever been. They're getting a dishwasher next month with the annual money from the Permanent Fund. And a new exhaust system for the car.

Every morning at nine o'clock Tammy does exactly the same thing. When she gets to Kroger's, she goes to the machines on the sidewalk in front of the store, buys a copy of yesterday's *New York Times*, the *Fairbanks Daily News-Miner* and the *Anchorage Sentinel*, takes all three over to City's Bagels across the parking lot, orders a plain bagel with a glass of tap water, and sits down to collect her cuttings. She'd rather smoke than eat a bagel, but it's illegal.

It's in City's Bagels she first spots herself, in an article in the *New York Times* about 'Madcap Lane', the lane with the houses that are sinking into the ground. She reads that article five times without stopping and then she looks up at the other customers in City's Bagels. It is as if the walls of the restaurant are telescoping away from her and everything in it – every person, every object – seems a little further away than a minute ago. As if a giant has lifted the roof of her life and peered in. No one looks back at her except a woman in a dirty coat who with one hand is feeding a bottle to a baby, while taking bites from a bagel held in the other. The mother smiles weakly. Behind the counter, the manager is leaning against the back wall, staring out the front windows. By the cash register, a girl with brown hair scraped back under her paper hat leans on her elbows. Tammy looks down at the newspaper again, spread out on the table.

When she gets back to her house that evening, walking through the half-light along the road from the bus stop, she finds a pair of scissors in the junk drawer to the right of the kitchen sink, cuts out the article, then pins it to the refrigerator door with an Arco Alaska magnet.

Her mother doesn't notice it until the next morning. She goes to the fridge for some milk to give to Jessica in her highchair and as she's closing the fridge door, super-size carton of milk in hand, she slows down, leaning in to peer at the clipping. 'What's this?' she asks.

Tammy takes the carton from her and gets Jess a plastic cup. 'You should read it.'

Beth sniffs; she's had a cold for three weeks. She walks over to the coffee machine and switches it on. 'Better take it down before your dad gets back,' she says.

In a few weeks, the fridge is covered.

*

On the journey up to Prudhoe Bay, in the Boeing 737 that ferries employees back and forth from Fairbanks, they don't serve any alcohol. But they do on the way down, which means Bill Ongtowasruk always comes home drunk. He works as a cook for Arco two weeks on, one week off. Two weeks pretty much dry, except for the bottle he's hidden inside some socks in his locker, is long enough. He's making more money than he's ever made – than anybody in his family has ever made. Sometimes on his week off, he likes to go hunting or fishing with a few of his buddies from work, weather permitting. But between Thanksgiving and mid-January, the sun never comes up at all on Prudhoe Bay, and he comes home to Fairbanks more often. He shuts down in the winter. He gets stupid, and slow – can't think right.

Bill, a small man, brown-skinned, with jagged teeth in a round mouth, still speaks English like a second language. When he was a younger man he was handsome, he had what it took, dark hair and sharp jaw-line. Even white girls went for him, and this time-limited sex appeal got him into places, jobs and homes, communities he might not have lived in otherwise. God help an ugly-ass Eskimo. The first ten years in Fairbanks were one long party, good, with all kinds of people coming round – white, brown, yellow, fancy and working-class – all-night drinking, bonfires out in the backyard, empty bottles in the sink, parkas piled up in the hallway. He'd lived in half a house, rented from the university where he had a job on the catering staff. It was near the campus, in a respectable neighbourhood. When Beth moved in, and a year later Tammy arrived, it felt like an OK family, like anybody else's.

Bill's Native background had been a novelty back then, until he started drinking like a Native too. A few months before they got kicked out of that house, he spent one memorable night on the roof directly above his daughter's bedroom, singing an Inupiat hunting song and aiming a broom handle for a harpoon at anything moving on the street below. Beth slept

16

through it all, but not six-year-old Tammy, lying back on her pillow, eyes open in the dark.

Beth's folks – not her real folks: she was adopted at birth by a white couple – started treating Bill differently after he lost the campus job. When he and Beth first got together, she had told him they thought he was good for her, because of her background. They were always squawking around – Native this, Native that – asking questions he didn't know the answers to. But when he, Beth and Tammy got kicked out of the campus house, and Beth wouldn't take their side over what they called Bill's 'problem', they stopped pretending to like him, and four years ago they'd moved back to Nevada. Bill throws the Christmas presents Beth's mother sends Tammy and Jess into the trash, unopened. He doesn't need her buying things for his kids now.

They're tough about security up in Prudhoe Bay, since all the terrorist stuff started. Any crazy kumaq could cause a hell of a lot of mess up there if he got a chance. Bill would never have got the job if one of the teachers from the university, one of the die-hard party-goers in this former time of all-night binges, hadn't written him a character reference, probably because he was worried about the things Bill might remember that he couldn't. So he'd been lucky, and sometimes he thinks he's one of those people who just gets away with things.

On Sunday nights when he's home, tradition is they all eat out. Bill never cooks anything off the job. He likes the food at the Thai House on Neville Street. Tonight, though, Beth declines the offer. She doesn't like Thai food much, plus the temperature's down and she doesn't want the hassle of getting Jessica trussed up for the cold weather. 'You and Tammy go,' she says, glancing at Tammy.

Driving down Fifth Avenue in his pickup truck, the snow is blowing hard and the headlights seem to be running out of juice; they surge and flicker, hardly cutting through the dark. First National Bank sign at the corner of Cushman shines out like a Christmas star in the night, flashing '−41°', in bright little ping-pong balls of yellow light.

'Tell you I saw a polar bear last weekend?' he says, shifting gears to slow down for the light on Lacey Street, and pumping his brakes. 'Right close up.'

Tammy is slumped down in her seat, hands in the pockets of her khaki-green parka. 'Where?'

'Kaktovik.'

'What were you doing in Kaktovik?'

'Uncle Frank – he's got a buddy lives there.'

Uncle Frank isn't really an uncle to Tammy, or anybody. He's a drinking buddy; he works the same shifts as Bill up in Prudhoe Bay.

'Took a couple of sno-gos up the airstrip, by this big old whalebone dump they got there. That's where any much bears hang out, nosing around for food in the trash.' The light goes green and he guns the truck forward, wheels spinning a little on the icy road. 'Seemed like nothing there at first, then the next thing we know this *mother* of a bear nearly jump on top of us! From behind a big ridge of ice. If Frank didn't have his gun ready, we'd have been goners.'

'Did he shoot it?' Tammy shuts the heating vent in front of her, putting a hand up in front of it to check if the air has stopped.

'Nah. Just a warning shot in the air. Scared it off good enough.'

Tammy presses her palm against the cold window, looks out at a bus wheezing past, going in the opposite direction. Its fogged-up windows are lit up from the inside, small circles of transparency like port-holes where people have rubbed at the glass to see out.

'You know they're all going to die, right?' she says. 'The polar bears? When the North Pole thaws out.'

'Aw, cut it out about all that. Ain't gonna *happen*, Tammy,' he says. 'You worry about nothing, too much all the time.'

18

He parks the truck illegally, right in front of the Thai restaurant with its red and gold façade and imitation Asian roof-tiles, but even the short walk to the front door sets the insides of his nostrils burning – all the exhaust fumes, winter-time, get trapped in the ice fog. Tammy takes her time, though, walking slow like a zombie. Halfway through dinner, he tells her that Beth thinks she should go stay with Uncle Cliff for a while. Uncle Cliff is a real uncle, Bill's older brother.

'In Shishmaref?'

'Sure in Shishmaref – where else?'

Tammy, for once in her life, looks surprised and this makes him feel good. 'When?' she asks.

A piece of chicken falls off his fork, spattering curry sauce across the white tablecloth. He spears it again, and shoves it in his mouth, still chewing as he answers: 'I'll take you out. End of next shift.'

Where Cliff lives is about a thousand miles to the west, on an island off the coast, tip of the Seward Peninsula, looking out over the Chuchki Sea. This is where Bill spent the first twenty years of his life. The people in Shishmaref, all five hundred or so, are Inupiat Eskimos.

'What about school?' she asks.

'You can go to school out there.' He nods at the waitress as she puts down the second Thai beer he's ordered.

'Why?'

He looks at her. 'Waddaya mean, why?'

'Why am I going to Shishmaref?'

He takes a sip of the beer, looks around the room and puts the glass down. The place is empty tonight, except for a couple of white men in business suits drinking at a table in the corner. He reaches round to the back pocket of his jeans for one of the toothpicks he always carries with him, leans back in his chair and begins picking his teeth.

'Mom thinks you need a change. Says you're driving her crazy, all this crazy stuff, night and day.'

'What crazy stuff?'

'You know. All that stuff on the fridge.'

Tammy stares back at him with a blank expression.

'And you never talk to no one – always in your room. Mom says you never say more than two words to her.'

'Vice versa.'

'Yeah, well, she's not such a talker.' He shrugs again and shifts in his seat, jiggling one of his legs up and down. 'I dunno – I mean, what kind of stunt was that? Out on the ice. Most people your age out having a good time, partying, raising hell, trying not to get caught. You walk around with a face like some kind of moose, grumpy about getting shot at! What the hell you *doing* out on that ice, anyway? Taking a walk? Hunting seals?'

He laughs and Tammy looks away. The Thai waitress spots the turn of her head and approaches to see if anything is needed. Bill shakes his head.

'Who's going to look after Jess? When Mom's at work?'

'I dunno – I think your mom got something planned. Mrs Kokeok, across the street. It was her idea – she must've thought of something.'

Tammy is staring down at the salmon-pink tablecloth, head resting on her elbows. There are spots of grease on it. She dips her fingertip in the glass of iced water by her plate and places it over one of the spots. The moisture spreads, leaving a damp ring around the mustard-yellow stain.

'What are you doing?'

Tammy looks up, eyebrows raised, head still in her hands. 'Nothing.'

'Trouble is,' Bill continues, 'you don't know what you got – life is good for us, lot better than for me when I was young. You got some special idea of what it used to be like, before TV or something. Like everything was good back then.'

'So you're sending me to Shishmaref? I hate to break it to you, Dad, but I think Uncle Cliff gets cable.'

He waves a hand at her. 'You know what I mean. Let's see how you like it, living out there on that island for a while, living *real* Eskimo way, way Cliff likes it. You'll be screaming heebie-jeebies, no time.'

'The real Eskimo way? What, you mean like shooting hoops, and cooking with Crisco?'

Bill's not listening. He lights a cigarette. 'Busting your butt get a couple seals, maybe a whale every year, what's the point of that? This is the best it's ever been for us. The best.' The waitress puts the check on the table. 'You finished?' he asks Tammy.

In Golden Heart Park there are people hoping for a look at the lights, but the sky's too overcast. Bill leaves the engine running, pulls out a bottle of Jim Beam from under his seat and takes a few bolts. His hair, which tends to stand straight up from his scalp like it's charged with electricity, is going grey. He catches sight of it in the rear-view mirror. With the end of a sleeve, he wipes at the fog their breath is making on the windshield.

'Want some?' he asks Tammy, offering the bottle.

'No, thanks.'

'Go ahead! Keep you warm.'

He keeps looking at her but she's staring straight ahead. A bunch of Japanese tourists are standing in the middle of the square, in a tight clump by the Unknown First Family statue. They're wearing identical white and yellow-panelled snow-suits, which look brand new they're so spotless – probably bought specially for the trip. They're all standing motionless, a flock of strange birds, necks craning skywards. Tammy reaches over and turns off the car heater, and immediately the joints of the truck start to creak like the cold is working at them, trying to tear them apart and get in.

'Crazy Japs,' says Bill, motioning towards them with his bottle. 'They try and make babies under the lights – they think it make good luck for them.'

'*Makes. Makes* good luck for them,' Tammy murmurs. 'Who says?'

'I read about it sure. In the paper.'

They sit there for twenty minutes, watching as the tourists give up and head off in a clump towards the centre of town and their hotel. Bill looks over at Tam. She's sitting with her gloved hands tucked under her legs.

'You're a good girl, Tam,' Bill says. His voice sounds like it's coming from a long way off. 'You're a good girl,' he repeats. 'But too much thinking about bullshit. That's what screws you. You gotta stop thinking about bullshit all the time.' He takes her hand and places it on his thigh.

Tammy arrives in Shishmaref in the middle of a family crisis: George, the eldest of Uncle Cliff's four children, has disappeared. Two weeks ago, he walked out of the front door to head for the local tannery, where he's been working since graduating from Shishmaref High School, and he never turned up. George has always been a loner, not so much at ease with people, not very happy in a crowd. One of only two teenage boys on the island who never showed interest in playing on the high-school basketball team. But he isn't the sort to run off without warning. The close-knit community has been searching for him, out at the fishing holes, over walkie-talkies, bush pilots cruising low over the shore-fast ice. So far there's nothing: no broken-down snowmobile, no smashed-up dog sled, dogs running loose, no frozen body under the ice. The only way off this island is by plane, and Uncle Cliff knows all the pilots like they're family, which most of them are.

'Had he been acting any different?' Tammy asks her cousin Stacey.

They're standing on top of a bluff by the shore on the north-west side of the island, looking out across the ice. Stacey shrugs and snaps the chewing gum she has in her mouth. She is wearing a pink parka, with artificial fur around the hood, pushed back off her head. Her long black hair is pulled back in a ponytail, pushed flat by a wool headband covering her ears.

'No different than usual,' she says.

Cousin Stacey had come to stay with Tammy's family in Fairbanks five years ago while her mother was having cancer treatment at the UAF hospital. Back then, she and Tammy had got along fine, but now it's not as easy. Tammy doesn't know what to say to her. Stacey doesn't like being asked difficult questions, and she doesn't like bad news either. She always complains about living on Shishmaref, but it's all she's ever known. While Tammy's body is still thin and relatively un-developed, Stacey's has already begun to settle, giving in to thickness, closer to the ground than it was even a year ago.

'What about Anchorage?' Tammy asks.

'What about it?'

'Maybe he went there.'

'How'd he get there?' says Stacey. 'Nobody flew him out. Anyway, George hates cities; he hates all that kind of stuff. He even walks out when Pete and Mikey start playing on their video games – if it was up to George, he'd have banned them in the house, he's that harsh. But Dad just lets stuff like that go, thank God. George never even watches TV, unless it's the news or something. He's weird.' She crosses her arms, slipping her hands, in white mittens, under each armpit.

'How is he weird?'

Stacey raises her shoulders. 'I dunno. He's just . . . hardcore.' Her shoulders drop. 'He's always been like that. When he was a kid, he went to the *same* tribal skills camp five summers in a row – I can see once, we all did that, but *five*! To George, there's only one way to do things and that's it. That's why he has such a hard time – because he's a pain, if you want to know the truth.'

'So he has a hard time.'

23

Stacey glances at Tammy, frowning slightly, her jaw working the gum hard. She shrugs. 'Not everybody wants what he wants. *I* don't, for sure. But he acts like everybody should.'

Tammy kneels down and pets the head of Oshim, one of Uncle Cliff's dogs, cupping her hand under his chin and taking her glove off so he can lick her brown fingers with his warm tongue.

'Maybe he just needed to get away for a while.'

Cousin Stacey snaps her gum. 'Maybe. Come on, let's go in: it's cold.'

Tammy isn't cold.

Uncle Cliff takes Tammy to pick up some muskrats from Art Lowell's hut on the eastern end of the island. Art's hair has gone completely white since Tammy last saw him, but he's still wearing the same old red checked shirt, with a white T-shirt underneath, and even the same trucker's cap – *Eagle Pack Super Premium Pet Foods* written across its front.

'Hi, Tammy,' he says, the teeth in his mouth crowding out of it like a door's flown open and they want to exit.

'How does he remember?' Tammy asks, as she and Cliff walk back along the shoreline in the frozen ruts of snowmobile trails.

'Remember what?'

'Me.'

Uncle Cliff looks at her. 'What do you mean?'

They stop to watch a bush plane coming in to land on the ice.

'Jimmy,' says Uncle Cliff, squinting and shading his eyes with one hand.

Passing by two wooden posts hung across with hundreds of stiff tom-cod left out to dry – their frayed tails curling upwards as if they have been caught that way mid-swim – Uncle Cliff stops at the foot of some bluffs. A few yards along, the remains of an old post office cling to the edge. A power-line pole has toppled over and some underground cables are protruding from the side of the cliff below.

Tammy can see someone's been trying to prop up the bluff with a line of cement sandbags, but it still looks very unstable. 'Is it getting worse?' she asks.

'Maybe,' says Uncle Cliff. 'Hard to tell.'

Cliff is a tall man, as physiologically different from her dad as he is temperamentally. His square grey moustache takes up the whole space between his upper lip and nose, and his eyebrows slant downwards, giving him a mournful look, even when he's smiling. He's lived on the island all his life, except for the years he spent at an Indian Bureau school down in the Lower 48. He'd come back as soon as he could, as soon as his schooling was finished. Everywhere he goes on Shishmaref, people stop him to talk.

'Uncle Cliff?'

He turns to her.

'You sure this is a good time for me to be here?'

He plunges his hands into the pockets of his parka. 'Sure, sure. Everyone likes having you here.'

Tammy looks down at her boots. 'I'm sorry about George.'

Cliff nods. 'So how's things going for you?' he asks. 'Things going OK in Fairbanks?'

She shrugs.

'Your dad?'

'He's OK. He's up in Prudhoe Bay a lot.'

'Yeah. That's good money, huh?'

Tammy scans Cliff's expression, but it's hard to read.

'And you? School?' He waits a while for an answer.

'I was testing the ice,' she says finally, looking down. 'On the river. That's all it was – an experiment.'

Cliff keeps his gaze on her, his eyes clear, smiling faintly.

'The break-up . . .' Tammy continues, faltering, 'I read it's coming earlier every year. I wanted to see if it's true.' She turns her head away, concentrating on the cliff with the underground cables protruding from it.

'I dunno,' he says, a few minutes later. 'It can be dangerous.

Worrying too much about one thing like that.' He sounds like he's talking for himself, like no one else is listening. 'Because you can miss other things, you know? At the same time.'

Another plane passes over, buzzing like a horsefly. Cliff looks up at it and laughs, the sound of his laugh clapping up into the cold air. He shakes his head and laughs again. 'Crazy,' he says, but the smile on his face is fading.

The gymnasium at Shishmaref High has been decorated in school colours for the dance, yellow and blue, with hand-painted banners that read GO HUSKIES! or HUSKIES # 1! Basketball is big business in Shishmaref, same as it is in every Alaskan high school. It looks like they've spent a shit-load of money on this gym. In one corner is a DJ system being set up by a skinny guy in jeans and a T-shirt printed with the skyline of Seattle. He's got an Eskimo crewcut, half an inch short all over, and he's wearing the sort of glasses the ahnas wear, the Eskimo grandmas, old-fashioned glasses with thick black frames along the tops of the lenses.

'Who's the DJ?' Tammy asks.

Stacey is taking her parka off. Underneath, she's wearing white jeans and a red T-shirt with POSSIBLY . . . printed on it in red letters. Her breasts look big. She looks round to see who Tammy means. 'That's Luke – Iyatunguk. Big basketball star – they always get him to do the music. His brother moved down to Seattle and sends him stuff.' Then as if it's an afterthought: 'He's George's friend.'

'Really?'

Stacey shrugs. 'Yeah. Since they were real little.'

Stacey's warned Tammy the dance will be pretty lame, because it's always chaperoned and everyone knows everybody anyway. But Tammy doesn't mind; it's so completely remote from anything she would do in Fairbanks. At home, there are a lot more places to go, but she never does. Half the Native

boys her age in Fairbanks are border-line alcoholics already. They spend their weekends puking on the roadside or sniffing petrol out of brown-paper bags. The kids here look a lot happier to Tammy. At one time every Eskimo kid from a bush village got shipped out somewhere else to go to high school. Bill had ended up in an Indian Bureau school in Oklahoma, where he got beat up by the teachers, he always says, every time he forgot to speak English. Only since the oil money started flooding in had every Native community got its own million-dollar school. The money hadn't stopped the heating in the schools from packing up every winter, though, and a lot of the first generation of naluaqmiu teachers – 'pipeliners' they called them, flown up from the Lower 48 – didn't last more than a year.

Earlier today, there had been some talk about the dance being cancelled because of George, but Cliff told everyone it was OK. The chaperone ladies are laying out the buffet, kids are starting to pile in – all ages from eight to eighteen – discarded boots lined up by the double doors, puddles of melting snow on the gym floor. The kids try on a succession of bored expressions.

'Is Mick here yet?' Tammy asks Stacey. Stacey's been going with a guy called Mick. Mick, seventeen, is an interscholastic wrestling champion. Last year, his dad got killed in a plane crash, flying back home in a blizzard from Point Hope.

Stacey shakes her head. She's wearing powder on her face, over foundation makeup. She's pressured Tammy to put on some makeup too, but Tammy told her no.

'Vicky's got some booze,' she says. 'Mick's going to slip some into the punch, when he gets here.'

Tammy nods. She notices that people on Shishmaref talk about other people on a first-name basis, as if everybody automatically knows who they mean.

The overhead lights go off in the gym and kids begin to move to the centre of the floor.

When Mick arrives, Stacey wanders over. Tammy watches them make their way to the refreshment table and pretty soon Mick's tipping a bottle into the punch bowl while Stacey and another girl stand in front of him for cover. Tammy's surprised how many people are dancing. There are a few older people in the crowd too – young men in their twenties, a few older girls. No one seems to mind them being there. She leans back against the wooden bleachers, retracted into the wall. She is used to being invisible in situations like these.

Stacey comes over to her after about half an hour. Her face is sweaty and a few strands of her curled hair have started to droop. 'Are you OK?' she asks. 'I told you it would be lame. Aren't you gonna dance?'

Tammy shakes her head.

'I'm going outside with Mick for a while. OK?'

Tammy watches them slip out of the side exit, crouching down behind other people so the chaperones don't see them leaving. The music stops a few minutes later and the overhead lights snap back on. Everyone looks around like they've been woken too fast from a hectic dream. She wanders over to the snack table and finds herself standing next to Luke, the DJ.

He looks at her. 'Hi,' he says.

'Hi.'

'You're not dancing.'

'No.'

His hands, hovering over the food, are long and wide. 'You visiting for a while?'

'Yes.'

'Stacey's cousin, right?'

She nods. 'You're a friend of George's, right?'

Luke looks at Tammy like she's accused him of something nasty. One foot tapping on the gym floor, he keeps glancing over at his sound system as if someone might steal it.

Tammy glances down at the left front pocket of his

black jeans; the top of a plastic bag is sticking out of it. He's starting to drift away. 'So where do you think he is?' she asks.

Luke switches his gaze to her again, his mouth slightly open. He frowns. 'I don't know where he is.' Then he smiles. 'Do you?'

Tammy looks away, and Luke turns to the floor again, nods when someone waves at him. 'You know what?' he murmurs, after a while standing there watching the crowd. Tammy isn't sure if he's talking to her or not. 'I'm *always* in this fucking gym. I spend more time in here than I do in my own house.' He falls silent. 'George'll be all right,' he adds, abruptly, a few moments later, still not looking at Tammy.

'How do you know?'

He picks up another hot dog off the table, takes a big bite out of it. 'Just do . . . I better get back to the music. Natives are getting restless – ha ha.'

Tammy goes in search of the girls' toilets. She has to go through the kitchen and two of the chaperone ladies, sitting in plastic garden chairs with their feet resting on turned-up cardboard boxes, beam at her. They say something to each other in Inupiaq and one of them points towards a door at the far end of the room, so Tammy goes out that way. She finds herself in a hallway with glass trophy cabinets along one side. From the gym, she can hear the muffled sound of the music starting again. Two girls come down the hallway towards her. Tammy trails one hand along the breeze-block wall to her right. Her fingers bump over bulletin boards, picture frames, glass. She can see the entrance to the girls' bathroom ahead. When her fingers knock a picture askew, she stops to straighten it. *Class of 2001*. There they all are, in the gymnasium under a flimsy wooden arch wound in blue and yellow crepe paper. She moves to the next photograph. *Class of 2002. Class of 2003* – George's class. She finds him in the back row, second from the right. Maybe she's looking at the photograph of a dead person.

He isn't smiling. Luke is in the middle of the back row, his hair much longer than it is now, hanging forward over his face. Tammy wants there to be something noticeably different about George, but nothing stands out. He's tall, like Cliff, with a broad, square face. She stands there for quite a while, fingering the shape of the cigarette packet inside the central pouch of her sweatshirt.

Much later that night, when she and Stacey are lying in bed together in the bedroom Stacey shares with her two younger brothers, Tammy tells her what Luke said about George. 'Does he always act like such a big shot?' she asks.

'Luke?' Stacey murmurs. 'I dunno. Sometimes.' She's almost asleep; she's come home pretty drunk. 'He probably liked you.'

Tammy can't sleep. If she were home, she'd be rolling things down the table. In the dim light from the hallway, she can see the humps that are the sleeping bodies of Pete and Mikey in the bed at the other end of the room. A bare arm is hanging over the edge of the mattress. The night before, one of them had been snoring, but it's quiet tonight.

'He said George knows how to take care of himself.' She tells Stacey this thinking it might make her feel better, but Stacey must be asleep because she doesn't respond.

Bill hates the final approach to Shishmaref. He's not used to these little bush planes any more; he likes the jets the oil company use, with a stewardess on board to take care of you, instead of being strapped in with your luggage next to some old guy reeking of fish oil. Native cowboy at the controls telling the passengers to take a seat in the front so they balance the weight of the cargo jammed in the back. These bush pilots don't know shit.

The plane dips one wing as it turns to set itself up for the new landing strip. The old landing strip cut across the island horizontally; it still gets used sometimes when the weather's good. At its widest, Shishmaref is only half a mile across, so the runway makes more sense the way it is now, vertical, laid out south of the town, at the bottom end of the island. Bill remembers when he was twelve, coming home on his first summer vacation from the shit Bureau of Indian Affairs boarding-school. They'd flown into a summer storm and the clouds over Shishmaref were so low the pilot was flying blind right up to the last minute. Bill had been sure the plane wasn't going to be able to stop, that they were going to shoot out onto the weak sea ice, too weak in the first week of June to support a plane. He'd been feeling superstitious because, after six months of homesickness so bad it made him as nauseous as the strange food they served, he wasn't actually going to believe that he was home until the moment his feet touched solid ground.

There are no clouds today. As the plane touches down, Bill is still thinking about his boarding-school days, and one time in his first year when he got mad at another student and yelled at him, in Inupiaq. The teacher brought the whole class in from the playground and made Bill stand up in front of them. She placed a strip of tape over his mouth, explaining to the class what she was doing, and made him sit in the corner for three hours, so that he would remember to speak English. As the plane touches down, he shakes his head clear of the memory. In the seats directly behind him, a couple of women are gossiping in Inupiaq – something about a stolen purse. He leans forward to look out of the window. He wants a drink.

When he gets off the plane, lots of people are milling around on the tarmac. It's the weekend of the Shishmaref Spring Carnival. He sees Tammy standing off to the right of the main crowd, her hands in her pockets. She's wearing a man's coat, too big for her, probably one she's borrowed from Cliff or one of her cousins. As always, the way she's just standing there doing nothing starts to bug him. He tramps over with his bag. 'Hey,' he says, nodding his head once, and they start walking into town.

31

A team of dogs passes, heading out to the end of the island to do a circuit. Bill doesn't recognize the guy on the sled.

Tammy turns her head to watch the dogs pass. 'Uncle Cliff says you used to have a team,' she says.

Bill nods.

'Did you race?'

'Sure.'

They walk on. When they reach the first line of houses, Tammy asks about Beth.

'They changed her shifts again at the hospital. She's working days now.'

'Who's taking care of Jessica?'

Bill shrugs. 'Day care.'

Cliff's invited a couple of people over for a caribou roast that night, including Steve Nayukpuk, the mayor of Shishmaref, and Joe and Evelyn Schroeder who run the Native Store. Steve grew up on the island but Joe and Evelyn are new, having moved here only fifteen years ago. There are ten of them all told round the kitchen table – with Stacey, her two little brothers, and Cliff's mother-in-law, Grandma Minnie – sitting on mismatched chairs gathered from every room of the house. Cliff's youngest, Mikey, sits on Minnie's lap.

'What's with the funny new houses?' Bill asks, halfway through the meal. 'Down by the shore.'

Cliff looks up from where he's carving some more meat and loading it onto people's plates. 'Whaddaya mean, new houses?' he says, looking up.

'Ones on car-jacks – look like they're having their tyres changed.'

'Movable foundations,' Steve Nayukpuk says, with his mouth full. 'We want to get everybody on them next few years, until one of these government agencies comes up with some relocation money.'

Cliff and Joe Schroeder nod their heads in agreement.

Bill laughs. '*Relocation* money? What – you gonna move? Where you gonna go? Other side of the island?'

'It's no joke,' says Cliff. 'Community voted on it last month: 161–20. Herbie's been working with the US Army engineers, figuring out what it would cost to move to a place on the mainland. Evelyn here's on the Erosion and Relocation Committee.' He gestures towards Evelyn and she nods. 'We lost a hundred twenty-five feet of ground in the last big storm, all in one night.'

'So you're gonna just *leave* the island? You can't do that – been Eskimos living here for ever. Hey, man, these things go up and down! The ice will build up again – shit, we had a snow-storm in Fairbanks – *May* – last year, didn't we? Tam?'

Bill looks across at his daughter, fork halfway raised to his mouth. She's been quiet the whole meal, like she always is, but now she looks up, her eyes dark and too serious for their own good. She begins to talk in a low tone.

'Well,' she says, 'actually, Dad, in the last fifty years, the largest ice shelf in the Arctic – the Ward Hunt – has lost ninety per cent of its surface area. The sea-ice volume has declined fifteen per cent, and thinned from ten feet to six feet in some places. Alaskan meltwater accounts for half of the worldwide sea-level rise of 7.8 inches over the past hundred years.' She pauses and looks down at her plate. 'So I would say it *is* a problem.'

After a brief silence, everyone except Bill and Tammy – even the little boys, though they don't know why they're doing it – bursts out laughing.

'Does she *always* talk like that?' asks Evelyn, looking around at everyone else at the table and reaching out to chuck Tammy under her chin. 'Talks like she's forty years old!'

Bill goes back to eating. 'Don't listen to her. She don't know what she's talkin' about. I don't know where she gets this stuff from, crazy stuff, people talking never even set foot in Alaska.'

'It's not crazy, Bill,' says Steve Nayukpuk.

'She sure knows a *lot*!' says Grandma Minnie, her wide bosom still shaking with laughter under her flowered blouse.

Bill pushes his empty plate away and shoots Tammy a look, underhand.

Tammy knows she's going to pay for what she's said and sure enough the next morning her dad suggests they take a little trip to Nome, overnight, just the two of them. He's got a cousin there he says he wants to visit.

'What about the dog races?' she asks. 'Isn't that what you came to see?'

'We'll be back by tomorrow. Big sprint doesn't start till twelve.'

Mid-morning they walk down to the airport together. Some snow is falling, but Shishmaref's having a warm patch and they end up getting their boots soaked walking through the slush on the road passing behind the washeteria and the general store. As usual, there are two or three snowmobiles and a couple of pickup trucks pulled up onto snowdrifts around the store. Bill goes in to get some cigarettes and a meat sandwich for the journey, and she follows him in. The pale yellow linoleum floor is muddy. She wanders around, and ends up picking out a postcard of the Tannery to send to Jessica.

When she gets to the counter, it's Erik serving – the white guy from California who's been hanging around in Shishmaref for a few months, helping out the Schroeders at the store in exchange for bed and board. Stacey says no one likes him much, and he's always trying to make friends with everyone. Tammy can see her dad's got nothing to say to him so they just pay for the stuff and go. When they're passing the post office, she tells him she'll catch up. 'I want to mail this postcard to Jess.'

Bill shrugs and pulls down the flaps of his hat. 'Make it quick – I'll try and get us on the next plane out.'

Luke Iyatunguk is in the post office. He's standing at the little counter to one side, putting stamps on a long, thin package. She says his name and he spins round so fast it's as if she's snuck up on him in an empty house.

She raises a hand. 'I didn't mean to scare you.'

'You didn't. Tammy, right?'

She nods. 'I thought you were playing basketball today.'

'I am. First game's not till three o'clock, though.' He checks the time on the clock over the counter, and Tammy glances down at the address on his package. HYDRAULIC TRANSPORT REFRIGERATION, LLC, it reads, with a Nome address. 'So you coming to the game?' says Luke, placing his arm on top of the address label on the package, even though this means his body is twisted in an awkward way. His parka falls open and underneath he's wearing a Shishmaref High School sweatshirt and baby-blue sweatpants with white stripes up the sides.

'I can't. My dad's taking me to Nome.'

'Oh.' Luke drums his fingers on the side of the package and looks at the woman being served by the postal clerk. 'Too bad.'

'Yeah.' The woman finishes at the counter and steps between them to get to the door. 'I better write this postcard – my dad's waiting.'

'Sure,' says Luke. He heads to the door, still holding his package so the label's covered.

'Aren't you going to mail that?'

He looks down at the package as if he's forgotten it's there. 'I guess I'll walk it down to the plane myself. Save them the trouble.'

The flight to Nome is uneventful. Tammy looks out of the window. There are rolling ridges of sea ice down below, as if the waves have been caught mid-swell, just that second, and frozen that way. Every so often there's a very high ridge, crumbling at the top, where two sections have crashed into each other, pushing upwards like battling continents. The ice should reassure her. But the white goes on and on and on and if she stares too long at it her eyes start to lose focus and she feels as if she's falling.

'Tammy,' her dad calls back.

'Yes?'

'What are you doin'?'

As they approach Nome, the sun is already starting to set to the right of the plane. The boxy, squat buildings look like a toy town.

Bill turns round in his seat. 'Got your seatbelt on there?' he asks.

Bill's so-called cousin Kenny runs the Polar Bear Saloon, on the main strip of Nome, and they head right there. Walking along Front Street, the town looks like it's the day after a big wedding and nobody wanted to clean up. A few isolated flakes of snow are falling. There are telephone poles on both sides of the road, about every four cars or so, and the wires sag across, tangled up with old Christmas lights, making a mess in the white sky. The Polar Bear Saloon and Liquor Store is a red building with a two-dimensional, old-fashioned saloon façade. Bill opens the rickety storm door, walks in and throws his pack down on the wooden floor.

'Kenny!' he calls out. The lights are on behind the bar, a strip light shining on the rows of coloured bottles. To the left of the bar, a flight of stairs goes up to the apartment above. In the corner of the room there's a jukebox; Tammy wanders over to look at it.

'Hey! Where is everybody?' Bill calls.

He goes behind the bar, starts poking around. He's standing in front of the cash register when someone says in a low, even voice: 'What the hell d'you think you're doing?'

Tammy turns. There's a man standing in the doorway at the bottom of the stairs and he's pointing a Kalashnikov at Bill, his finger curled round the trigger.

Bill straightens up. 'Hold on, guy,' he says, raising his hands. 'There's no problem here. Is Kenny around? I'm a friend of Kenny's – I'm his cousin.'

'So why you behind the bar?'

'No reason. I told you – I came to see Kenny. He's waiting on me.'

The man keeps his rifle aimed right at Bill's heart. 'Better not be any cash missing.' He glances over at Tammy. 'Who's the girl?'

'That's my daughter. Tammy.'

'Ain't meant to be any kids in here.'

'I told you – we're staying. We're visiting. You go and ask Kenny. Tell him Bill and Tammy here for a visit. Bill Ongtowasruk.'

The man looks over at Tammy again, then back at Bill, squints his eyes through the sight and raises his shoulders as if he's going to shoot after all. Then he laughs, lowers the rifle, turns and replaces it third gun up in a rack on the wall behind him.

'Sorry 'bout that,' he says, walking over to Bill. 'We had a couple robberies last year. And since I didn't know ya . . .' He extends a hand with fingers thick and brown as cigars and Bill shakes it.

'Sure, sure,' Bill says. 'Lot of desperate people out there, do *anything* for a drink.' He moves round to the front of the bar and plants himself on one of the stools. 'But, hell, tell you what, though, I could use one *myself* after that show-down!' He laughs a couple of loud laughs and slaps the bar with his hand. 'How 'bout it, huh? You serving?'

'She old enough to be in here?' asks the guy.

'She'll be fine,' Bill says, without turning his head Tammy's way.

He doesn't move from the bar again until eleven o'clock that night, when Kenny helps him upstairs and onto a sofa in the living room upstairs. Tammy leaves the Polar Bear a couple of times during the afternoon. She goes out and buys three papers, reads them in a diner, and cuts out two articles. Late afternoon, she walks down to the shoreline, where the sand is meant to be black but of course she can't tell this time of year.

37

She heads back to the Polar Bear again about six o'clock and takes some cash from her dad's wallet.

'Hey, Tam,' he greets her, his eyes bright and stupid. 'How ya doing? Have a drink! What you want, a Coke?'

'I'm going to get something to eat.'

'Good plan. Bring me something – what you getting?'

'I can't bring food in here, Dad,' Tammy tells him, but he's already turned away from her to a sad-looking white lady sitting on the next stool. She's one of those ladies with dyed hair and polyester clothes: one look makes you figure they've ended up where they are for a very good reason. And they've probably left a whole lot of mess wherever they were last. Why else would they want to hang out with a bunch of drunk old Eskimos? Bill is leaning towards the lady, his arm resting on the bar between them. Her eyes look half-shut; she's smiling and laughing too loudly whenever Bill cracks a joke.

After eating in a place called the Glue Pot – Tammy orders three courses, spends all of her dad's money with satisfaction – she doesn't feel like going back to the Polar Bear. The snow starts to fall again. She wanders around the town, figuring if she waits until midnight the bar might be a bit quieter and she can slip upstairs and find a place to sleep. Halfway down Bering Street, a short, deserted street in an industrial section of town, she looks up when she hears the sound of a siren a few streets away. To her left, a small sign over the garage door of a warehouse catches her eye. HYDRAULIC TRANSPORT REFRIGERATION, LLC, it reads, the name she had read on Luke's package. She's just standing there – frowning at the coincidence, wondering if the package had come on the same plane with her and her dad, and whose job it had been to walk it down here and what it had contained – when the steel garage door rolls up and Cousin George walks out from under.

She knows who he is right away, even though she can see only a small section of his face within the enclosed space made by the peak of his hunter's cap and the hood of his sweatshirt.

He stops, surprised to find someone there as if waiting for him. He keeps one arm raised, hand still holding onto the steel door he's just pushed up.

'Yeah?' he says.

'George?'

'Who's that?' he says, turning his body away.

'It's Tammy. Your cousin.' George doesn't move. 'Remember? From Fairbanks? Uncle Bill and Aunt Beth?'

Finally, George starts to move. 'Oh, sure. Hi.' He pulls down the steel door and locks it, puts the keys in his parka pocket and turns to face her. 'So what are you doing in Nome?'

'I flew down with my dad.'

George nods his head a couple of times.

'How about you?' she asks. 'What are you doing? Down here in Nome.'

He starts to walk, and she falls into step beside him. 'I'm working,' he says. 'I've got a job in town.'

George is moving fast, but he's not heading anywhere; that becomes obvious. His steps are steady and relaxed, but they keep turning right corners until Tammy thinks they must be heading back the way they came, and Nome's not really a big enough town to get lost in.

After about fifteen minutes of this, walking in silence in the pale orange light of the street lights, flickering, glowing in the falling snow, Tammy stops. 'George.' She stops halfway up an alley, near the back entrance to a restaurant, and the air smells like grease, grease burnt on a griddle.

George slows down ahead of her and then he stops too, a few feet in front. He turns round. 'What?'

The snow is coming directly at her face, blowing horizontally like it's threading through a wind soc.

'I know about you.'

George's face is impenetrable.

'I've been staying on Shishmaref, last couple of weeks.'

George still doesn't say anything. He takes a few steps

towards her. She hasn't noticed until now that he's not wearing any gloves; she's surprised his fingers haven't turned white.

He sniffs. 'Were you looking for me? Is that why you were standing outside the warehouse?'

She shakes her head, eyes blinking against the snow. 'It was a coincidence.'

Very close now, he looks down at her, frowning. His thick black eyebrows are threaded with ice particles, like little slivers of white paint someone has left there to dry. 'Why would you be standing outside a trucking warehouse in Nome, all by yourself, at night, in the middle of a snowstorm?'

Tammy turns her head away. 'I don't know. Why would *you*?'

'That's not an answer.'

'I wasn't just standing there. I stopped because I heard a siren and then I saw the name on the sign, the same name I saw this morning in Shishmaref, on a package Luke Iyatunguk was sending—'

'Luke showed you?'

'No. I just saw it.' She waits a few seconds. 'And then you came out.'

George wipes the snow off his face. 'So where's your dad?'

'He's in a bar. He probably hasn't noticed I'm gone.'

George is listening hard every time Tammy speaks and he keeps scanning her face with his eyes, like it's a computer screen he's proofing for data. It's as if he's looking for something he can analyse – a birthmark, a scar – and he can't find it anywhere. After a while, he looks away. 'We should get out of this snow,' he says.

'OK.'

They head back to the HTR warehouse and duck under the steel door. George leads the way into an office at the back and switches on the fluorescent lights. Inside, a large metal desk with a wood-veneer top sits in the centre of the room. Along the opposite wall is a row of filing cabinets and, hanging on the wall behind the desk, a calendar open to a picture of a leaping king salmon. The desk-top is empty: no paperwork anywhere, no piles of invoices, just a black phone and a computer.

'Is this where you work?' she asks.

'Yes. Sit down,' says George. He pulls over a metal chair for her and seats himself behind the desk. For the first time since meeting him, Tammy feels apprehensive. Despite unzipping his parka when he came into the room, he's still got the hood of his sweatshirt pulled up, the strings tied up tight so only his face is visible. He picks up a ballpoint pen on the desk and draws a few sharp, straight lines down the page of a little memo pad with the HTR logo printed at the top. 'Look. I need you not to tell anyone about seeing me,' he says.

Tammy pulls off one of her mittens and checks her fingers, curling and uncurling them a couple times, watching the pink-ness returning to the tips each time. George repeats what he's just said.

'Tammy?' he says, when she still doesn't reply.

She puts her mitten back on. 'I heard. There are a lot of people worrying about you. They're not saying, but they must be wondering if you're dead.'

George pulls at the strings of his sweatshirt hood and yanks it back off his head. His hair is dark black and long, pulled back into a ponytail. There's a small section of white hair running through it, like a skunk mark. Tammy suddenly feels short of breath.

'How did you get here?' she asks. 'Without people knowing.'

'I drove.'

'You drove?'

He nods. 'An old snow machine – across the inlet.'

'All the way to Nome?'

'Teller. Hitched a ride from there. It's no big deal. People used to do it with dogs all the time.'

'Wasn't it risky in the middle of winter?'

George shakes his head, pursing his lips. 'No.'

His gaze on her is too focused, invasive. Tammy looks down at her hands.

'What are you going to do?' he asks.

She rubs her hands along the tops of her thighs. 'Couldn't you at least let someone know you're OK? That you're alive?'

'I can't. I understand what you're saying,' he continues in a low voice, 'but how could I do that? How could I just let them know I'm OK, like you say, without them wanting to know more?'

'Of course they'd want to know more.'

He nods. 'And that's the problem.' He pauses, putting the pen down. 'You'll just have to trust me. Or not. But if you don't, then you won't see me again, and neither will they.'

She looks up at him, and laughs. 'Is that some kind of threat? I feel like I'm on TV.'

George's brows come together; he shakes his head. For a second, he looks embarrassed. 'A threat?' He stands up and walks across the small office. 'No. I wouldn't threaten you. I didn't plan on anyone else getting involved.'

'I didn't plan on it either.'

Tammy holds herself still, looking at the leaping king salmon on the calendar until she can almost smell the cold river water. The calendar's still on March – no one's turned the page over.

A few moments pass before George speaks again, and his voice is soft, right behind her. 'Do you believe in anything?'

'What do you mean?' she says, straightening her back against the chair.

'Is there anything that you believe in?' he repeats, more slowly. 'Something you know is right to do, even though lots of people around you don't see it the same way.'

Tammy shrugs. 'I guess.' She pauses. 'But if Cliff were my dad, I'd never do it to him.'

'Do what?'

'Leave him hanging.'

'I'm doing this for him.'

42

'Doing what?'

George comes round behind the desk and sits down again in the chair, covering his face with his hands and digging his fingers up through his hairline.

One of the fluorescent panels in the ceiling has started flickering. Tammy squints up at it. She thinks about the fluorescent lights in her school in Fairbanks; there's one that always buzzes right above where she used to sit in Science class. She thinks about the picnic tables by the banks of the Chena river, where she'd gone out onto the ice; the slatted wood they're made from is always damp, always rotting. She thinks about going through the ice, the giving way, the moment of subsidence, what it felt like. She sees herself falling through the fluorescent panel above, the glass shattering like ice and a foot coming through.

'OK,' she says, still looking up.

'OK what?' His hands still covering his face.

'OK, I won't say anything. I won't tell anybody for a while. But I can't promise, if Cliff asks me directly.'

'Why would he ask you?'

'I dunno. But maybe he would.'

George nods. 'OK.' He runs a hand over his scalp, taking the ponytail out and then scraping back all his hair and putting it in again. 'Thanks,' he says, standing up and reaching out a hand across the desk. She's not sure if he wants her to shake it or just hold it, so she just takes it, over-handed, and his fingers grip round her palm. 'I love my dad, you know.'

'OK,' says Tammy, dropping the hand after giving it a loose shake. His eyes are matt brown like damp driftwood.

'It's strange,' he goes on, 'meeting you tonight. I hardly ever come into Nome.'

THE POLAR BEARS

Luke is standing by the magazine rack in the Native Store. He's reading a magazine with pictures of motorcycles on the cover, and his hair looks wet as if he's just stepped out of the shower. Tammy goes down one aisle and up another, picking out a box of cereal on the way. It's the first time she's seen Luke since her trip to Nome. Aisle by aisle, she gets closer to where he's standing. She picks a newspaper off the magazine rack.

'Hey,' Luke says, looking around to see if anybody is with her. A couple of girls are loitering over by the case with the sodas in it. They've been looking over at Luke, but they start to talk to each other as soon as he glances their way. 'How's it going?' he asks, shifting his glasses back up his nose, still holding open the magazine.

'OK.'

'Not going crazy yet?'

'No. Why would I be going crazy?'

He shrugs. 'On the island – nowhere to go.'

She shakes her head. 'I don't mind that.'

'How's school? Everyone being nice to you?' he asks, nodding his head towards the girls by the sodas.

'I'm not going to school.'

Luke raises his eyebrows, but he doesn't comment.

'How was the basketball tournament?' she asks.

He nods. 'Yeah, good. We won.'

'Is that what you want to do?' They're walking up to the counter, and Tammy puts her things down, hands Evelyn some cash. 'Play basketball?'

Luke shrugs. 'I dunno. Sure, maybe. If I could make some money out of it, which I probably couldn't. How was Nome, anyway?'

Tammy looks at him. She's not sure how frequent the contact is between him and George.

Evelyn is standing behind the counter with Tammy's change in her outstretched hand, looking back and forth at the two of them. The phone's in her other hand, pressed to one ear. 'You wanna *buy* that magazine, Luke?' she says.

Luke smiles at her. 'Nah, I'm gonna put it back.'

'Thought so.' She looks at Tammy. 'I wondered what he was doing up here by the cash register.'

Tammy lingers by the counter with her paper bag, wondering if she can ask for some cigarettes. She walks slowly towards the exit.

'Sort of dead this time of year in Nome, I bet,' Luke says, opening the door for her. 'George and I—' He stops as the same girls who left the store a few moments earlier come back in again, laughing as they pass through the door Luke is holding open with his foot.

'You and George?' Tammy asks, when the door is shut again and they are outside.

'What? Oh, yeah. George and I went down to the sled race this year. It was excellent – you ever been skijoring?'

She shakes her head.

'You attach skis to the dogs. You should try it – it's a kick.'

'Is that what you did with George?'

'With George?' Luke frowns, shaking his head. 'Nah.' He looks at his watch just as Evelyn switches on the lights inside the store. The moon's rising, faint white in the grey sky around

45

it. 'Do you want to do something sometime?' he asks. 'Go out on the ice? I've got an iron horse I like to take out.'

'An iron horse?'

Luke grins, teeth flashing white. 'Sure. Snow machine. You can get way out on the sea this time of year. I thought you might want to see it out there.'

Tammy runs her finger through the snow on the hood of a pickup truck next to her. 'Isn't the ice starting to soften? This time of year?'

'No way. There's lots of time left. I'll let you know when I'm going out next. Maybe this weekend, if the weather's right.'

A creak in the ceiling above makes Tammy click the computer mouse, sending away the search-engine window. She looks up, her eyes still, eyebrows raised. By the time she gets out of bed each morning, everyone else in the family has usually left the house. She rises from her chair quietly, goes to the bottom of the stairs and listens again. Pete and Mikey's dirty running shoes are tumbling down the treads. She steps over them, climbing the stairs, the slippers Grandma Minnie made for her making no sound on the wooden floor. She stops in the hall-way outside George's bedroom.

'Hello?' she calls.

Knocking first, she opens the door to George's room and goes in.

There is a feeling of recent absence, of objects in the room holding their breath. The room is not much larger than a tool shed, and there is no window. Tammy is struck by the same emptiness she had witnessed in the office at the HTR. A single bed is covered in a thin brown blanket. A table sits against one wall, with a chair and a two-drawer filing cabinet next to it. There is nothing on the table, though when she looks closely at its surface she can see scratches and indentations in the wood caused by years of homework. There is nothing in either drawer of the filing cabinet. Under the bed she finds two cardboard boxes: a few sweaters in one, and an old pair of boots in the other.

She lies down on George's bed, lowering herself to a flat position. Her hands lie on the blanket, twitching slightly. Posted on the wall at the foot of the bed, right next to the door so not obvious to anyone when first entering the room, is a handwritten poster, presumably in George's hand. When Tammy sees it, she sits up and leans forward to read.

Inupiat Ilitqusiat

Every Inupiat is responsible to all other Inupiat for the survival of our culture spirit, and the values and traditions through which it survives. Through our extended family, we retain, teach and live our Inupiat way. With guidance and support from Elders, we must teach our children Inupiat values.

Below this is a list, written out at different angles and in different inks, as if it has been added to over a period of time: *Knowledge of Language, Sharing, Respect for Others, Co-operation, Respect for Elders, Love for Children, Knowledge of Family Tree, Hard Work, Avoiding Conflict, Respect for Nature, Spirituality, Humour, Family Roles, Hunter Success, Domestic Skills, Humility, Responsibility to Tribe.*

Tammy stares at the handwriting, imagining George kneeling on this bed, writing on the poster at different times and for different reasons. There's no way of telling how old the poster is, but the handwriting isn't that of a young child. It's the only thing up on the walls. She lies back again and stares at the ceiling, the same ceiling George must have stared at most of his life. She smells something, slightly rotten, like ice in a freezer that has picked up the smells of the food it is keeping cold. There is a knock on the door.

Tammy sits up, balancing her weight on her fingertips in

47

order to make no noise as she swings her legs off the bed. She places her feet on the floor. 'Yes?'

The door opens and Cliff walks in. His face is pale and he is frowning, but the frown disappears when he sees Tammy, the only trace of his expectations a few drops of sweat that have broken out on his forehead.

'I'm sorry,' Tammy stammers, standing up in a rush. 'I shouldn't have come in here.'

'You can come in here,' says Cliff. 'Nothing wrong with coming in here.' He looks around. 'Not so much to see, huh? He used to have a couple other posters up – schoolwork, things like that – but he took 'em all down last year.' He pauses. 'Likes it better plain, I guess.'

Tammy gazes around the room and nods a few times. She can't look at Cliff. If he asks her right now where she thinks George is, she will tell him. She swallows and runs her tongue along the back of her lower front teeth.

Cliff notices the handwritten poster on the wall behind them. He takes a long time looking at it, then he turns and smiles at Tammy. 'How're the Inupiaq lessons going?'

Tammy smiles a small, twisted smile; her chest is aching. 'I've just had one. So far.'

Cliff nods, patting her arm. 'You keep going with it,' he says, and walks out of the room. 'Sue Tocktoo says you're doing real good.'

A family is passing, riding three abreast on a snowmobile, and the man driving raises his hand. The ends of his black moustache reach down to his chin, like a Mexican bandit's.

'Hey Clarence,' says Stacey, in an uninterested tone.

They are driving down the main gravel road through town in a four-wheeler with a wooden trailer behind, two empty water barrels and a large bag of laundry on it. It's snowing, mild flurries.

'So, did he?' Stacey asks. 'Ask you out? Are you gonna go out with him?'

Tammy shifts in her seat. 'How do you "go out" on an island?' she asks.

'You know what I mean.' She shoves the gear into place.

'Could you teach me to drive this?'

'Sure – if you want. What did he say exactly?' They pull up by the water pipe. Stacey sticks the plastic tube hanging from it into the mouth of one of the barrels on the trailer and turns on the water. 'Tell me what he said,' she says.

'He asked me if I wanted to go out on the ice sometime, that's it, take a drive in his snow machine. What does he do, anyway? Does he have a job?'

'He helps his dad down at the airport, fixing planes. Connie Stenek's sure gonna be pissed off. She's had her eye on Luke since the first grade – they were in the same class. She's not going to like it, some iqlaaq turning up and stealing her guy.'

'Some *iqlaaq*?'

'Some stranger.'

'Am I a stranger?'

Stacey looks at Tammy. 'Sure. To her you are.'

'I'm not stealing anything.'

They drive the four-wheeler with its water barrels full now to the washeteria and unload the bags of laundry. The inside of the washeteria is decorated in wood-veneer panelling with a bulletin board on the wall near the door, next to a painting on towelling of Jesus standing among a flock of sheep. Two large washing machines and one industrial-size dryer stand against the far wall; there are two public showers and a large sink at the right end of the long room. In the corner, someone's left a mop standing in one of those buckets on wheels. A woman is sitting on a chair near the two showers and a toddler is play-ing peekaboo in the shower curtains. After loading the clothes into the machine not in use, Stacey and Tammy sit down on some metal folding chairs and Stacey unzips her parka.

'Do you always do the laundry?' Tammy asks.

Stacey nods, and takes out a packet of gum. 'Since Mom died . . . Want a piece?'

'No, thanks.'

Aunt Ginny had died five years ago, six months after she came for treatment in Fairbanks. She had a tumour in her pancreas. Aunt Ginny's funeral had been one of the only times Beth ever visited the island and Tammy remembered how, in private, she had criticized the coffin, a basic white box built by a neighbour in a workshop two doors away. Tammy was nine; she'd never been to a funeral before. She had found it all disturbing. It had taken the men in the village four days to dig the grave in the middle of February, thawing out the soil layer by layer with a fire of coals, moving the coals and digging a little, then replacing the coals over the new frozen layer, moving and digging again. Watching this process, with the rest of the kids from the village, Tammy had thought to herself when she died she wanted to be laid out on the sea ice, as far out as possible, away from everybody, and then when the ice broke up in the summer she would simply sink down, gently, bit by bit, with no one there to watch.

Stacey's staring blankly at the linoleum floor, popping her gum.

'How's it going with Mick?' Tammy asks.

Stacey looks up and smiles. 'Good.' She glances over at the woman sitting near by, and shakes her head at Tammy, putting a finger to her lips. Tammy wonders if Stacey's still a virgin. 'So you going to be here all summer?' Stacey asks.

Tammy pulls off her wool hat, and rubs a hand through her hair. 'I don't know.'

'It's pretty good here, in the summer. Everyone stays up all night.' She pauses. 'What's it like in Fairbanks?'

'Hot. Lots of mosquitoes.'

The woman next to them starts talking to her toddler in Inupiaq and Tammy tries to understand.

'Maybe you can come out to camp with us, in August,' Stacey says.

'Yeah, maybe.'

Stacey stands up to put another load in the second machine being emptied by the woman with the child. Tammy watches her carry the bag over, stand there and wait, while the woman pulls out the last of her wet clothes. The little girl, standing quietly behind her mother, stares unblinkingly at Tammy, as if seeing an alien. Tammy stares back, until the girl is called by her mother and the two leave the laundromat.

Stacey sits down again and watches the laundry spinning round. 'I've been emailing this guy,' she says.

'What guy?'

She smiles and shrugs. 'Some guy. In a chat room. He lives in Anchorage.'

Tammy coughs. She gets out her cigarettes and asks Stacey if she can smoke in the laundromat.

'*I* don't care.'

The cigarette feels good, the first in a while. She hasn't been sure about smoking in front of people on Shishmaref.

'How long have you been emailing this guy?'

'Couple of months.'

Tammy looks around for somewhere to flick the ash. 'How old is he?' she asks.

Stacey shrugs. 'I don't know.'

'Is he a white guy?'

She laughs. 'I don't know anything about him. He could be Chinese, for all I know! He says he's an Eskimo.'

'That's what he called himself? An Eskimo?'

Stacey looks at her. 'Yeah. Why not? A lot of people use that word.'

Tammy nods and swallows; her throat is feeling sore from the cigarette. The machine with the first load in it finishes and Stacey goes to transfer the clothes over to the dryer. Tammy

51

gets up and stands next to her, offering to help. 'Do you do that a lot?' she asks.

'Do what?'

'Email people you don't know.'

Stacey bends down to pick up a wet athletic sock that's dropped onto the floor. 'Sometimes. I want to go there, to Anchorage, after I graduate.'

'Why?'

Stacey makes a face. '*Why?* So I can get a job – what else? There's nothing to do around here – why do you think George left?'

Tammy pretends she is reading the instructions on the machine. 'So you think he's OK?' she asks, a few moments later. 'George.'

Stacey shrugs. She goes back to her chair and picks up the magazine. 'You wanna know what I think?' she says, looking up after turning a few pages. 'I think he's gone up to live in the middle of nowhere. With a pack of wolves. And I think he'll be better off there.'

Bill organizes another trip to Shishmaref on his next week off and takes Tammy to Kotzebue for the weekend. Tammy wants to go back to Nome, but since Bill didn't actually settle the tab with Kenny before he left he thinks he'll wait on that. End of the month, he'll have the cash in hand to revisit the Polar Bear. They can go then, he tells her. They go to Kotzebue with Cliff and a couple of the other islanders. Kotzebue's up the coast, still a Native village but a hell of a lot bigger and no one jumps on a guy if he wants to have a drink. Bill has scored a bottle of whisky in the airport at Fairbanks, waiting for his connecting flight, because he knew how much it would cost him out in the bush. The day they get there, Cliff takes them down to this hardware, fishing-supply sort of place run by a friend of his, because he's looking to replace his old rod with something more up-to-date, and everyone just hangs out there the whole afternoon, which is starting to bug Bill, until about six o'clock when a lot of other people start turning up for an all-night poker game. If there's anything Cliff can't resist, it's a good game. All his life, front row in church every Sunday, vacation Bible school, confirmation classes, the only sure-fire way to get Cliff to look Bill's way was to throw down the cards. Bill taught him: games he'd learnt at boarding-school, games played for money or contraband late at night after the dormitory lights had been turned off. Every vacation, he came home with a new variation, and Cliff took no time to learn. Cliff could get on Bill's nerves – always had – but he wasn't a bad guy to meet over a gaming table.

A couple of people turn up with bottles. Kotzebue's a damp town officially, so even though people can't buy alcohol here, it's not illegal to bring it in or possess it.

'How much you pay for that?' Bill asks a guy at the poker game, cracking open a fifth of bourbon. 'Fifty bucks, right?' he says, grinning. 'Maybe more, huh?'

He studies the other players as they sit down; he's learnt you can tell a lot about your opponents before the first card is dealt. Turns out the player he has to watch is Irene, the lady shacked up with the guy who owns this place. He keeps an eye on the zipped pockets of her down vest to make sure she's not slipping cards into the pack. Bill doesn't trust the friendly, happy Eskimo thing they're all signed up to in this town, same as Shishmaref. All of Cliff's buddies are losers; it's the Native community show. Save it for the tourist, because it's all a crock of shit once you scratch the surface. Give any man a little, and he's gonna want more if he can get it – it's only natural. Cliff can take his chances, but Bill'd rather live in the real world. They got a regular poker game going now up in Prudhoe Bay, mostly Eskimos, except once in a while one of the white guys from Personnel joins in. One game, the head of Catering sat down and played a couple of hands, but no one could relax and no one felt comfortable about fleecing him the way they knew they could.

Cliff's not up to his usual game level tonight. He's making stupid mistakes, keeps glancing over at Tammy, sitting by herself in a corner of the room watching the TV that's suspended from the ceiling. Bill doesn't see why Cliff has to keep looking at her.

'Call it, Cliff,' he says. 'What you waiting for – relocation?'

Cliff throws his cards down. 'I'm out.'

'Why don't you leave her here, Bill?' Cliff had suggested before they left Shishmaref. 'With Minnie. She'll keep an eye on the kids.'

'I came to *see* her, aren't I?' Bill said. 'She's my daughter. I don't wanna leave her behind.'

Pretty soon the Eskimos not so used to their drink are getting plastered, and Bill starts gaining an advantage even though he's drinking twice as much as anybody else. Cliff clears away Bill's glass about midnight, so he switches to straight out of the bottle. Like so often, he gets the feeling – about halfway up the buzz – that he'd like to go flying. That he'd like to be in a plane right about now, flying low at twilight over a field of deep snow, or circling a range of summer tundra, hot as thunder, colours like gobs spat up in your eye.

'Bill?' says Cliff.

'Anyone here know how to fly a plane?' Bill asks, looking round the table. No one answers; they're all studying their cards. Bill picks up two blue chips, scooping them up with the backs of two fingers and ferrying them over that way, balanced. 'I'm gonna see you there, Irene.'

At about two in the morning, Cliff pushes his chair back from the table and goes over to Tammy. Bill glances over, holding his cards tight against his chest. The last two games have gone against him and he knows that somebody's cheating. 'Where?' he hears Tammy ask.

'Ed Lyon's place.' Cliff's deep voice takes up too much space in the room. Bill twists his mouth, grimacing at the sound of it.

'He's the basketball coach in town – out on an away game. It's a nice place, no problem. Want me to walk you over?'

Tammy is getting up now, rubbing her eyes. Bill can remember her doing that when she was a little runt, rubbing her eyes, standing on the carpet in the hallway outside the upstairs bathroom, in her Snoopy pyjamas. He reaches for the bottle and notices the wet ring it's left on the table.

'Tam?' he calls. 'You all right? What you doing?'

'I'm taking her over to Ed's place,' Cliff answers.

'Raise you fifty,' says Irene. Her flat cheeks are dry and red. Bill doesn't like the way she grins all the time. There's a wad of dollars sitting on a plastic saucer next to one of her fat hands. All these Bush women got these fat hands, skin so dry and flaky it's like looking at some kind of skin disease. Beth doesn't have hands like that; hers are smaller, thin-fingered, smooth and waxy like white skin.

'Bill, I'm taking her back, OK? I'm walking Tammy over to Ed's.'

Why Cliff is talking like he can't hear him, Bill doesn't know. 'No problem,' he says and gestures to the guy dealing that he wants another card.

The noise of the heater over the door is bugging him. He runs a hand across the small of his back where his shirt is damp and pulls his shirttails out of his pants. He's lost track of where they are with the bets. He looks up at the sound of the front door being pulled open; he thought they had left already.

'Behave yourself there, Cliff,' he says, laughing and elbowing the guy sitting next to him – stupid loser hasn't had a winning hand all night. 'That's my little girl you got there.'

'Ready to go?' Luke yells over the sound of the engine.

He's driven up on a gleaming Ski-doo; there's not a scratch on the bright yellow paintwork, the red flame patterns breaking over the front and down the sides, the neon yellow runners.

He hands Tammy a pair of tinted goggles like the ones he is wearing. It's a bright day, sun bouncing off the snow like a super-ball out of control.

She climbs on.

'I like to go pretty fast. Just holler if you're freaked.'

Tammy can't hear him very well with her parka hood up over her sweatshirt and hat. 'Where are we going?' she yells back.

'Out there.' Luke points towards the sea. 'All the way to Russia, if you want!'

'Cliff says the ice is thinning already.'

Luke turns his head her way and revs up the engine. 'Don't worry!'

She puts her arms around his waist. Though she's aware of the warmth coming off Luke's body, and the occasional pull of his muscles as he ploughs the machine through a crest of snow, once they get going Tammy feels like she is alone. Her head-wear muffles sound. Away from the land, the cold feels different: solid, thick. She feels it pressing against her. She's known temperatures this low before but never this clean, this pure. They pass a large pool of sea water, out in the middle of the ice. She has forgotten – momentarily – that they are not on solid ground. After about half an hour, Luke stops the machine and they climb off. She pulls back her parka hood and takes off her goggles, just to see what it will feel like; the temperature closes in on her like a hot iron pressing against her cheeks until they burn. This is good cold.

There isn't anything to look at. Not a single landmark any-where, 360 degrees around. Sun high in the sky, small and fierce.

'How do you know where we are?' she asks.

Luke points to a compass stuck to the inside of the Ski-doo windshield. 'No problem. I know my way around.'

Their voices sound strange, like they shouldn't be talking.

Luke lifts up a section of the snowmobile seat and brings out a thermos. 'Want something to drink? It's hot.'

She nods. He hands her the plastic cup, steam rising off it, and she takes a sip. It's straight alcohol.

'Like it?' he asks, grinning.

She hands back the cup without answering and walks away across the ice.

'Want some more?' Luke calls after her.

Fifty feet away from the snow machine, she turns a slow full circle, shading her eyes from the glare of the snow, the goggles Luke's lent her hanging loose round her neck. She calls back to him. 'Do you ever get any polar bears around here?'

Luke is leaning against the snowmobile, watching her. He's put away the thermos. 'Not so much,' he calls back. 'Pilot saw one last month, about thirty miles off the coast – that's nearer than they usually come.'

She turns another complete circle. 'None today,' she says in a quiet voice.

Luke is walking over, slowly. He's got a rifle in one hand. 'They have to be major hungry to come this close to shore.'

'Are we close to shore?'

He shrugs. 'Ten miles.'

She keeps turning round and round on her own axis and when she comes full circle for the fourth or fifth time Luke stops her with his hand.

'You'll get dizzy,' he says.

She's breathing deeply. The cold air feels right in her lungs. This is the best she's felt in a long time.

Luke leans the rifle against the side of his legs so it's resting on the snow, the thin barrel pointing towards the sky. He looks ahead at the horizon, barely visible. 'I used to drink a lot – couple a years ago,' he says, his face serious.

Tammy turns her head. She squints, not sure what he wants.

'But I don't any more.'

'OK,' says Tammy, after a little while.

Luke scratches the back of his head. 'Your dad drinks a lot, huh?'

She frowns, staring down at the snow. 'Who told you that?'

'George, I guess. Sometime. I mean, it's his uncle, right? Your dad.'

Tammy looks up at Luke again. 'Right.'

'Why'd they send you to Shishmaref? D'you get into trouble back home?'

Tammy steps away from Luke and turns another circle, more slowly this time, her arms spread wide.

Luke sticks one hand in his coat pocket and hangs onto the end of the rifle with the other. 'I was just wondering, you know. People don't come here a lot by choice – not our age people, anyhow.'

'I wouldn't have come if I didn't want to.'

She starts to run across the ice, surfing across the little bumps and ridges, sliding, arms outstretched like aeroplane wings. After a little while Luke starts to run too, whooping up a noise, arms by his side, until they both skid into the same high ridge of snow, falling forward. They turn onto their backs and, cushioned by the snow, they lie with their eyes closed against the glare of the sun.

After a while Tammy reaches inside to the inner pocket of her parka and pulls out a pack of cigarettes. She has to hunch forward to get the match lit. 'I wish there were some polar bears out here,' she says, leaning back on her elbows.

Luke turns his head, squinting. 'Why?'

'I want to see one, before it's too late.'

'Too late for who?'

Tammy looks at him. She shrugs and turns away again. 'Too late for everybody.'

'How old are you anyway?'

Tammy doesn't answer.

'Can't be much more than fifteen.'

She lies back again in the snow and exhales the white smoke up into the cold air. 'Polar bears have to come ashore every summer when the ice breaks up,' she says, picking a piece of tobacco from between her lips and reciting the facts as if she is in a classroom delivering a report, 'and the break-up is happening ten to fourteen days earlier than it did twenty years ago. The bears that are coming ashore aren't fat enough yet to survive the summer without food, especially the females, and then they don't have enough milk for their cubs. They're coming to shore on average about forty pounds lighter, and it's also getting later and later before the ice re-forms and they can start hunting again.' She takes another drag of her cigarette. 'So, basically, they're dying out.'

Luke has sat up while she's been talking. 'Where'd you get all this from?'

Tammy looks at him. 'It's basic information.'

When her cigarette is finished, she extinguishes it in the snow and places the butt in the gap between the cellophane and the packet. She stands up, brushing the snow off her clothes. The snowmobile across the snow looks very small; they've run further than she realized. She jumps up and down a few times, aware of the ice underneath her.

'You getting cold?' Luke asks, standing up as well and walking towards Tammy. 'We should go back.'

When Tammy turns, he bends over and kisses her. Her arms drop to her side. When he draws back, she takes a step away, her eyes fixed on the ground. Neither one of them says anything.

Halfway back to the snowmobile, Luke stops to pick up the rifle he dropped when they began to run. 'I didn't bring you out here to try and do that,' he says.

'It's OK.'

As they're approaching Shishmaref, Luke slows down near the airstrip and points at a plane parked on the ploughed tarmac. 'State trooper plane,' he yells, over the sound of the engine. Tammy leans forward to understand him better. 'They only fly out if somebody calls 'em.'

'What do you think it is?'

He revs the engine, turning the handle with his right hand. 'Could be George, I guess.'

By the Native Store, there's a crowd gathered and a state trooper is speaking to Erik and a couple of other boys Tammy recognizes from the dance in the gym. With a tightness in her chest, she imagines the crowd opening up to reveal George in the centre.

'What's up?' Luke asks an old guy on the edge of the crowd.

The guy turns, smiling with cracked lips in a face whose skin looks like it's been stretched over a rack and dried in a cold wind. 'Buddy Cleveland.' He chuckles. 'They got him locked up in the basement, up at the church.'

'What did he do?' asks Luke.

The old man lifts a brown, age-spotted finger and points. 'Chased those boys with a machete. Chased them into the store and scared the tanik half crazy. He called the cops.'

'Tanik?' Tammy asks.

'Erik,' says Luke. 'The white guy.'

'Where's Joe and Evelyn?' he asks the old man.

'Juneau – wedding anniversary.'

Luke drives on towards Cliff's house. The fairy lights above the porch are on, strung around a pair of caribou antlers on the flat roof.

'There you go,' says Luke, turning the engine off.

'Thanks for taking me out there.' Tammy hands back the helmet and goggles. 'It was good.'

'No problem.'

He turns the machine around and heads back to the store.

Stacey is standing halfway inside the hallway closet. 'Where's the ice auger?' she is shouting as Tammy comes in. 'Dad?'

Uncle Cliff comes tumbling down from upstairs in his jeans and flannel shirt, his white hair unbrushed. 'Hey, Tammy.'

Stacey turns. 'Hi.'

'What's all the yelling for?' Cliff continues. 'What you looking for?'

'I can't find the auger.'

'What you need that for?'

'I wanna take Tammy out fishing.'

Cliff turns to look at Tammy. His face is a little damp, as if he's just been washing it. 'I thought you were out with Luke.'

Tammy coughs into her hand. 'I just got back.'

'Sure.' He nods, still looking at her. 'OK, let me look.' Stacey gets out of the way and Cliff goes into the closet, emerging a few seconds later with the auger in two pieces. 'Gotta know where to look,' he says, smiling, and hands it to Stacey. He goes into the kitchen while Stacey stuffs the rest of the gear into a dry sac, then hangs it over her shoulder.

'So do you want to go ice fishing?' she asks Tammy. 'I was gonna go with Vicky, but her mom needs her. We should get some snacks, if we're going.'

'Where are the boys?' Cliff asks when they walk into the kitchen.

'I saw Mikey playing outside, by the store,' says Tammy. 'With that friend of his.'

'Eddie,' says Stacey. 'Yeah, they went down to the store for some candy.'

The kitchen counters are crowded with stuff: microwave, coffee machine, deep-fryer, plastic containers, cookbooks, and a large tin of Crisco without a lid by the stove. Cliff has tied a striped apron around the waist of his blue jeans. He reaches into the bread bin, pulls out some pilot bread and puts some slices in the toaster. The coffee machine is gurgling, spitting out coffee in angry bursts into the glass pot below.

'Where are the sno-go keys?' asks Stacey.

With his back turned, getting down some grape jam from a cupboard, Cliff tells her to take the dogs.

'The dogs? No way! It will take too long to get them

61

harnessed, and then we'll have to watch 'em while we're fishing.'

Cliff shifts over a couple of steps and gets a knife out of a drawer. 'They'll stay with you.'

'I haven't driven the dogs in a really long time.'

'So? I know that. They need exercise.'

Stacey turns away, opening the fridge door. 'They're not *my* dogs,' she mutters.

Cliff puts the knife down. 'What d'you say there?'

Suddenly the kitchen is silent; the coffee has finished brewing.

Stacey closes the fridge door. 'Nothing,' she says.

After a few moments, Cliff speaks again, in a low voice. There's so much sadness in it. 'Why d'you talk like that? Why do you talk so selfish? Who's teaching you to talk that way?'

Stacey shifts her weight, swallowing and looking down at the floor. 'No one's teaching me. I'm sorry. I didn't mean it.'

He turns back to the counter and picks up the knife. 'If you don't mean it, why d'you say it? Take the dogs out. George isn't here, so you'll take them out. I'm taking the snowmobile up river to Minnie's old fish camp. I'll take Pete with me.'

Stacey nods. 'OK.'

Before she leaves the kitchen, she goes over to her dad and puts her arm around him, pressing her round face against his shoulder. He reaches one hand back and pats the small of her back a few times, says a few words in Inupiaq that Tammy can't understand.

THE DEAD ZONES

On Memorial Day weekend, the Polar Bear Swim takes place in Nome and Uncle Cliff asks Tammy if she wants to go along.

'There is *no* way you're making me go in that water this year, Dad,' says Stacey. 'It's like a fucking freak-show!'

'Stacey!' says Uncle Cliff, glancing over at Grandma Minnie, who's standing by the stove in a sleeveless housecoat, plump brown arms with skin as soft as tissue paper.

'She doesn't understand English swear words,' says Stacey.

'She understands more than you think. Somebody get the boys,' says Uncle Cliff. 'Food's on the table.'

Grandma Minnie smiles as she approaches the table. Her mouth folds inwards over toothless gums; the skin above her lips is scored with vertical lines, like scorings on a walnut shell. Tammy squeezes past her into the living room, where Mikey and Pete are playing basketball with a little foam ball, bucketing it into a plastic hoop and net on a pedestal. The television is on – the little set sitting on top of the huge old wooden-cabinet TV that doesn't work any more. It's blaring out some NBA game. Uncle Cliff's gun rack hangs on the wall over the sofa, five guns lined up from biggest to smallest – triple-barrelled Drielling rifle down to the .22 he uses for small game.

'Time to eat,' Tammy says, watching the cheerleaders on the

television jumping up and down on the sidelines of the court. Mikey throws the ball on the sofa.

There are two plane-loads of villagers flying down from Shishmaref to the Polar Bear Swim; it feels like a school trip. On the flight, Tammy sits beside Luke's mother, who presents her with a new aktikluq decorated with bright curly tape at the hemlines and around the hood. Luke sits a few rows back; he nods at her when he passes but he doesn't smile. Once airborne, people pass around plastic tubs of newly thawed, fermented nuktuk, the final supply from last summer's hunting season. Everyone's joking and chatting: the noise is busy and loud. It's more like a rowdy bus ride than a plane journey. As they're walking across the tarmac into the airport, Cliff puts an arm around Tammy's shoulder.

Bill is standing by the gate, wearing a hat with plastic caribou horns coming out of the top. Standing next to him is his Filipino buddy from the oil fields, Ricky, with a stupid-ass grin on his face.

'Hey, Bill,' says Uncle Cliff, his arm still resting on Tammy's shoulders. 'We didn't know you were coming.'

'Polar Bear Swim? Wouldn't miss it,' he answers, nodding his head while he gazes at Tammy. 'How you doing, honey?' he asks her.

'I'm fine,' she responds, fingering the decorative hemline of the new aktikluq she is wearing.

Sometimes the Polar Bear Swim gets postponed if the ice hasn't broken up enough and conditions are dangerous, but this year is no problem. It's a beautiful day and the Nome Rotary Club has built a bonfire on the beach to warm up all the swimmers afterwards. Hundreds of people fly into Nome every year for the event, and the beach is packed with them, like the beginning of a marathon with the water's edge as the starting line: little flat-chested girls in tight Lycra bikinis, their skin covered in goosebumps; big fat Eskimo women, fully clothed, prepared to wade in that way; middle-aged, pasty-looking white men in shorts and running shoes; and local TV news teams, hoping to catch some local, feel-good colour for the evening show, bearing giraffe-necked, fuzzy microphones and wearing newscaster outfits that make them conspicuous.

The sea is deceptive; it doesn't look cold. It's sparkling in the sunshine.

'How cold you think that water is, man?' Bill asks Ricky. He and Ricky have been in Nome since last night, hanging out at the Polar Bear.

Ricky squints and looks out over the Sound. 'Beats me. Forty? Maybe a little warmer? How long since the ice broke up?'

'Last week, I think. A couple weeks.'

Ricky turns his head, and grins stupidly at Tammy, looks her up and down. 'Been having fun out in the boonies, Tammy?'

She keeps her eyes on the sea. 'Yes.'

'You're looking like a real Eskimo now – ain't she, Bill? Look at her clothes.'

Bill glances over at Tammy. 'I got some summer clothes Mom sent you, back at the Polar Bear. Hey, you know what?' he continues, ripping off the stupid hat with the caribou horns. 'I think I'm gonna take a little swim myself this year.'

'Don't,' says Tammy.

He turns to her, half-smile frozen on his open mouth. 'What d'you say?'

'I don't think you should go in the water if you've been drinking.'

'If you've been *drinking*! Shit.' Bill laughs and Ricky laughs too. He starts unbuttoning his shirt. 'You call one beer at lunch *drinking*? Hell, most of the people in the world be drunks if that's drinking.'

The crowd falls quiet as a man wearing a bright orange apron climbs on top of the lifeguard tower in the middle of the beach. He turns to face the crowd and begins shouting through a loudspeaker. '*OK, everyone. Howdy! Welcome to the 2004 Nome Rotary Club Polar Bear Swim!!*'

There's a huge response: big cheers, people banging things and blowing on tooters.

'Maybe I should drag you in too. How 'bout it, Tam?' says Bill, putting his arm around her shoulder and pulling her tightly to him. He's stripped down to his vest now, the tattoo of a wolf spreading across his left shoulder partly visible.

'*There are a few safety issues we'd like to warn you about, folks, to make sure this remains a fun day for everyone . . .*'

'How 'bout you, Ricky? You man enough?'

'Not *fool* enough, more like, man,' says Ricky. 'No way. I like to stay warm and dry.' He nods his head and winks at Tammy.

'* . . . so please don't let any kids under five in the water. We don't want 'em getting trampled, and, remember, this water's cold! Furthermore, any women out there expecting a baby – hey, it's* happened! *– or anyone with a pre-existing heart condition, we strongly advise you – we can't* stop *you, but we strongly advise you – to watch from the sidelines. The ambulance guys are here to help but they'd rather have an afternoon off, wouldn't you, boys?*'

Another big cheer from the crowd.

Bill hands Tammy his jeans and shirt, along with his wallet and keys. He's still got his oil company ID dog tag on a chain round his neck.

'The water will be cold, Dad.'

'What you talking about, *cold*? I been out in sixty below, two or three days running. My dad and I used to fall through the ice regular, end of the season. Hasn't killed me yet.'

'*OK, everybody. When you hear the bull horn, that's the time to get going. Is everybody ready? I said, is everybody ready? Five! Four! . . .*' People are joining in with the count-down. '*Three! Two! One! Everybody . . . in!*'

Tammy holds her dad's clothes, letting people push past. They're all trying to run but they can hardly move with all the other people in front. She wonders if Luke's gone in; she'd heard him say he wasn't going to swim this year. She wonders if he has plans to see George while he's down here.

When the first wave of swimmers start coming out of the sea, talking in high-pitched voices like the sea spray they've breathed in is helium, stretching out their arms for the towels held out by waiting relatives, Tammy scans the faces, trying to identify anyone from Shishmaref. The smell of cold is coming off people's bare skin. Ricky has disappeared. She thinks she spots Stacey standing near the bonfire, round the other side in the heat and smoke, so she heads over that way, still holding onto her dad's clothes. It's slow going, getting through the tangled-up crowd of people, bent over with cold, gasping and laughing.

Hearing someone shouting her name, she turns around but the sound stops and she can't tell where it came from.

'Tammy!' The call is nearer now; Stacey grabs her shoulder. She's breathing fast.

'Did you go in?' Tammy asks, but as she asks she notices Stacey's clothes aren't wet.

'It's your dad,' says Stacey.

They walk across the beach, and Luke is suddenly there as well, falling into step beside Tammy. She can't see through all the bodies, but as they get closer a lot of people are looking in the same direction and there's a little semicircle of people standing near the First Aid vehicles. The first thing she recognizes is Uncle Cliff's hairy back, leaning over somebody. He's on his knees, still in his wet shorts, a few drops of water about to run down the back of his neck. He should have a blanket covering him, she thinks. There's a paramedic on the other side of Tammy's dad, pumping at his chest.

Uncle Cliff has his eyes closed and he's repeating something over and over, in Inupiaq.

'What's he saying?' Tammy asks Luke.

'It's a prayer,' Stacey answers.

At the sound of their voices, Uncle Cliff opens his eyes. 'Tammy,' he says, reaching out for her hand. Tammy can't understand why he's so upset. There are tears in his eyes. 'I saw him going under. Crazy kumaq – he should never go in the water. Even when he was a kid, he never could take it.'

Tammy stands at her dad's feet, watching the paramedic trying to revive him. Suddenly he retches and starts to cough. The paramedic turns him over into the recovery position and a little green fluid seeps out of the corner of his mouth. He still hasn't opened his eyes.

'We'll need to take him to the clinic,' says the ambulance man. His co-worker goes to fetch a stretcher. 'Anyone coming with us?'

Cliff looks at Tammy and the paramedic turns his head to her.

'I'll come. He's my dad.' She wonders what happened to Ricky; he's nowhere around. 'What's wrong with him?'

'Come on,' the paramedic says. 'You can ride in the ambulance.'

Bill opens his eyes. There's a ceiling above him. He breathes in and out, twice, then turns his head. Tammy is dozing on a chair in the corner of the room. He watches her for a while; he doesn't think she is really asleep, but when she doesn't move after a couple of minutes, he looks up at the ceiling again. There's a sound, bugging him, like the rasping of sled runners over gritty snow, sled runners going back and forth over the same rut. Eventually he realizes it's the sound of his own breathing.

Tammy is watching the morning news.

'For the second time in three years,' reads the newscaster, 'an

68

oceanic dead zone has been detected off the coast of Oregon. Falling levels of dissolved oxygen in the water have created what scientists call a "hypoxic zone" incapable of supporting marine life. Believed to be the immediate cause is a huge influx of cold water, low in oxygen and high in nutrients, which causes an algae bloom responsible for absorbing the last of the oxygen in the water. The larger cause may be a much more widespread, global warming-induced change in Pacific Ocean circulation. Here's science editor Jane Lubbock with more on the subject.'

On screen now is a young female reporter, standing on a dockside overlooking an ocean view. She is wearing a lime-green dress, and the breeze is disturbing her hair.

Tammy looks at her dad. He's lying flat on his back, mouth slightly open. About an hour ago a nurse had come in and fitted an oxygen mask round his face, then changed the bag on his IV. He'd woken up once in the night, Tammy had told her, just for a little while.

Beth arrives at seven a.m., with Jess. Uncle Cliff picks them up at the airport and brings them straight to the clinic, then goes to arrange a motel room.

'Did you get those clothes I sent?' Beth says to Tammy, first thing.

'Not before Dad drowned, no,' she replies.

Beth looks ragged. The blonde hair colour she puts on her hair once a month is due for a touch-up; there's a green thread sticking out of the buttonhole on her pants, where the button's giving way. She approaches the bed, arms hanging by her side. There are tubes going up Bill's nose and another one connected to the back of his hand. The nurses have put him in a pair of pyjamas that make him look like a stranger. Sitting on the bedside table is the hat with the caribou horns he'd been wearing on the beach. Beth stares down at him.

'What was he thinking? Going into that freezing water.' She turns to Tammy. 'Is he going to need an operation?'

69

'*I* don't know,' Tammy responds.

Beth stares at her for a few seconds and then glances up at the television, still on CNN. She pulls up a chair to the bedside and sits down. 'You want to go have breakfast or something?' she says to Tammy. 'You been here all night.'

When Tammy is passing through the lobby, she spots Luke sitting in a chair by the main exit doors to the hospital, still wearing the clothes he'd had on at the beach.

'Hey,' he says, jumping out of his chair as soon as he sees her. 'How's your dad?'

'What are you doing here?'

He shrugs. The skin on his face is creased, like he's been sleeping rough. 'Thought I'd stick around. You hungry?'

She nods.

'I know a good place.'

The Glue Pot, the same place where Tammy had come to eat the first time she was in Nome, looks different in daylight. It's painted blue, a bright, rich shade coming away in damp patches. Two large windows look out onto the sunlit road, the passing cars and trucks reflected in the glass.

They walk in, choose a booth in the back corner of a side extension, and halfway through breakfast Tammy tells Luke what she knows.

'What do you mean?' says Luke, wiping some bacon grease from his lips.

'I know George is in Nome. I ran into him, last time I was here.'

He stares at her for a second, still smiling. Then the smile vanishes, he glances around at the tables near by, then looks back at Tammy. 'So what do you want me to say?'

'Are you planning on seeing him? Before you go back?'

He runs a finger through the syrup left on his plate. 'Maybe.'

'I want to come with you if you do.'

Luke pushes his plate away and leans back against the banquette. 'How come you haven't told anyone?'

70

'I promised him I wouldn't.'

The waitress comes over and takes away Luke's empty plate. He screws up the paper napkin she's left behind.

'Is there something going on between you two?' he asks.

Tammy sits up straight, drawing away from Luke. 'What do you mean? He's my cousin.'

Luke shrugs. 'Doesn't stop some people.'

Tammy slides out of the booth, reaching in her back pocket for some money and throwing it on the table.

'Where are you going?' says Luke, grabbing her arm, but she twists it free.

Outside in the car park the remaining patches of snow are dirty, veined through with exhaust fumes and tar and all the other shit that comes with the territory. Tammy wishes she had her break-up boots but they're in Fairbanks. She strides back to the clinic through the slushy streets.

Luke catches up as she's waiting for a line of cars to pass before she crosses the street in front of the clinic. 'George isn't in Nome any more,' he tells her, breathing fast.

'I don't care.'

She takes a step forward off the kerb, dangerously near the back end of the last car to pass. When she reaches the doors of the clinic, she leans against them instead of going in, holding onto the metal handle and putting her cheek against the cold plate glass.

'You OK?' asks Luke, catching up again.

Tammy nods, her eyes closed, but she feels so heavy, like her body's been packed with wet snow. She forces herself to stand up straight, releasing the door handle. Moving out of the way of somebody else entering the clinic, she turns to face Luke. 'Where is he?'

'He's staying about twenty miles out, on the Nome–Teller road.'

Through the glass doors, both of them watch two orderlies pushing a stretcher past the reception desk; there's a thin old lady on it, lying flat, her eyes closed. Tammy raises her hands to her face, covering her mouth and chin.

'I want to see him,' she says, through her fingers.

A few hours later, having told her mother she is going back to the motel to get some sleep, Tammy is waiting on some steps leading up from the sidewalk in front of a falling-down, clapboard establishment called the House of Bargains. The steps, two of them, concrete, remind her of the steps up to the loading dock at Kroger's, where she likes to sit and smoke, round the side of the store. The House of Bargains, past its sell-by date, is on a lot all by itself, where the long grass is beginning to straighten up again in the spreading spaces between snow patches. Its weathered boards, at one time probably bright pink, have faded in the Nome winters to a salmon grey. She takes up her habitual position, bringing her knees in close to her chest and making a circle of her arms around them, with a lit cigarette in the hand tying the knot. She looks up and down the street, sucking smoke in between turns of her head. An old man is sitting on the dilapidated porch of the House of Bargains and he displays no embarrassment about staring. Each time she looks back, he's still staring.

'Hi,' she says to him, once. He moves his jaw slightly and looks away, only to resume his watch a few seconds later. They sit there together for about fifteen minutes. The sun is wet in the sky, its light turning the damp concrete of the pavement a cardboard brown.

Luke finally pulls up in a muddy white pick-up, the same logo, HTR Inc., displayed on the side of the cab. There's a middle-aged man at the wheel. Luke opens the door and gets out to offer Tammy the middle space. 'Any problems?' he asks.

She shakes her head.

'He asked for you,' her mom had commented when Tammy had got back to the clinic after breakfast. 'He woke up. I told him you were out getting something to eat.'

'Did the doctors come?'

Beth nodded. 'They want to do some tests. It's his heart. They think he had a heart attack, in the water.'

'So when are we going back to Fairbanks?'

'A couple days, I guess. But he's got some stuff in his lungs too, from the water. They're worried about him getting pneumonia.'

Tammy had laughed. 'Pneumonia? An Eskimo with pneumonia? Dad will hate that. He'll never live it down.'

Beth had stared at her, as if she didn't know who she was.

The man who's driving the HTR truck doesn't say anything the whole ride out. He's wearing a blue bandana on his head and his face is scarred with the same kind of purple-black scars that run across Uncle Cliff's face: frostbite wounds.

'This is Mr Wyatt,' says Luke, after a few miles. 'George's boss.'

'Hi,' says Tammy.

Mr Wyatt doesn't speak, just cracks the window next to him a little. Tammy notices a few beads of sweat on his forehead; his cheeks are flushed too. He looks like a Native American, but she isn't sure. It's hard to tell how old he is – anything from forty to sixty.

Outside, the landscape is vacant, flat, its monotony broken up by the occasional piece of old mining machinery half emerging from under the receding snow, a sour yellow sky, empty horizon eventually bunching itself up into clumps of hills in the north. The sun is out, weakly beating through the cold. Tammy can see clumps of reindeer grazing far away across the tundra, but mostly she stares ahead at the grey tarmac of the road. At one point in the journey, Luke shifts his leg and leaves it where it re-settles, pressed up against hers. Presently, they turn down an unmarked gravel road that goes on for about two miles and ends in a clearing in front of a ramshackle cabin leaning in on itself, barely upright on its four walls. The felt on its roof is half torn off and hanging over the edge; the central wall sags in the middle, so much that a few of the grey, weather-worn planks have split in two in the centre, their jagged edges like the scar tissue of a puncture wound. Parked next to the cabin, on a flat area of gravel dotted with scraggy tundra plants poking through, is a very large container truck, with the same HTR logo on the side.

Mr Wyatt, turning off the ignition, speaks for the first time. 'Everybody out!' His voice is husky and high-pitched. He chuckles, kicks open the cab door and jumps down with a sudden burst of energy Tammy hasn't expected. Luke gets out too. He and Wyatt drop the back of the truck and start to unload some stuff, while she wanders over to the miner's cabin. The air smells of melting snow and diesel exhaust, with far away something sweeter – flowers on the tundra, on the verge of exploding into bloom.

'Hello?' she says, as she bends her head to go through the slanted cabin door.

There's no sign of life. An old iron stove squats in the middle of the floor, both of its stove lids missing, rust caked along the seams of its legs. In the corner of a room a single iron bed is tipped up on its side, springs broken, dirty mattress folded over on itself. The afternoon sunshine is breaking through the gap in the wall where the sagging planks have split in two. It doesn't look like anyone's living here.

Luke walks in.

'No one here,' she tells him.

'Nope. Guess not,' he says.

'What about the truck?'

'No one there. Mr Wyatt's doing some repairs on it.'

She looks through a sagging window frame – through a large hole in the murky pane of glass – back to where the vehicles are parked. Mr Wyatt is disappearing into the big truck's container, slamming the double doors behind him.

'So where d'you think he is?'

'I don't know. Hunting, maybe? Out hiking – he likes getting out.'

She turns to face Luke. 'How does he contact you?'

'Computer.'

'Email?'

'Sure.'

With the toe of his boot, Luke flips over a squashed plastic bottle that's lying on the cabin floor. Its green label has mostly disintegrated. She stares through the window in the opposite wall. The melting snow on the tundra has formed itself into a series of angular shelves, like miniature sea cliffs with thick forests of wet, mustard-coloured vegetation down below. She can't make Luke take her to where George is.

'What are you gonna do?' asks Luke. 'Are you coming back to Shishmaref?'

Tammy shakes her head. 'Probably not. My dad has to have an operation, in Fairbanks. My mom will probably want me home.'

Luke stamps down on the green plastic bottle, squashing it flat. 'What's wrong with your dad?' he asks, a few moments later.

'He had a heart attack.'

'Too bad.' He looks up at her, squinting, his mouth pulled up in a grimace. 'It's too bad,' he says one more time.

Uncle Cliff arranges with Kenny at the Polar Bear Saloon so Beth can use a vehicle while they're in Nome, if they need to for any reason. Tammy spends the next day down at the beach with Jessica. It's June, and when the sun's out it can feel warm. Jess loves to play on the hard, packed sand with the sea looking blue and pleasant, like it did on the day of the Swim. One day they see a fog-bow, shimmering way out, over the thawing sea ice. This time of year all the tourists migrate up from the Lower 48, sporty-adventure types, with their brand-new fishing equipment and spotless tents from L. L. Bean. They watch Jess and Tammy playing on the beach, pleasant smiles pasted onto their faces as if they're walking past a museum exhibit –

sometimes the really enthusiastic ones ask if it's OK to take photographs. Jess takes after Bill more than Beth – she looks like a bona-fide Eskimo baby, with her flat eyes and skin browned by the sun. She's still cute, like a cartoon character. There's a lot of amateur gold mining on the beach, too. Some of the dredges are state-of-the-art – miniature gold mines bobbing around fifty feet offshore on huge flotation devices – but Tammy and Jess also trip over the guy ropes of dirty canvas tents pitched by die-hard goldaholics who don't have the money for high-tech dredging. These people sit in their tents day and night under the near twenty-four-hour sun, sifting through layers of sand, foot by foot, inch by inch.

When her mom gets back from the clinic, Tammy heads to the public library to read the papers. She tells her mom that she needs to keep up with her schoolwork.

When Beth asks Tammy what it was like staying on Shishmaref, Tammy tells her she liked it.

Beth laughs. 'Yeah. For a couple weeks, maybe,' she says.

'I don't know why you're shocked,' Tammy says two mornings later in their hotel room when her mom is getting ready to go. 'It's a mystery something like this didn't happen months ago.'

'Something like what?'

'Dad having an accident.'

'What does that mean?'

'It means he was drunk when he went in the sea.'

Her mom bends down and picks up off the floor a paper bag from the burger place they'd been to the night before. She scrunches it up in her hand. 'You're making a big deal out of nothing. How come no one else is worrying?'

'Because everyone else figures you're embarrassed enough about it already. Uncle Cliff worries – you can see it in his face.'

'Your Uncle Cliff is too good to be true.'

'What does *that* mean?'

'It means he should mind his own business.'

Beth goes to fetch her coat from the chair, stepping over Jess, who's making a bee-line crawl to a toy she wants across the room. 'Don't let her get dirty like yesterday,' she says as she leaves.

Later on that day, eating dinner in the café on the ground floor of the clinic, Beth is pushing around the food on her plate. Her eyes are bloodshot – those blue eyes that had always fascinated Tammy when she was little because they were like Disney princess eyes, so different from her own – and she suddenly looks up and asks her daughter what exactly it is that Tammy finds so great about Shishmaref. Jess is laid out on the booth bench next to Tammy, asleep after a whole day outside, coat unzipped and pulled open to give her some air.

'People take care of each other,' she says, after some thought.

Beth drops her fork onto the plate and the noise makes a lady at a nearby table look round. 'And what do *I* do? I spend my *whole* life taking care of . . . Jesus, you think I work for kicks?'

Tammy shakes her head, looking down at her plate. 'No.'

'*Jesus*,' Beth repeats, lighting a cigarette.

A few minutes later, when the plates have been cleared away, and Beth has ordered some coffee, Tammy tries again. 'They take things seriously.'

'What?' says Beth.

'On Shishmaref.'

Beth snorts. 'Oh, yeah, right,' she says, closing her eyes and pressing a hand against them, which smears her mascara.

Tammy can see a line on the side of her jaw where she's forgotten to blend in her makeup. She looks down at Jess next to her on the seat. She lays a hand on Jess's belly. It's rising and falling. 'You know what I was thinking about yesterday?' she says.

'What?' says her mom, sighing and opening her eyes again.

'The caribou.'

Beth's fingers tense. She brings them down from her face and lays them carefully on the table, palms down. 'What caribou?' she says.

Tammy shrugs and takes a drink of water. 'All of them. The ones up north. On the slope. This past winter, they cut up their legs on the weird icy snow, because of all the rain out of season. That kind of snow, when it rains, they drop right through – it can't take their weight – so when they try and walk their legs get split open by these lacerations.'

Beth is staring at Tammy, her head tilted to one side, eyebrows slightly raised. After a while, she moves. 'Let's go,' she says, picking up the bill.

'What do you do all day?' Bill asks, when they are alone.

Tammy won't look at him. 'Not much. Hanging out with Jess.'

'Where?'

'On the shore.'

'Lots of people around?'

'Some.'

'Tourists?'

Tammy nods.

'Mom says you go to the library.'

'Sometimes.'

'Why d'you do that?'

'So I can do my schoolwork. I don't want to be behind next year.'

Bill stares at Tammy for a few moments, then he turns his head. 'What's the motel like?'

'It's OK.'

A few seconds later, without warning, he starts bawling again. The feeling is like being sick, a sort of low-grade blue nausea every hour or so and there's nothing he can do about it. The nurses say it's just a side effect from the drugs. He hasn't cried that he can remember since he was a little kid in the

78

Bureau boarding-school. He grabs for Tammy's hand, like he's drowning, and she sits there, letting him hold it, her head turned away as if he smells bad. His eyes roll, trying to find something to look at, something he can rest on. The curve of his beer belly, making a little foothill under the yellow blankets, is quaking.

'Anybody say they want to die,' he sobs, 'don't know what they're talking about.'

'You'll get better,' says Tammy, with no emotion in her voice.

'Tell me something,' he says, a few seconds later, when he's managed to calm down.

'What do you mean?' She takes her hand away.

'Tell me about something.'

Tammy is quiet for a moment, looking down at her hands. Then she lifts her head and, in the same weird, flat voice she uses whenever she talks about this stuff, she starts to talk. 'Three people have been bitten by sharks in Texas this year, along the coast – which is a high number considering there's only been eighteen shark attacks in the twenty-five years before that.'

Tammy pauses, and when she doesn't continue Bill asks her why the shark attacks are happening, just to keep her talking. 'They think there are a lot more sharks in the waters near the coast now, because they're searching for water with more oxygen in it, away from the dead zones.'

'The what?'

Tammy opens the hands resting on her thighs. She studies her palms. 'The dead places, where there's no oxygen in the water, because of pollution and the way it's affecting the temperature of the ocean. The sharks need a better place to live.'

Bill's attention wanders off along the tube coming out of his hand, up to the bag hanging off a pole next to his bed. He watches the clear liquid dripping. Tammy is still talking but he can't listen any more. He shuts his eyes, feeling the tiredness that he tries to ignore crowding in and beating him down, again.

At the Polar Bear Saloon, when Tammy tells Kenny her mom needs to borrow the car to take Jessica to a doctor's appointment, he throws her the keys without any questions. She sits behind the steering wheel and takes a deep breath before turning the key in the ignition. Before she left Shishmaref, Stacey had given her a few lessons on a four-wheeler, up and down the dirt road by the shore. Kenny's car is just a little bigger and more enclosed. To her right is the lever marked D for Drive, P for Park, R for Reverse. She pulls down the indicator stick, and looks behind her. With her foot on the brake, she changes the gear to Drive and heads out of town, going slow.

At the old miner's cabin, nothing's changed. There's no one around. But the HTR truck is still standing like a strange dinosaur in the middle of the empty landscape. She walks around it once, all the way round. She pulls herself up by the door handle and looks inside the cab, which is empty except for a couple of maps on the passenger seat. Hanging from the side of the truck, though, she feels a vibration, a sort of low hum, which seems to be coming from the waffle-textured piece connecting the cab and the container.

Tammy lowers herself back down to the ground, walks up to the thing and puts a hand on it to test the vibration; it feels hot and cold at the same time, like it might burn her with cold, and she quickly pulls her hand back. Something is switched on, that's certain. Drifting down to the back of the container again, she suddenly gets a whiff of the sea, a hint of fish and salt in the breeze, as if the wind that has picked up is coming off the water to the west. She knocks on the back doors. At first there's no answer. She shivers and, as she does, one of the handles on the big back doors slots downwards and the heavy door is pushed outwards, cracked open a few inches. A figure appears in the small gap.

'George?' She takes a step away from the truck. 'It's Tammy.'

George opens the door a little bit wider, puts a hand up to shade his eyes from the sunlight and leans out so his face is in the open air. He looks at her. 'What are you doing here? Is anyone else with you?'

'No.'

'How'd you get out here?'

'I drove.'

George looks over at Kenny's car, and then back at Tammy. 'Hold on.'

He disappears back inside the truck for a moment, then re-emerges, jumping down onto the ground and slamming the doors behind him. George is dressed in full Eskimo gear, wolverine-skin parka with wolverine fur round the hood, whitish-grey sealskin leggings, mukluks, even wolf-skin gloves. He's like a Native exhibit come to life. In the sunshine, he strips off the parka to reveal a bright blue ugligluk over a plain white long-sleeved T-shirt.

He walks a circle around Kenny's car. 'How old are you?' he asks.

'Sixteen.'

George stops moving. 'You're not.'

Tammy smiles, trying not to. 'No. I'm not.'

To her surprise, George smiles too, though he turns his face away so she nearly misses it.

'How did you know I was here?' he asks.

'Luke brought me here – about a week ago. But you weren't here.'

George frowns. 'Luke? When?'

'Eight days ago. We came with Mr Wyatt. They brought out some stuff. And Wyatt fixed your truck.'

He continues to stare at her for a few moments, then he nods. 'I wasn't here . . . Has something happened?' he asks.

'My dad's in hospital, in Nome. He had a heart attack.'

George's eyebrows rise. 'I'm sorry.'

'He's OK.'

'So that's why you're in Nome.'

'Yeah.'

'And you drove out here all by yourself?'

'I told you.'

Another faint ghost of a smile passes across his face.

The same breeze comes up, with the smell of the sea in it, and George glances back at the doors of the truck. He flexes his hands, encased in the wolf-skin gloves. For the first time, the idea comes into Tammy's mind that maybe someone else is in the truck, someone George doesn't want her to meet. Maybe he's got a girl in there, living with him inside the truck, seven months pregnant.

'Are you still working for the trucking company?' she asks.

'Sure,' he answers, dismissing the question. He stands there on the gravel, still and silent, legs in a wide stance, frowning slightly as if she's set him a riddle he can't solve. 'Do you want to come in?'

Tammy looks around. 'Come in where?'

He nods towards the truck doors.

'Oh, sure. OK.'

George puts his parka back on, zipping it right up and pulling the hood tight. Then he opens both truck doors, jumps up onto the ledge and leans over to give her a hand. He stops, arm still outstretched, frowning again. 'You got anything warmer to put on? In the car?' he asks. 'It's cold inside – refrigerated.'

Tammy looks down at her clothes. 'No,' she says.

'I'll lend you something.'

George's hand grips hers; he pulls her into the truck fast and slams the heavy doors again behind them, shutting out the daylight, as if he wants to do it as fast as he can. It's freezing inside the truck; Tammy's breath comes out in foggy exhalations. She's surprised to step onto a surface like snow, and it takes her eyes a few moments to adjust to the darkness. Standing in the centre of the container, its curved walls lit up from the inside so it's glowing a sort of translucent, pale blue – the seams of each block brighter than the centres – is an igloo. Its walls are glistening, so they look like they're wet, but she somehow knows if she reaches out a hand to touch them they'll be solid, dry, very cold. It's a large edifice, taller than she is, reaching at the uppermost height of its dome to the roof of the truck container. All around her, the walls, the floor and the ceiling of the truck are also tightly packed with snow, and there's a sort of misty fog hovering in the upper air. Directly in front of her is the entrance tunnel to the igloo.

'God,' says Tammy.

George has ducked around the igloo into an unlit corner at the back of the truck and he comes back with a parka, its ruff white round the edges then black and brown on the inside. He hands it to her and she puts it on, though it's far too big.

'It's so cold.'

George nods. 'Twenty below. It's warmer inside the igloo.'

'What is it doing here?'

'What do you mean?'

'Where did it come from?'

'I built it.' He gets down on all fours and climbs into the entrance. 'Follow me.'

After a few seconds, he emerges in the centre of the dome. From outside, she can see his shadow, tall and still, waiting for her to follow. He is standing as if he can see her through the thick walls, as if he is looking straight at her and can see her expression. Inside the tunnel the walls are glistening, the ice catching the light of candles George has placed in little niches carved out along the way. Reaching the centre, the first thing she feels is the change of temperature; it must be nearly twenty degrees warmer. George has taken off his parka. In the corner of the room on a ledge of snow is a saucer filled with oil, the wick in the centre of it burning with a steady flame, and, rigged up above it, a tin saucepan. On the floor, scattered about are plastic tubs full of meat and jagged, knife-like pieces of frozen-solid fish. At the far end of the space, a low platform is carved out in snow; it's covered by a blue waterproof mat, with a sleeping bag laid on top of that, along with some other blankets and a caribou fur. Near the head of the sleeping bag, pinioned into the snow itself is a wall thermometer, the mercury hovering at about 32°.

'Why doesn't it melt?' Tammy asks.

George is standing by the saucepan over the oil flame. 'The snow's been seasoned. You warm it up so the insides of the blocks melt, then you let the cold air in again and the snow freezes into ice. You keep melting and refreezing until you've turned the snow blocks into ice blocks, from the inside out. There's a hole up there – see?' He points with a knife to a little hole the size of a ski-pole basket, right above the stove. 'That keeps the ventilation going.'

'But that just leads to the truck.'

'There's a hole in the truck too, in the ceiling. The stove-pipe goes from this hole straight to the outside.'

'Where did you learn to do this? From your dad?'

George shakes his head. 'Inupiats don't make igloos. Do you want something to drink?' He goes over to a sleeping bag that's folded up in a pile at the end of the low platform and takes out a bottle of water from inside it. He puts the saucepan over the flame, pours a little water into it, then leans down, scoops up some snow from the floor and adds the snow to the water. 'I'll make some coffee. OK?'

Tammy nods and looks down at her feet. The shoes she has on are lightweight, canvas tennis shoes. They look out of place; she bends down and takes them off. She places them neatly by the entrance to the tunnel and bends down to remove her socks. 'Where'd you get all the snow from?' she asks.

'Outside. I built it in March.' He stares at Tammy's bare feet.

'I want to feel it,' she says.

'It's dangerous. You'll get cold.' He kneels down and pulls

back a little piece of plywood that's lodged in the snow at ground level. Behind, there's a mini-larder with rows of tins and zip-loc bags. 'You're shivering already.'

'I'm fine.'

'Get under one of those sleeping bags. No sense in getting cold.'

In her bare feet, she walks over to the sleeping platform and climbs up. With her legs hanging over the edge, she carefully dries her feet on a blanket and then places the blanket over her legs. Along the wall above the sleeping platform, George has carved more of the niches with candles set into them. The coffee he brings is black and oily and way too strong for Tammy, but the harsh taste of it on her tongue makes sense. She imagines its blackness going down into her insides, like it can be seen through a heat-sensitive camera, standing out in the middle of all this white.

George leans back against the edge of the sleeping platform, a few inches away from where her legs are hanging over. 'In Mexico,' he says, 'poor people steal these refrigerated trucks and live in them. Like air-conditioned trailers, to get away from the heat. Wyatt told me.'

From where she is, Tammy can see the hollow in his throat, between the collar-bones. A few delicate black hairs are visible above the neck of his white T-shirt. The stubble on his chin is thick – must be a few days' worth.

'What do you do all day?' she asks. 'In here.'

George looks at her. 'Who wants to know?'

Tammy takes a sip of her coffee.

'How about you?' asks George.

'What?'

'What do *you* do all day?'

She thinks about it. 'Not much.'

'Why were you staying on Shishmaref?'

Tammy hesitates. 'I needed a break,' she says.

'From doing not much,' says George. 'Do you go to school?'

'No.'

'Why not?'

She pulls the blanket further up her body and strokes the fabric with one hand. 'I stopped.'

He takes her empty cup away and puts it in the corner by the stove. He walks back over and leans against the edge of the sleeping platform again, his legs, long like Uncle Cliff's, on a straight incline.

'It's quiet in here,' says Tam, after a minute or so. 'You can't hear the engine.'

'Sometimes you do.'

'Has Luke seen inside here?'

George nods. His reindeer leggings are wet where they've been leaning against the snow. Some of his hair has come loose from its ponytail and is hanging down over his cheek. Tammy turns her head. Cramponed into the wall to the right of her is a kind of chart, protected in a waterproof casing. She looks at it more closely and sees it's a sort of Inupiaq calendar, circular, based on the moons. *May*, it reads: *'the moon when rivers flow'*. *June*: *'the moon when animals give birth'*.

'Don't you miss things?' she asks.

George is looking down at the floor. 'Not much. I don't think about it that way.' A few moments later he adds: 'I'd like to show Dad this.'

'He'd like it.' Tammy strokes her fingers back and forth on the blanket over her knees.

'How is he?'

'He says you're not dead.' George turns his head. 'Because he would have felt your spirit pass if you were.'

George nods, and Tammy's not sure if the nod means that he believes that too, or if it just means he understands Cliff would think that way.

'Could you bring me my shoes?' she asks, folding up the blanket and laying it carefully on the sleeping platform, behind George. 'Do you sleep here?'

George hands her the shoes. 'Yes.'

'It's not too cold?'

He shakes his head.

'I should probably get back to town. It's not my car.'

She rubs her hands together and George reaches out for them, bringing them close to his mouth and blowing. His breath is warm and, if such a thing were possible, it feels sweet.

'Come back,' he says. He drops her hands. 'If you want to.'

Tammy reaches out and with one finger tucks back a strand of the black hair that's hanging in front of his face. She expects it to feel rough, but it's soft and cool. 'OK,' she says.

When she steps outside, the temperature, the light, feels obscene. George has stayed in the igloo and she likes thinking of him inside that white as she carefully drives back into Nome.

THE HABITATS

All week she holds the memory of the igloo inside her, like a heat sink at the back of a refrigerator, keeping her cool. At lunchtime the day after meeting George, she goes to the hospital with Jess and her dad smells something different about her right away. He sits up on his elbows, the toast crumbs from a club sandwich falling down his pyjama front.

'You're going to pull out your IV, Dad.'

He leans towards her and she concentrates on the faded green stripes of his pyjama top. 'What were you doing yesterday? You didn't come. Mom said she didn't see you most of the day.'

'I didn't feel good. I went to the library.'

There's a plastic bag on the floor near the chair where she's sitting, with a six-pack of beer inside. 'Where'd these come from?' asks Tammy, pointing.

He looks at the bag. 'Your mom. They won't let me drink them, though. Waddaya mean, you didn't feel good?'

She looks him square in the face. 'Wrong time of the month.'

Bill pulls his head back, grunts and switches on the remote. ESPN. There's a baseball game going, and every so often he says the name of a player as they come up to bat. Tammy picks up a newspaper off the floor and starts to read.

'Don't think you're getting away with nothing,' says her dad, about twenty minutes later.

'What?' She's been reading about floods in South America.

Something catches in Bill's throat and he clears it with a lot of effort, coughing and swallowing before he can speak again. 'Me being out of action, in this hospital here – it won't be lasting much longer.'

'Uh-huh.' She still has the newspaper in front of her face. 'So when are they sending you home?'

'Couple of days. When the chest X-ray's clear.'

Tammy has noticed that he does look a little better today. She can hear him breathing; he's watching her. She puts down the paper and closes her eyes. The frogs. The amphibians. Salamanders, newts, toads, dying mysteriously all over the world. She tries to concentrate on their names, but she finds she is getting a headache. Missouri's hellbender vanishing from Ozark streams. Gastric breeding frogs in Australia. Chinese crocodile newt. Fleischmann's glass frogs and the golden toad in Costa Rica. The scientists think it might be greater ultraviolet light exposure from a thinning ozone layer, but some are just disappearing with no apparent cause, in presumed protected environments.

'What?' he says. 'What did you say?'

She opens her eyes and he's squinting at her, shading his eyes with one hand like she's a bright light he's looking into. 'I didn't say anything.'

'Come over here where I can see you.'

Tammy slowly shakes her head. Neither one of them breaks the eye contact between them, Bill straining his neck forward away from the pillows. Without expecting it, they are suddenly at a standstill.

'Crazy,' her dad says finally, falling back against the pillows and returning to the baseball highlights. 'Where'd I get such a fucking crazy daughter?'

'How are we doing, Mr Ongtowasruk?' the nurse asks as she walks into the room.

Tammy stands up.

'Hi there,' says the nurse.

Tammy lifts a hand. 'Hi. OK, Dad,' she says in a pleasant voice. 'I'm gonna go find Mom. You take care.'

He calls after her as she walks down the hallway, but she pretends she doesn't hear.

'Your sister sick again?' says Kenny. He's serving a customer but he leans back and gets the car keys off the hook while the beer is still rising in the glass.

'Yeah – she's got some kind of bug.'

He throws the keys onto the bar. 'Sorry to hear that.'

Tammy nods. She picks up the keys with one finger and turns to go.

'You're too young to be doing that.'

Tammy stops and slowly turns round. Kenny is smiling. He gestures for her to turn her back to him again and points to the back pocket of her jeans, where the top of a cigarette packet is showing.

When she knocks on the HTR truck doors, there's no answer. She calls a tentative hello, afraid of the sound of her own voice. She sits on the hood of Kenny's car and waits. Just as she's about to go, she spots someone, standing far off across the tundra, still and quiet on a small rise. It's George. He raises an arm and Tammy begins to walk towards him, keeping her eyes on the ground to avoid tripping over the stiff tussocks of grass.

'What's wrong?' he says when she's near enough to hear. He's holding a white cloth bag, streaked with mud, and a canvas gun case is slung over one shoulder.

'What do you mean?'

'I thought something had happened.'

Tammy reaches him, and stops. 'No,' she says. Her chest is tight; she can't breathe enough. 'Why?'

He shakes his head. 'I don't know. You didn't come for a while. I thought maybe you'd gone back to Fairbanks.' He turns and looks towards the foothills on the horizon behind him. Then he turns back, takes two sudden steps towards Tammy, stops himself, turns to the foothills again. 'I'm checking my traps. You want to come with me? Either be something or there won't.'

The air is warm, everything is moist, spongy; the vegetation is springing with colour and in between each twisted shrub or low-lying smudge of flora the earth is dark brown and grainy.

George walks a few steps ahead, one hand flexed and held slightly behind, as if he might warn her to stop any minute. 'Are you OK?' he asks.

She takes a few rapid steps to catch up. 'Yeah.'

'Your dad?'

'He's the same.'

George motions to her to stop. He listens, then kneels close to the ground, pulling Tammy down as well.

'What is it?' she whispers.

Taking her face in his hands, he looks into her eyes, but he is listening more than he is looking. His focus crosses from her left eye to her right and back again. The back of his windbreaker is sticking out where the gun bag is protruding. Tammy tries to turn her head slightly when she hears a scratching sound in the dirt, behind a small group of shrubs twenty feet away. The sound comes in short bursts, stops and starts.

'It's one of my traps,' George whispers.

'There's something caught in it.'

He nods. A deep growl, nasty, coming from the same place, makes Tammy's stomach drop.

George still has her face in his hands. One of her knees is beginning to hurt where it is pressed down against a root or branch.

'Are you OK?' he asks. 'You know what I heard?'

Tammy doesn't speak.

'This space machine some scientists have set out into space – you know what this spaceship is supposed to be doing?'

Tammy shakes her head, rubbing her lips together.

'It's chasing a comet. It's supposed to catch up with this comet and land on it, so people on earth can find out what it's made of. But to do that—' The animal suddenly screams, a high-pitched scream, making Tammy jump. 'To do that,' George repeats, 'the spaceship has to land on the nucleus of the comet, dead centre, which they think is all made up of ice. Can you picture that? Trying to land on a nucleus made of ice? Trying to land on a shooting star? Wouldn't that be hard? As big as space is?'

Tammy shifts her weight. She waits to see if he'll say more.

George is listening again. He releases her face and slowly stands, leaving one hand on her shoulder. With the other, he reaches back into the gun bag and draws out a rifle. 'Wait here,' he tells her.

Tammy nods and looks down at the ground, her fingers spread, keeping her balanced. A few seconds later, the sound of a rifle shot makes her duck. She looks up to see George alter his aim by a few centimetres and fire again. He is standing just beyond the clump of bushes. Carefully he replaces the rifle in the gun case and reaches inside his coat for a hunting knife. Then he takes a few steps forward and he kneels down close to the ground. Now Tammy can no longer see what he's doing.

'George?' she calls. She turns and looks back at the cabin. Kenny's red car is where she left it, pulled up alongside the truck.

After a little while George straightens up, spits a few times on his knife and wipes it on his leggings, then puts it back in his pocket. He walks over to Tammy, dragging the cloth bag stained across one side with blood. 'Not what I expected,' he says.

'What was it?'

'A wolverine.'

Tammy stands up, the knee that has been bothering her making her lean to one side.

'Must've been eating the rabbit that was caught in the trap,' George continues. 'I thought I smelt something when we came up – could you smell it?'

Tammy shakes her head.

'Sometimes they can get nasty if you disturb them while they're eating.'

'Isn't it a little close to town for wolverines?'

He nods.

'Are you sure it's dead?'

'Yes.'

When they get back to Kenny's car, the weather has gathered and it's starting to rain. Standing by the passenger door, they both look upwards as a flock of geese pass overhead. Drops are running down George's face.

'Do you want to go inside?' He points to the cabin instead of the truck.

'OK.'

Once inside, George takes the gun case off his shoulder, slips off his coat and offers it to her. She shakes her head. Someone has turned the iron bed on its feet again, unfolded the dirty mattress and put it back on top. The rain is coming down heavily now; it drips through holes in the cabin roof. George stands near one of the drips, cleaning under the nails of one hand with his knife.

Tammy sits down on the bed and pushes down with her hands on the damp mattress either side of her body. 'Who left this here?'

George looks up and shakes his head. 'I dunno. It was here when I got here.' His long legs are in black jeans today, with sealskin mukluks reaching halfway up his shins.

'Remember that time we played Monopoly all night in your kitchen,' Tammy says, 'when we were kids?'

George doesn't answer right away. Then after a while he nods. 'Yeah. I'd forgotten about that.'

'I just remembered it, all of a sudden.'

George walks over to the window and looks out at the rain.

'I'm sorry about your mom,' Tammy says. 'I never said anything.'

'Don't have to.' He walks over to the open door. 'A hundred years ago, two hundred, Inupiats used to die of old age and that was it. No one got cancer, or heart attacks, or all the other stuff. That's why she didn't recognize any of the symptoms.' He pauses, then: 'How old are you?' he asks, turning. The question comes suddenly, in a different tone of voice.

Tammy looks at him. 'Fourteen.'

'I keep dreaming about you,' says George.

Tammy starts to come every day to the cabin. Each time she sees him, at first there is a strong feeling of ambivalence. She wants to turn her head away as much as towards. Every time she turns onto the clearing, wheels crunching on the gravel, the door to the back of the truck is opening and George is standing in the gap. 'Did you hear me coming?' she asks. George shakes his head.

He waits for her to walk over and reaches out his bare hand to help her up. She notices a lot of tiny cuts and scrapes across the back of it, and how warm it is, even gloveless. He shuts the doors behind her. Inside, the igloo is lit up but sometimes they stay outside it while George, lit by the beams of several electric hurricane lamps laid out on the snow, finishes transferring fish from crates into large top-loading containers running along one side of the trailer.

'Your fish?' she asks.

'No. HTR – transport job.'

Tammy hadn't noticed the containers before. There are five or six of them, like the kind they use in the lock-up at Kroger's to store the big frozen turkeys. While George is occupied, she takes a walk around the circumference of the igloo. Towards the front end of the container, nearest the driver's cab, is a small graveyard of stiff animal carcasses – reindeer, ptarmigan, hare – whose blood has drained into the icy snow. Round plastic tubs are piled up near by, the meat inside identified in black magic marker: walrus, seal, whale. From far off, she hears a clatter on top of the truck roof and looks up at the ceiling, at the hole with the sectioned stovepipe end plugging it up.

George has finished his work and comes to stand next to Tammy.

'Does the rain come in?' she asks.

'Sometimes.'

'These all yours?' she asks, pointing to the corpses.

He looks around. 'Yeah.'

'What about the wolverine?'

'I sold it in Teller a couple of days ago, hide and all, when I was picking up the fish . . . Do you want to go inside?'

Once, when they emerge into the central dome, the sleeping ledge is strewn with a mass of printed paperwork, some of it loose, some in plastic zip files. George hurries over and bundles it all up, sticks it in a dry bag and then into a canvas backpack leaning against the platform. Tammy waits, at a distance, then scrambles up onto the bed and puts her legs inside one of the sleeping bags. George is lighting the wick of the oil lamp.

'What was in the package Luke sent you, the day I met you outside the warehouse?'

He blows out the match. 'Can't remember. What shape was it?'

'Long. Thin.'

He considers this, pushing his lips forward, then shrugs. 'Dunno. Could have been something for the truck. Machinery, probably. Mechanics in Nome always try and rip you off.' He looks at the flame. 'I'm running low on oil.'

'On what?'

'On seal oil. I need it to cook. And for the lights.' He puts the pan on the stove, crouches down to get a plastic tub out of the mini-larder, then dumps its contents into the pan with

95

a little water out of a thermos. 'You like reindeer stew?'

Tammy is feeling a little sick. 'Sure.' She puts a hand on her stomach. 'So this is what you live on? Whatever you kill?'

George is looking down into the pan, stirring its contents. 'Yes,' he answers. 'You don't eat fresh meat in Fairbanks?'

'No. My dad works – he doesn't have much time for hunting.'

Bill had learnt to cook in the army, on a base in West Virginia. He favoured ribs with barbecue sauce, fried chicken, inch-thick steaks. He never cooked Eskimo meat, as he called it; hated the smell of walrus and seal.

'He works up in Prudhoe Bay, right?'

'Yeah.'

'Here,' George says, walking over with the pan and handing Tammy the wooden spoon he's been using to stir.

She sits up. The chunks of meat are hot and tender. They take turns with the wooden spoon until it's all gone and George puts the empty pan on the snow next to him.

Tammy looks at George and notices he is trembling. 'What is it?' she asks.

George shakes his head and shifts his body away from her. 'Nothing.'

She picks up a blanket. 'Here, take this.'

'I'm not cold.'

'I didn't say you were.'

He glances at her and another spasm of shivers passes through him. Grabbing the blanket, he climbs onto the sleeping platform, over Tammy, who pulls up her legs to make room. He lies down next to the wall, covers himself up to the neck with the blanket and closes his eyes.

Tammy looks down at him. She wants to touch him. 'Maybe you're getting sick.'

He shakes his head, eyes still closed.

'How do you know?'

He doesn't answer; his body has gone still, as if he's in sudden hibernation.

She looks up at the dome above them. 'Sometimes they use heat to destroy cancer cells, did you know that? They use heating rods, or lasers, or else they get people to take these things called pyrogens that make you have a fever.' She glances down at George again. 'But I don't think it's right. Heat is bad for you. Look at all the diseases there are in hot places. People stop sweating when they get too hot, just like people stop shivering when they're too cold.' She pauses again. 'So it's probably a good thing, your shivering.'

Tammy rests her chin on her knees and closes her eyes. She sits this way for a while, wondering if George has gone to sleep, then she lies back on the sleeping platform a few inches away from the edge of his body.

'Why have you been coming to visit me?' he asks.

Tammy brings a hand up to her mouth and chews on the skin near her thumb, without noticing she is doing it. 'What do you mean?'

'It's a pretty simple question.'

She looks up at the little skylight window cut into the snow above the sleeping platform and wonders why George has taken the time to make such an unnecessary thing. It's not as if they can see the sky through it. George raises his arms and folds them behind his head and Tammy is very aware of the proximity of his left elbow to her right shoulder. She is still feeling nauseous.

'I used seal gut to cover that window,' he says. 'I saved it from last summer's hunting – all that time.' He pauses. 'Wonder how it's going this year.'

'What?'

'The hunting.'

Bill's hand drops onto the bedcovers, still clutching the TV remote control. He's been watching some home-improvement programme but his head is hurting now. He looks around the room and his eyes can't find anywhere to rest. Where is everybody? He places the remote on the tray across his bed, pushes the tray back and then the bedcovers and gets out of bed, yellow feet flat against the cold floor.

In the corner of the room, near the chair for visitors, is the plastic bag Beth brought for him. Bill wanders over to it, taking a circular route as if he doesn't want to give away his destination. He sits down in the chair, pulls the six-pack of beer out of the bag and onto his lap. The aluminum is cold against his leg where his dressing gown falls open. He takes one can out of its plastic ring and puts the rest back in the bag. Tammy sits in this chair, he thinks, every time she comes to visit. She never sits by the bed: it's like heart attacks are catching or something. Sits over here like a lump, no expression on her face, no feeling. She never used to be that way, not when she was little. People get the wrong idea about her because she never talks, she never gets excited about anything. Bill knows what she's really like underneath. He wants to bring that other Tammy out more, the one who used to run around naked in the backyard and hold his hand whenever they went to the store to get something. She needs to relax. Otherwise what kind of life is she gonna have?

His head is hurting even more now. He closes his eyes, raises the can of beer to them and presses its cold surface to their lids.

Tammy closes her eyes. She thinks about her dad, lying in his hospital bed. She hasn't been to visit him in two days.

'What's it like in Fairbanks?' George asks.

'What do you mean? You've been there.'

'Not for a while. What do you eat?'

She frowns. 'We eat what everyone else eats.'

'So it's all store-bought.'

Tammy draws her knees up. 'Yup,' she says. She senses George turning his head towards her, still lying flat, but after a while, when she doesn't open her eyes, he turns his head away again.

'And you like living that way?'

'I love it.'

A few minutes later, he speaks again. 'I didn't mean to bug you. I think there should be a choice, that's all.'

'Lots of people don't have a choice. That's just the way the world works.'

In a niche in the wall above their heads, one of the oil lamps goes out and Tammy, sensing the change in light, opens her eyes. Feeling very tired suddenly, she turns onto her side and rests her face on one hand.

George is looking at her. 'You're right about most of the world,' he says. 'But Inupiats didn't always live in that world. I don't know about your dad – maybe he's different – but for lots of people . . . How would you feel if all your life you'd trained to be a carpenter and then suddenly you're told there's no more wood? There's only plastic, but you're going to have to pay for the plastic, and it costs a lot more. What should that carpenter do? Get some other job to pay for the plastic he doesn't even want? So he can make plastic chairs and plastic tables? My dad, all he's ever wanted to do was live on the island, hunt, fish, get enough food to feed us all, enough furs to trade to buy the other things we need – oil, fuel – just enough to share out with everyone else and get by. And that's not even saintly behaviour or anything, that's just the way it's always worked, the systems that have been in place for hundreds of years.' He shuts his eyes. 'But that kind of life's impossible now. What about Luke's dad? Last year, he spent five months away from home working in construction in the Red Dog Mine because they needed the money. He missed all the summer hunting. And the rest of us didn't have his help. Sorry.'

He's started to shiver again.

'Why are you shivering?' Tammy asks, sitting up. 'We should go outside.'

George pulls her towards him, turning slightly so that his arms are around her. She holds herself still at first, eventually relaxing her arms so that her hands come to land lightly on his

99

back. When George feels her touch, he hugs her more tightly, his mouth against the side of her neck, just under her hairline. They stay this way, hardly breathing.

After a few moments, his hold on her weakens and he rolls away. 'It's you,' he says. 'I'm shivering because of you.'

Tammy stays lying on her back. Even though she knows above the skylight window is just the metal roof of the truck container, she imagines they are out on the ice, a hundred miles out on the Chuchki Sea off Shishmaref, and what she is seeing through the seal-gut window is a steely-grey sky, chock-full of snow about to fall.

After a few minutes, she begins to take her clothes off, piece by piece, until she is entirely naked. She pushes away the sleeping bag and the other blankets, exposing her skin to the temperature. George turns his head and watches her as she does this. Neither one of them speaks. After a few seconds, she is shivering too. George picks up one of her hands, brings it to his mouth and blows on it, like he had the first time she visited the igloo. Then he kisses her open palm, the inside of his lips wet and warm against her skin.

Tammy watches him, his head bowed and the hair falling across his face. He looks at her; he never smiles. 'This would be a good place to be when the world ends,' she says.

'Where?' he whispers, reaching out to examine her cheek with a hand that is trembling.

'Right here. No one would suspect. It would be quiet.'

He nods. 'Worlds' endings should be quiet.'

Tammy looks at him then and something bursts inside her, behind her breasts, like the lighting of a gas flame in a heater. It's not comfortable, it's involuntary, it begins to spread downwards. 'Yes,' she says.

A few more minutes pass. Tammy can hear the low murmur of the truck refrigeration unit. She realizes she has been accepting it as a natural sound, the sound of weather, wind, outside. The oil flame on the stove has gone out now and the only light is coming from two wax candles in the niche at the other end of the sleeping platform.

Tammy leans forward and kisses George, holding his head in her hands. His hair-line is damp with sweat. They fuck for the first time that afternoon, in the half-dark, under the sleeping bag and the caribou rug, both of them shivering and sweating.

When Tammy gets back to the motel room, she finds her dad sitting in an armchair in the corner of the room.

'Look who's here,' he says.

'Hi, Dad.'

He's struggling to get up from the chair. Under a new bathrobe, he's still in the pyjamas the hospital provided.

'How come you're out?'

Beth comes to the bathroom door, her hair in a towel. 'The doctors let him out. We have to go back tomorrow morning for a final check-up and then we're flying back to Fairbanks tomorrow afternoon. I would have told you if I knew where to find you— Just take it easy, Bill. You promised the doctors.'

He is standing now. 'I'm fine,' he says, keeping his eyes fixed on Tammy. 'Is this the kind of time she's coming back every night?'

Her mother shrugs, rubbing her hair with the towel. 'I can't keep my eyes on her every second.' Tammy looks around for Jess, but there's no sign of her.

'You don't have to,' she says, walking over to the cot. Jess is fast asleep inside, lying on her side.

'Kenny came by,' Bill continues. He crosses the room, hands in his bathrobe's pocket, strolling as if he were taking a walk for pleasure. 'Asked where his car was. First time we've heard anything about it, I told him.' He's standing a few inches away from Tammy by now, one hand on the cot rails. 'As far as we know, Tammy can't even fucking *drive*!'

The spit from his mouth hits her right eyebrow and Tammy

closes her eyes and thinks about cold places: snow, ice far out on the sea. She opens her eyes again and looks straight at him. 'What are you angry about? That you didn't know where I was? Or that you looked like a fool in front of Kenny?'

He shoves her so hard she falls over against the cot, and then he starts to cough.

'Bill,' her mother says. While Tammy gets up off the floor, checking to see if Jess has been woken, Beth comes over to Bill and he lets her help him to the side of the bed. Tammy reaches into the cot, her hands shaking, and pulls the blanket up over Jess's shoulders.

'Leave her alone!' Bill shouts from where he is on the bed, and Tammy laughs, putting her hands up like an apprehended criminal. Her dad is swearing and Tammy crosses in front of him to the bathroom, taking off her coat on the way and dropping it on the floor. She locks the bathroom door and sits on the toilet for twenty minutes, the bath water running until the tub is full and she turns it off. She pushes back the sleeve of the blouse she is wearing and smells the skin on her forearm. It still smells of seal oil, of him. She takes off all her clothes and lowers herself in the hot water. When she comes out of the bathroom, her mom has disappeared and her dad is lying flat under the covers, his head propped up on a pile of pillows.

'Where's Mom?' Tammy asks.

'She went out.'

Dressed in a large towel, Tammy walks over to her single bed and lifts her suitcase onto the mattress. She hears the bedsprings squeak behind her. She goes back into the bathroom and gets dressed in a T-shirt and sweatpants.

'Come here, Tam,' Bill says, when she comes out again.

'Is Jess still asleep?' She goes over to her suitcase and puts away the clothes she'd been wearing in the igloo, leaving her hand pressed against them for a moment.

'What are you doing? Looking for something?'

She picks up a pair of jeans and turns to face him. 'I'm packing.'

'Why?'

'For Fairbanks, tomorrow.'

The sun is low in the sky, where it will stay all night, and it's bouncing off the mirror on the wall opposite the bed straight into Bill's eyes. He raises his hand to shade them. 'Come over, this side of the bed. I can't see you where you're standing.' Tammy takes one step to the left. 'We gotta talk.' He squints, ducking his head down until it's out of the sun. 'You can't just go around doing whatever, Tam. I mean, sure, I remember your age. It's natural go wild, go a little crazy sometimes, but Nome's not Shishmaref. You coulda got killed driving a car round here, your age – some drunk guy come along and crash into you.'

Tammy lifts one hand to scratch the side of her nose. 'You're right,' she says.

'Where'd you go to?'

She shrugs. 'Nowhere special. Just round town. Up to the train.'

'What train?'

She wishes she hadn't said it. 'Old miner's train, little way out of town.'

Bill nods his head and pulls up his blankets. 'Oh yeah.' He coughs a couple of times, and it seems like any energy he had has suddenly run out. He looks old and sick. 'I gotta talk to you, Tam,' he says quietly, almost like he's talking to himself. 'About a lotta things. This thing, this heart problem – it made me see lot of things clearer. I want to make it right, things I done wrong in the past.'

Tammy resumes her packing. 'What kind of things?'

'I know I'm not always being such a great dad.' He pauses, as if he can't talk because he's getting choked up, but Tammy doesn't believe it and she doesn't look at him. 'Lately – I'm up in Prudhoe Bay all the time with the job. I don't know what's going on. I been away way too much. But that's gonna change. I'll be off work for a while now, I guess, so I'll be home more, in the house. I can do some work on it, like you said needs doing.'

Tammy starts picking up clothes that are lying around on the floor.

'What you doing? You don't do that. Your mom can do that.'

'It's OK.'

'No, come on, come over here and sit down – can't you sit down for a *second* and talk to me? You're right – you're not a kid more now. I can see that. So don't *act* like a fucking kid. Sit down, why don't you? Can't you do me that nice thing for once?'

Tammy puts the clothes on her bed, pulls over a chair from the table and places it five feet away from the bed, on the side near the bathroom.

'Thanks,' Bill says. He nods at her, and runs his hand back over his scalp. 'Like I said, when we get to Fairbanks, we can hang out, do some time.'

'I go to school.'

He shakes his head slightly in an irritated way, like he's trying to get a noise inside his head to stop. 'Yeah. I know you go to school. I'm not *talking* about that.' He looks at her and he licks his lips, rubbing one lip over the other.

Great Skua. Leach's storm petrel. Northern Fulmar. All the bird species that are going extinct because sand eels, their staple diet, are disappearing from waters getting too warm for sand eels. Tammy can see her dad's mouth moving, but she's managing to zone out the sound of the words completely. Black-legged kittiwake. Guillemots. European petrel. Something moving on the bed distracts her for a moment and she scans the cover. It's her dad's hand moving up and down under the sheets. She looks away again as fast as she can, but he's seen her see it – he has his eyes glued on her face. She can't remember any more birds.

'I sure love you, Tam' – his words are coming through now, like someone's turning up the volume – 'you know how much I love you. You're so beautiful: your hair, your eyes. Why d'you wear those baggy jeans all the time? You should show off your legs, you should let me see them. And your tits – they're growing now, aren't they? They're getting bigger—'

Tammy stands up, but Bill lunges out and grabs her arm. Awkwardly, still holding onto her with one hand, he kicks the covers off so his pyjama bottoms are exposed, untied and loose, then he forces her down onto him, pressing her face against his stubbly cheek, spreading his fat hands across her back, and then turning her face so he can kiss the side of it with his thick, wet lips. Tammy's body goes limp.

'I shouldn't shout at you before,' he whispers, while his hips are working down below, pressing himself against her. 'When you got in.'

'It's OK.'

He tightens the pressure against her back. 'You're not a kid no more, are you?' he says. 'You're growing up.' He strokes the side of her waist. 'I was wrong there, to yell. You know what they say – spanking hurts the skin, but shouting hurts the soul.'

This is an Inupiat saying – Tammy thinks of George and shuts her eyes tight. Bill is still, breathing heavily, keeping hold of her with an arm across her back. Tammy turns her head and looks at the cot where Jess is sleeping, putting herself there instead of where she is.

'I'm gonna try be a better dad from now on, Tam. I am – you see.'

Then his shoulders start to shake, and Tammy realizes he's weeping. Her hands grip the sheet beneath them.

'You see. Lot of things going to change.' His speech is slurring, like he's on heavy medication. 'This is like a warning for me, this hospital time. I'm not gonna do this any more. No

105

more no way, I promise.' The arms around her go limp and he turns his body, pushing her off him and curling up in a ball.

As she's climbing off the bed, he reaches out a hand and holds her wrist, lightly. 'Just tell me where were you today,' he says. He turns his face to her, tears making tracks down its crevices. 'Huh? Please?'

'Nowhere.' She detaches his fingers from around her wrist. 'I told you.'

There is the sound of a key in the door and Tammy walks over to her bed, resumes packing.

Beth is carrying a brown-paper bag, hair covered up by a wool cap. She puts the bag down on the counter by the TV. 'You two sort things out?'

'Sure,' says Bill. He's wiped his face, hitched up the bed-covers and is lying back on the pillows, his arms resting on top of the covers. 'We had a talk – everything's sorted out now. Ain't it, Tam?'

Tammy looks at her father and counts to thirty before answering, noticing her mother's lips getting tighter the longer she waits.

'Sure,' says Tammy.

Later on, when they're watching the Jay Leno show, Bill bare-chested, the covers tucked up under his flabby arms, same pyjama bottoms on, Tammy asks what time their flight goes.

'Afternoon sometime,' says Bill, intent on the television. He's ordered a steak from room service and it's laid out on a tray in front of him, stinking up the room.

'And I'm coming back to Fairbanks, right? That's where you want me now?'

Beth looks up from the magazine she is reading and glances over at Bill.

'Yup,' he says, without looking away from the TV.

Tammy wakes early the next day. Six a.m. – no one else up yet. The room's filled with the weird mustard-yellow light of midnight sun, reaching into its corners like a kind of poisonous gas. She sits up and looks around from the viewpoint of her fold-down bed, crammed into one corner. Halfway across the room, Beth stirs in the double bed.

'What is it?' she mumbles, as Tammy gets up.

'I'm going to the bathroom.'

Beth turns over and pulls the covers over her shoulders.

Inside the bathroom, Tammy dresses quickly, turning on the tap so only a trickle runs out, and washing her face with water from two fingers held under. She uses her mom's hairbrush to scrape her hair back in a stubby ponytail and feeds herself a little toothpaste with a finger. She doesn't have an exact reason for rushing through all these things, but her body is anxious, needs to hurry. She stops, staring at herself for a few moments in the mirror. Though she looks the same, since yesterday, since being with George, she is a different person.

When she opens the bathroom door, a light is on in the room and Beth is reading in bed, a TV magazine propped up against her knees.

'You dressed already?' she says to Tammy in a low voice. She peers at the digital alarm clock by the bed. 'Not even seven.'

'I couldn't sleep,' says Tammy, going back to her bed and lying face-up on top of the covers.

Beth flips a few pages, and sighs.

Tammy looks up at the ceiling. One of the end-of-the-world scenarios that keep her awake at night is based on the rate of fertility in men and women getting lower and lower because of all the chemicals in the air and water, until only a very few people can actually conceive any more, and those few have to interbreed so they produce more and more genetically screwed-up children and eventually everyone dies out. Once the humans are all gone, it will take nature about fifty years to grow over everything humans ever built, it's reckoned.

The ceiling above her is textured and painted white. There's a smoke alarm directly above her head, and someone has made a mess of painting around it.

'I'm not exactly looking forward to going back to Fairbanks either,' Beth says. 'Back to work, and your dad needs looking after, and Jess.'

Tammy turns her head and looks at her mother. 'Why go back, then?' she asks. 'Why don't we stay here in Nome? You could get a job out here. Dad would be close to his doctors. Our house is falling apart anyway. I could get a job. I could help out with money and take care of Jess.'

Beth lowers her knees and stares at Tammy. 'Why the hell would we wanna stay in Nome?' she says. 'What are you talking about?'

'She doesn't want to go back to Fairbanks, that's what she's talking about,' Bill announces in a loud voice, still curled up in a ball under the covers, facing the other direction. 'She doesn't like it at home. Not *good* enough for her.'

Beth laughs, more like a grunt than a laugh. 'Maybe she should spend some more time on Shishmaref!'

'Nah,' says Bill, rolling over onto his back and rubbing his eyes. 'They all got crazy out there. They're all acting weird, bad as Tam. We should never send her – it's like catching something. What time we supposed to be at the clinic?' he asks, still on his back, his eyes closed again.

'Nine-thirty,' Beth answers.

'Better get up if we're gonna get breakfast.'

Waiting for almost an hour before the doctor is ready to see him, there's nothing to do but sit in a row, on orange plastic chairs, staring at the posters about Aids and all the other fucked-up diseases, or reading some shitty magazines, months out of date. At least he's got the plane tickets home in his pocket. The baby starts to wail.

'Should I take her outside?' says Tammy.

Bill looks up from his *Auto Trader*. 'You go, Beth,' he says.

Beth looks up. 'Why me?'

'Baby's better with you.'

Beth's lips tighten, but Bill doesn't see it because he's gone back to his *Auto Trader*. There's a 1957 Chevy truck advertised for a thousand bucks.

Finally the receptionist calls his name.

'About time,' says Bill. 'Come on, Tam.'

'Your daughter can wait out here,' says the receptionist, smiling, her narrow head held like a bird's on the end of a stiff, long neck.

Bill looks at her, blank-faced. 'I want her to come with me.'

When they enter the treatment room and Dr Pattillo asks Bill to strip down to his underwear and put on this robe, Tammy says she needs to use the bathroom. She leaves quickly without looking at her father.

'How long's this gonna take?' Bill asks.

As Tammy is passing back through the waiting room, she sees someone familiar sitting on one of the orange chairs. It's only when she's returning to Dr Pattillo's office that she suddenly realizes who it is: Mr Wyatt, from HTR. He looks different, like he's cleaned up to come to the doctor's. He's wearing a pale brown T-shirt and black jeans, and his black hair is slicked back flat over his head, with a clean side parting. He glances up at her as she passes but shows no sign of recognition.

Tammy sits down in a chair opposite, her brain buzzing. For just a moment, she wonders if George has sent Mr Wyatt to find her. Wyatt has got a sad face: the deep lines in his brown, hound-dog cheeks slope downwards and his thick eyebrows are like black clouds gathering over his eyes. He's slumped in the curve of the chair, brown and grey running shoes on his large feet.

'What are *you* looking at?' he says, without looking up from his reading material.

Tammy glances around. There's no one else in the waiting area. The receptionist is talking on the phone. 'Nothing.'

Mr Wyatt's jaw moves from side to side as he slowly shakes his head, still reading his magazine.

Tammy glances at the clock on the wall above the receptionist's cubbyhole. She's been gone from her dad's side for about ten minutes. 'I think I know you,' she says. 'I rode out with you to Teller one day, with Luke Iyatunguk.'

Mr Wyatt doesn't respond.

'To an old miner's cabin?'

Now he twists his mouth like he's running his tongue around his teeth, slowly lifts his head and looks her up and down. Quickly she moves across to sit in the seat next to him. Wyatt swivels his body around and away from hers, as if she's got a sickness.

'Do you remember?' Tammy continues, in a low voice.

Mr Wyatt shakes his head. 'Nope.'

After a pause, she speaks again. 'I've been back there a couple of times since, but I have to go to Fairbanks today.'

Mr Wyatt is still looking at her blankly, heavy-lidded.

'I need to get a message to our friend out there.'

He lifts his magazine and recommences reading. 'I don't know anybody lives in Teller.'

'The person I mean doesn't live in Teller. It's on the way—'

'I never even been to Teller.'

'Well, like I said, it's before you get to Teller, where this friend lives—'

'*What* friend?' says Mr Wyatt in a loud voice and the receptionist looks up.

Tammy flushes, glancing over at her. 'George,' she says, turning away from the receptionist.

Mr Wyatt smiles for the first time.

'George,' she repeats. 'You know a George, don't you?'

He looks at her sideways, scratching his stubble. 'Maybe.'

'He works for you. He works for HTR, right?'

Mr Wyatt nods, still looking straight ahead. 'Could be.'

'Could you give him a message for me?'

He doesn't answer right away. Then he turns to face her. 'You looked different before. Your hair was different.'

110

'Miss Ongtowasruk?' It's the doctor's voice.

Tammy looks up. Dr Pattillo is standing in his white coat at the end of the row of chairs. There behind him is Bill, still in his paper gown.

Bill leans his body to one side so he can see round Dr Pattillo. 'Tam?' he calls.

Dr Pattillo turns to look back at his patient, and two people, who have just sat down in the waiting area, raise their heads from their reading material.

'Let's go back to the room, Mr Ongtowasruk,' says Dr Pattillo, as Tammy gets up to join them.

'See ya later,' says Mr Wyatt, raising a hand to Tammy and smiling, as if they've been having a good chat.

'Who was that guy?' Bill asks her when they're back in the examining room.

'I dunno. He asked me how long we had to wait.'

'Why did he ask you? What was he, an Indian?'

'I don't know. I didn't ask him.'

'Looked like an Indian.'

Tammy can feel the doctor trying to catch her eye, but she looks down at her hands.

Bill goes over to the receptionist as soon he gets out of the appointment. He's sent Tammy to find her mom. 'You know that guy that was waiting over there?' he says.

The receptionist frowns slightly, the movement affecting only her pale, well-groomed eyebrows, not her smile.

'Sitting over there, the Indian guy.' Bill turns and points to the chair where Mr Wyatt had been sitting. 'I used to go to school with him.' He smiles, lowers his voice. 'Haven't seen him for a *hell* of a long time, if you know what I mean.'

When Tammy and Beth get back to the waiting room ten minutes later, Bill has disappeared. They sit down and wait. Tammy watches her mother fussing about with a broken fastening on the diaper bag. Jess has woken up and is standing by Beth's chair, little fingers gripping onto the knees of her mother's jeans.

Tammy stands up. 'I'll go ask if she's seen him.'

The receptionist glances over towards Beth and Jess. 'He's probably gone to the bathroom. Have you checked?'

Tammy takes a step back and looks up at the clock on the wall above the receptionist's cubbyhole. 'We've been waiting twenty minutes.'

The receptionist, who's gone back to her paperwork, looks up at the tone of Tammy's voice. She smiles, slowly.

'What about Mr Wyatt?' asks Tammy.

'Who?'

'Mr Wyatt. He was sitting right there, wearing a brown T-shirt and black jeans. The Indian guy.'

The receptionist still looks vacant. Following the line of Tammy's pointing finger, she frowns at first and then suddenly brightens up, lifting her sharpened pencil off the page where it has been poised. 'Oh, *I* remember. It's just that an *awful* lot of patients come through here in a day. Your dad was the one who came out in the middle of his appointment, wasn't he?' She looks at Tammy. 'Looking for you.' She points her pencil at Tammy. 'Then he asked me about Mr Wyatt and I told him he probably wouldn't be very long.' She pauses, as if she expects Tammy to be satisfied with this. 'They went off together, I think,' she adds, pleased with the information she's already given. 'Maybe they went to the coffee shop.'

When Tammy still doesn't say anything, the receptionist's eyes narrow very slightly. 'Is there a problem?' she asks.

PART TWO

THE FOREST FIRES

George's return to Shishmaref is quiet. Cliff embraces him once in the police station, then he asks nothing more. They catch a late-night plane from Nome, and father and son walk back to Cliff's house at one in the morning, through the neighbourhood busy like a noonday lunch break. Everybody is out on the streets, all ages in the midnight sun. George walks with his head down, and though the people who recognize him whoop and holler, even jump up high in some cases and clap their hands together in the air, no one approaches them or interrupts their journey home. Teenagers drive by, piled onto their four-wheelers. They turn their heads to stare at George.

The rest of the family is lined up in the living room, waiting. Minnie gives George a fierce hug, stretching up on her toes to kiss his face twice, and then goes into the kitchen to warm up some food. Pete has his orange foam basketball in his hands, which he squeezes as he watches Minnie kissing George. Stacey gets up from the sofa and stands a few feet away. She's wearing a denim skirt with horizontal rips across the front and a pink T-shirt. She looks different, thinks George; he realizes, with a shock, that she and Tammy are the same age. Stacey doesn't say anything when Mikey, sitting on the back of the sofa with his feet on the cushions, starts to quiz George about where he's been. George looks around the room, at all the family photographs crammed onto the walls, so many of them that it's impossible to tell the colour of the paint underneath. He feels overloaded with sensation; his attention doesn't rest on any one thing for long.

'Pete made junior varsity,' Mikey tells him.

George looks over at Pete.

'He's playing rear guard.'

'No, I'm not,' Pete says, throwing the foam basketball at Mikey's head.

As soon as he can, George retreats to his bedroom. He puts his pack down on the bed; it doesn't contain much. The police in Nome kept all his paperwork. They asked him why he had blueprints of proposed drilling sites in the ANWR, why he had copies of the minutes of the last Senate meeting in Juneau on rural transportation systems and of the Denali Commission report to the US Congress on its energy programmes. They asked him why he was so interested in Senator Stevens' addresses to the Alaska State Legislature, and the Alaska Federation of Natives' presentation to the Denali Commission. George had told them he was interested in Native issues, that he was considering going into local government.

The last two weeks in the igloo had been confusing; not what he had planned. He should have felt angry with Tammy for screwing things up the way she has, but he just wants to talk to her. This is a new thing, wanting to talk to a girl, wanting to talk to anybody. When Luke and he were younger, and Luke had told George stories about trying to feel up girls behind Art's smoke shed, about the magazines Evelyn Schroeder kept under the counter at the Native Store, about how far Connie Stenek had let him go the night before in her bedroom, George had felt nothing but a faint disgust. He couldn't join in with these conversations. There had been other things on George's mind at fourteen; his mother was dying.

Lying back on his bed, he wonders what his mother would have thought of Tammy. He's aware his memories of his

116

mother are circumspect, are filtered through the eyes of the boy he was when he lost her, and is no more. As the years pass, he begins to suspect she is turning into a sort of half-remembered saint. It seems strange to think that of course she had known Tammy. The Tammy he knows now, the one he's just met, seems unrelated to the one occasionally present in his childhood.

He sleeps with his clothes on; three months in the igloo have made it a habit. The heat inside the house is uncomfortable. Halfway through the night – or it could be day: there is no visible difference and he is disoriented – he wakes up from a dream about Tammy. He puts a hand on his erect penis. The house is silent. He wonders where she is at that moment.

The worst of all the many bad things about the discovery of George is the way Uncle Cliff refuses to look at Tammy when he turns up at the Nome police station. He walks right past her and asks the policeman behind the desk if he can see his son, George Ongtowasruk. Tammy is sure that he has seen her. She moves her feet on the tiled floor and considers going over to him. He is standing very upright, as if he has a stiff neck. After a few moments, an officer takes Cliff down a long hallway and into a room off the right. The police don't allow Tammy to leave the station until they have verified that the gun-toting histrionics of her dad haven't added up to anything illegal. She never sees Cliff again that night.

Bill had followed Mr Wyatt out of the hospital, eventually ending up at the HTR warehouse, where he left him long enough to pay a visit to the Polar Bear Saloon, have a few long-anticipated drinks, borrow the car – which he asked for – and a .30-06 Sauer carbine from the gun rack on the wall – which he didn't – and head back to the HTR, where he set up an Indian stakeout. He didn't have to wait long, because very shortly afterwards Mr Wyatt came out of the warehouse, got into his pickup truck and drove out to the miner's cabin, where upon arrival he was confronted by the barrel of Bill's gun. When Bill's nephew George appeared out of the back of the large truck parked on the gravel area, Bill was momentarily confused. In a mental leap fuelled by the whisky running through his brain, he presumed Mr Wyatt to be not only the low-life Indian seducer of his fourteen-year-old daughter, but also the kidnapper of his missing nephew. Making a citizen's arrest, he insisted that Mr Wyatt drive them all back into town at gunpoint for a visit to the Feds. George went along for the ride, at the same time trying to convince his uncle in quiet tones that he'd got it all wrong. The police, confused by the meandering thread of Bill's accusations against Mr Wyatt, went back to the cabin, and that's when they discovered the truck and the igloo inside it.

Tammy's dad is released about midnight, when he's sobered up. Mr Wyatt is let off with a warning about health and safety, and the police make do with a statement from Tammy about what did or didn't take place between her and Mr Wyatt, and what she was up to visiting George at the miner's cabin in the first place. Tammy's family fly back to Fairbanks the next morning. She writes a letter to Uncle Cliff as soon as she gets home, asking him to forgive her for not telling what she knew about George. Instead of Cliff, it is Stacey who writes back, wanting to know exactly when Tammy first found out about George, and what was going on between them. Tammy doesn't write back. She doesn't know what to say.

Mr Asawa is happy to see Tammy back in Kroger's, where everything is just as it was, except there's a new batch of high-school kids working the checkouts during the vacation. The summer of 2004 is shaping up to be the hottest in history, and Mr Asawa complains about the money he's being forced to spend on air conditioning. The electric fans go off the shelves as quickly as he can stock them.

'Now *everyone* wants to sit in the cold room with you, huh?' Mr Asawa jokes. 'This crazy weather!' He pauses, then: 'You look nice,' he adds. 'Something different. Vacation suits you.'

Tammy starts keeping a record of the temperatures in a small spiral notebook. In August, there are twenty-two days above 80° and lots of these would register much hotter if it weren't for the smoke from forest fires filtering the sunlight. At the end of June, just after she returns from Nome, high winds fan small forest fires in the Haystacks subdivision north of town, resulting in the evacuation of its residents. By the first weekend in July, 481,000 acres of Alaska are on fire. One day, when her bus doesn't turn up, Tammy walks home from Kroger's by the side of the highway. There's no pavement, and the gravel on the side of the road is loose, banking down to shallow ditches either side. Smoke from the forest fires has descended into the town; the air is thick with an orange fog all the way down to shin-level. Headlight beams of passing cars – people driving home from work – shoot eerie cylinders of light through the mist and Tammy wonders if the drivers can see her. Reaching the town centre, she comes across people walking around wearing gas masks; it looks like the aftermath of a chemical attack. At least the smoke has chased off the mosquitoes. At home, the bath water turns black when Tammy puts her body in it.

NASA scientists, she reads in a copy of *New Scientist* at the public library, have discovered that as well as carbon dioxide and the other greenhouse gases, soot may also be having a 'significant warming impact on the Arctic'. Tiny soot particles both warm up the air and darken the surface of the ice. The darker surface then absorbs more sunlight, causing the ice to melt faster. But this process doesn't depend on local forest fires. One-third of the soot affecting the Arctic is actually coming from South Asia, where the smoke from millions of cooking fires emits a cocktail of poisonous chemicals responsible for killing 2.2 million people a year, before it lifts into the upper atmosphere and heads to the North Pole.

To Tammy her time away from Fairbanks seems like an extended daydream. She spends a lot of evenings lying in the bath with the bathroom door locked. She considers the water, wondering whether the angle of the surface line has increased. She wants to draw a line in indelible ink along the side of the tub. Hours can pass – Jess sitting on the dirty bath mat playing with a set of plastic cups and plates Tammy bought her from the reduced shelf at Kroger's – Tammy in the water, staring at the pine-board walls oozing condensation. She re-works George over in her mind, like a fact she needs to remember, a set of data from the internet. Her memories of the visits to the igloo make her belly cramp, make her sink down lower in the water, gripping the edges of the bath with both hands.

On Sundays, she takes Jess on a Red Line bus to the UAF Museum and pushes her around the Native Cultures displays. Tammy's been before, brought here on school trips all through her years at elementary school, but it didn't interest her much then. She'd always disliked the museum trips because of the attention it invited upon her and the other Native kids. She buys a carton of juice for Jessica in the restaurant and reads the display notices aloud as they go round. They sit out on the green lawn in front of the building until the mosquitoes get too bad. There's a good view of the rest of the town.

Fairbanks is flat; the roofs are flat, the tallest building is only eight storeys high. On top of the flat buildings, things have been abandoned: old satellite discs, broken heating units, upside-down shopping carts, coils of plastic tubing, empty cardboard packaging, soggy from rain and snow. The winters take their toll and only buildings built the same summer ever look new. All the rest have something going wrong: paint peeling off, rust starting to seep out from the seams, patches of damp in the middle of concrete walls, doors that stick, burst pipes, rotting window frames. During the summer, without the snow to cover its sins, the city is at its ugliest. In the southeast corner of Kroger's, there's a brown stain spreading across the ceiling tiles, and one tile is beginning to sag. Tammy imagines it dropping out one night, brown water rushing down in a flood onto the fresh lettuces piled up below.

On her breaks from bagging groceries, she sits on the steps near the loading dock round the side of Kroger's to smoke. The steps fit her body well. She watches people walking to the car park behind the store, wheeling their carts with the brown-paper bags of shopping inside, keys in hand ready to bleep the central locking on their cars. Life has become so easy, she thinks, people have lost their ability to endure it less so. People will never want to give up all their things.

A beetle following a twisted crack in the pavement by her feet catches her eye and she takes in another breath of smoke. She wonders what George is doing right now.

She isn't sure yet what effect cigarette smoke has on the atmosphere. Smoke rises, she knows, because it is hotter than the surrounding air. But in a warm atmosphere, cigarette smoke – which quickly cools – rises and then descends until the lower air is saturated with it, second-hand. Inside her is different, though; there is no rise or descent, more of a general spreading out, a dispersal. She takes breaths of carbon monoxide, hydrogen cyanide, nicotine, tar and ammonia. She blows them out again.

'Tammy?'

Standing there in a bright red windbreaker and black cycling trousers, his wire-rimmed glasses a little bent in the middle, is Mr Dervish, her former science teacher at Lathrop High. It takes Tammy a few seconds to place him. There's something different about him, and it's only after they've spoken for a while she realizes that he's shaven off his beard.

121

'Hi, Mr Dervish.'

'How are you, Tammy?' He seems actually interested.

'I'm fine.'

He nods towards Kroger's, behind her. 'Do you work here?'

She nods. 'Yeah.'

Mr Dervish used to post his homework assignments on a personal web page in the school website, and expected his students to look them up. Tammy remembers a picture of Mr Dervish's wife on the web page, sitting next to Dave on a sofa, wearing a cranberry-red sweater over a white turtleneck. She remembers a crocheted quilt thrown over the back of the sofa, pine-clad walls behind; it looked like the kind of photo taken for a Christmas card. There had been pictures of his husky dogs too, spread across the page, superimposed as little cut-out heads.

'I'm sorry we lost you at Lathrop,' he is saying. 'Where did you transfer to?'

Quickly she names another school, one she passes every day on the bus route to Kroger's.

Mr Dervish nods. 'That's a good school. I know you were having some trouble at Lathrop.'

He's holding a brown-paper bag of groceries in his arms, a bag of Fritos sticking out of the top. To Tammy, he looks sort of lost.

'How's Mrs Dervish?' she asks.

Mr Dervish cocks his head to one side and smiles faintly, as if the question surprises him. 'Well, that's nice of you to ask, Tammy. She's fine. We're expecting a baby.'

'Congratulations.'

'Do you have any brothers or sisters?'

'A sister.' The ash on her cigarette is about to drop off.

'Did she go to Lathrop too?'

Tammy shakes her head. 'She's a baby.'

She takes a quick drag from the cigarette, then stubs it out on the steps. One of the guys from the delicatessen section walks by on the upper level of the loading dock, passing behind Tammy. His apron is streaked with greasy stains.

'I should probably get back to work,' Tammy says.

'Is this a summer job?' Mr Dervish asks.

Tammy stands up. 'Sort of.'

He chuckles. 'Where's your apron?'

She puts her hands in the pockets of her baggy jeans and looks at him, unsmiling. 'Inside.'

Bill is sitting on a tree trunk out in the woods near the house. He isn't feeling so well, not like he thought he was going to feel by now. The medicines the doctors put him on are clogging up his thinking, making changes inside, like he's some sort of guinea-pig. He's come out here to chop some wood but after a few swings of the axe his chest starts to hurt, so he takes a break. Last night Beth forgot to buy the chocolate milk he likes on her way home from work, which is still pissing him off. He pulls out a small airline-size bottle of vodka and cracks the twist top. Lately he's been drinking vodka more than whisky or rum: it feels cooler, better for him, cleaner going down.

It's fucking humid in the woods. He swats at a mosquito on his arm, leaving a splat of blood behind. Sitting still like this, after a while all the animals start to come out. He should have brought his gun with him . . . just a little target practice, got to keep in practice for hunting season next autumn. Every year, Cliff gets a cabin with some other folk in Denali, but Bill doesn't know if he's going to go this year, not after what happened between Cliff's boy and Tammy. He wouldn't trust himself around the boy, who's always been kind of a weirdo. He finishes the mini-bottle of vodka on the third slug and leans down to plant it upwards in the soil, only the top sticking out of the thick green undergrowth. The air smells rank, like too many green things gone to mush. It reminds him of the woods down in West Virginia, outside the army base where he'd done his stint of service. Once he'd had a girl out in those woods, a black girl who'd worked in the bar in town, laid out on the brown and yellow bracken. She'd already been done by half the soldiers on the base, but she'd never been with an Eskimo, she told him. Somewhere far down below, his cock gets a little plumper at the memory, except it doesn't feel like his cock any more, not since the heart attack.

A ground squirrel wanders by, climbing across the exposed roots of a nearby tree. When Bill coughs, it sits up on its haunches and freezes. Its small glass eyes beat, blink, like a bird's. Bill reaches down, yanks the empty vodka bottle out of the ground and throws it at the squirrel.

When he gets back to the house Tammy is in the bathroom, brushing her teeth. He starts to unzip his pants for a pee and she goes out. When he's finished he goes into the kitchen, where Tammy's got Jess in a highchair, giving her some lunch.

'Where were you?' she asks, directing a spoon into Jess's mouth.

'Out in the woods. Cutting up some logs.'

'Jess was in the yard, all by herself.'

He opens the fridge, looking for the chocolate milk Beth was supposed to have bought. 'So?'

'Weren't you meant to be looking after her? I just got back.'

Bill closes the fridge door. 'I *was* looking after her. She's OK, isn't she? Anything wrong with her?'

He considers eating something but feels a little sick. He goes into the living room and turns on the TV, tripping over an empty cereal box on the floor by his chair. After a little while, Tammy walks into the room. She's got a sandwich on a plate. She doesn't sit down, just stands there eating her sandwich.

Bill looks up at her. 'Yeah?'

'Mom says you're starting work on the house.'

Bill looks back at the TV and switches the channel. 'That's right.'

'What are you going to do?'

'You should be *happy*. Way you're always complaining about it. I'm gonna get it straight, fix it up. I'm gonna underpin it.' He tries to say the words carefully but his tongue isn't working like it should, so he demonstrates with two hands, sliding one palm under the other. 'That's what they call it, underpinning – have to pour in a new foundation.'

'Who have you got to do the work?'

Bill slaps his hands down on the arms of the chair and swivels his whole body round, his shirt twisting round his torso so it lifts up, exposing the belly above the belt-line. '*I'm* doing it. That OK with you? Maybe you think your friend George do a better job.' He's got her there; she looks away. He smiles. 'Or maybe it's just *igloos* he can do.' He turns back to the TV. 'Couple of buddies from work say they gonna pitch in, on their off-weeks.'

Bill's surprised to hear Tammy come back at him for more. 'A couple of buddies?' she says. 'What – for free?'

Bill sighs, and slaps his hand down on the vinyl arm of his chair. 'No, no, I'll sure pay them. I been looking into it – there's money you can get from the Corporation, for improvements, for your house, especially this kind of thing – permafrost subsidence, they're calling it.' These words feel good in his mouth, feel easy. 'Permafrost subsidence. It's happening all over. Government's onto it. You just gotta fill out some forms.'

Bill is right about the money available. There's a new scheme and he talks to some lady on the phone and she tells him there shouldn't be a problem. Someone from the Permafrost Foundation will come out to assess the property. When he tells the lady he's planning to do the work on the house himself, there's a pause and the lady asks him if he works in construction.

'I work up in Prudhoe Bay, but I'm off work a little while, so I got extra time right now.'

'The work will have to be done by a registered contractor, sir,' she says, 'in order to qualify for aid.'

So Bill calls up his friend Frank, Uncle Frank, who used to work for a construction company, and asks him to make up some estimates for him on company letterhead.

'You'd think they like you trying to save them the money,' he says, shaking his head as he puts the forms in the envelope and seals it. He laughs. 'Hell, I'm charging the kumaqs more than I *need* now!'

On the first Saturday in August the weather is perfect for starting the job. Bill gets out in the yard by eight-thirty. Beth's taken Jess off to the mall to get some shoes and then she's going over to her friend Judy's. Bill stands at the lower end of the house, his house, sledgehammer in hand. The sun is already pretty high in the sky and he's wearing an Arco cap on his head to shade his eyes. The day before he's had his hair cut, buzz cut right down to the bone, and his scalp is itching. He takes off the cap, has a good scratch and then replaces it. He's not sure what to do first.

The house is all on one level, resting on a four-foot cement base with wood construction above. It's long and thin, so if you a fired a gun at one end the bullet would pass in a straight line through nearly every room in the house. At the near end, someone added an extension about ten years ago, housing an extra bathroom, a utility store-room and another bedroom, Tammy's. A wooden porch clings to the side of this extension, with steps leading up to the front door.

Bill admits the house has seen better days. Even when they moved in, the roof had started to split in places, two planks curled back like a cow-lick on a young boy's head. Since the building began tipping, two legs of the front porch are bowed out in the middle, as if the whole thing were attempting a slow curtsy. All in all, there's probably about a 15° slope, and it feels like it's even worse some nights when he gets in late.

The short wall at the lower end of the house has been propped up by four thick logs. Bill approaches this wall, braces his legs and sets his shoulder against it, as if he is going to heave the whole house back into position. He steps away again and takes a packet of gum out of his pocket, unwraps one stick, puts it in his mouth and begins to chew.

A few moments later, he picks up the sledgehammer he's dropped in the long grass and whacks at one of the wooden props, just for the hell of it. He does it again, harder. The impact reverberates up his arm and shoulder and the sledge-hammer drops out of his grip.

'What are you doing?' Tammy is standing in her bare feet in the grass. She is wearing a pair of white shorts and a Nanooks sweatshirt. She walks over to him, her bare feet picking up little bits of wet grass. 'What are you doing?' she asks again.

'What's it look like?'

Tammy looks at the sledgehammer on the ground. 'I don't know. Where's Mom?'

'Went shopping. With Jess.'

Bill ducks under the wooden props and kneels down close to the ground near the side of the house. He leans forward and peers at the cracks in the cement foundation.

'How are you going to do it?' Tammy asks.

The sound of her voice has been bugging him lately. Every time he sees her, he thinks about her with that George boy, yakking away about all the weird stuff she always talks about. Yakking away about all her so-called problems. She wouldn't know a problem if it punched her bloody.

'Without the whole house falling down,' she adds.

'I'm not worried about it falling down.' He backs away from the house again and takes his cap off to scratch his head. 'Just got to dig it out, bit by bit, then pour in more foundation underneath. Guy from the permafrost place is coming round Monday to drill some holes, get a picture what's actually happening down there.'

Tammy walks around him to look at the other side of the house. 'If you lift one side, won't you need to drop the other side a little? To stop it breaking in the middle?'

Bill stares at her. 'That is the dumb-assest thing I ever heard. You think building a house is like some cartoon? You don't know nothing about it. Shit, we're not gonna lift it so it's *higher* than the other side! There's a way to do this kind of thing.'

Tammy doesn't seem bothered by what he's saying. It's like she never even hears it. 'Wouldn't it be easier to just start over?'

Bill snorts. 'Start over! And who's gonna buy it looking like this? Huh?' He moves in again, crouching near to the ground and running a dirty thumb along the seam where the cement base ends and the wood begins. 'You're pretty dumb some-times, ain't you, Tam?' he calls over to her as she's walking away. 'All that stuff you're always looking at, all that stuff outta the papers. All a lot of jim-jam.'

Tammy stops and turns back. 'What if the ground keeps on sinking after you pour in the new foundation?'

Bill turns away without answering.

In the afternoon, Tammy comes out of the house again, an orange in her hand. She can't see Bill anywhere. She sits down on the porch steps and starts to peel the orange. A couple of weeks ago, Beth had bought some plants in plastic pots and put them by the front door. The plants are growing but their flowers have shrivelled up and faded. Tammy kneels to examine them and wipes away a thin film of ash from the green leaves. From up on the porch, she can see a yellow deck chair which her dad picked up a month ago in a garage sale, collapsed in one corner of the lawn. She puts the last orange segment into her mouth and walks over to it. There's a glass lying on the ground next to it, tipped over on its side, half hidden in the long grass. She looks up at the blue sky, not a cloud in sight. It's warm.

A little way into the woods, round the back of the house, Tammy's tacked a yellow tape measure to the trunk of a birch tree. An increase in the extent and density of vegetation growth in spruce forests along the tree line is being attributed to rising temperatures in Alaska, on average 1.8°F per decade over the last three decades. It's been a few weeks since she last checked the tape measure. After looking around for a while, she thinks she must have lost her bearings. There are clouds of mosquitoes in the woods and it's hard to concentrate. Eventually, just as she's about to give up, figuring somebody's ripped it off, she spots a little bit of yellow halfway up a white trunk. The tape measure is almost entirely covered by new growth. She kneels down to examine the dark leaves growing up the tree; they feel warm, puffed up with heat and moisture.

She waves a hand to clear away the mosquitoes in front of her face, but they fan out and immediately regroup. Tammy pulls out the drawing pin that is holding the tape measure to the trunk and re-attaches it a foot higher up. When she emerges from the woods onto the lawn again, she hears female voices coming from around the front of the house.

Bill is standing by the edge of the road talking to a pretty girl in a red top and blue denim shorts. The girl is part of a larger group, but the rest of her friends have walked on, down the road to where it begins to curve. They don't look like they come from this part of town. Realizing their friend has stopped to talk, they've stopped too, looking back at her with a range of irritated expressions on their faces. One of them, in a pink waist-length denim jacket, sees Tammy and, leaning over to another, whispers something that makes the whole group laugh.

'Dad,' calls Tammy, standing close to the wooden porch supports, in the white painter's overalls she put on to go into the woods.

Bill is laughing, leaning towards the girl on the handle of a garden rake he's picked up.

'Dad,' Tammy calls again, and he turns his head. The girl looks at Tammy too, smile fixed on her face.

'What?'

'Lawnmower's not working.'

'Yeah, OK,' he answers, turning his head back to the girl, but she's seen her chance and skipped on after her friends. They're halfway round the bend in the road now, a gaggle of migrating birds. Bill watches them get away, then throws the rake to one side and tramps up the porch steps and into the house. Tammy decides to mow the lawn.

When she goes in an hour later, after putting the lawnmower back in the garage, Bill is sitting at the kitchen table riffling through the Yellow Pages, a bottle of beer open on the table and an empty one next to it. Tammy kicks off her grass-stained shoes in the utility room. She gets the feeling it would be better to go straight to her room, but she's hungry. She walks quickly across the kitchen floor and, avoiding any eye contact, opens a cupboard, standing up on tiptoes so she can get a better look past the tins and the cereal boxes: double-helping jars of Gerber's baby food stacked up in rows, next to a box of Graham crackers; microwave popcorn; a six-pack of diet 7Up; sachets of Taco Bell chilli mix.

Bill shuts the phonebook with a thud and reaches for a different one. He knocks a pile of papers and unopened mail off a little side table that's propped up with bricks under two legs to keep it level. Tammy walks over to the fridge and opens it, pushing Jess's highchair out of the way so it's wedged up against the wall. In the freezer there are a lot of items wrapped in foil, furred over with ice; they look like they haven't been touched for years.

'You gonna go hunting this fall?' As soon as she says it, she knows she shouldn't have said anything.

'What?' Bill's tone is mean, tight.

Tammy's fingers tighten around the rubber lining of the fridge door, and she tries to keep her voice sounding normal. 'I asked if you were going hunting this fall. With Uncle Cliff, like you usually do.'

He hacks, clears his throat. 'I dunno. Why? You want to sneak in a visit to your boyfriend while we're gone?'

Tammy closes the fridge door, quickly and softly, and turns to leave the kitchen. But as she turns, Bill stands up in her way, forcing her backwards against Jess's highchair, which folds into itself, tips over and crashes against the wall. Tammy stumbles and falls backward on top of it, hearing something crack.

'What broke?' she says.

Bill reaches out an arm, as if to help her up, but instead of yanking her to her feet he grabs her shoulder, pulls her head towards his crotch and begins to undo the silver buttons of his jeans. Steadying himself first on the side of the white fridge, the other hand gripping Tammy's shoulder, he takes out his penis. It's only half-erect; Tammy's never seen it before in daylight. She looks away and Bill rubs it against her cheek. Soft. The hair above it grazes against her closed eyelids as her father moves, holding her head now, carefully, almost gratefully. His eyes are closed, his head slightly tipped and turned to one side.

Her father's penis catches on the side of Tammy's shut lips, pulling them to one side. Inside the kitchen, everything is silent, just the hum of the fridge. From the woods comes the screech of a grey jay, then a flapping of wings.

She tries to think of something else, to not be there. On the plane to Nome, the day of the Polar Bear Swim, Luke's eighty-year-old grandmother had sat across the aisle from Tammy, squeezed into a seat next to a family of young brothers, all her own grandsons. She'd refused to take off her parka throughout the trip – it was covered with a pattern of little blue flowers, with a dark brown wolverine ruff. Never saying anything, she'd sat there for forty-five minutes, smiling like a Buddha, her rough cheeks the colour of tobacco, shiny and criss-crossed with dozens of lines, crow's feet fanning out from her squinty eyes, shiny stubby teeth with gaps in between them, wet, sometimes catching the light. Whenever she felt Tammy looking at

131

her, she would turn and nod her head, smile even harder.

'Fuck,' says Tammy's dad. He steps back suddenly, rubbing himself across the front of his chest. 'Shit.' He backs off, putting his limp penis back inside his shorts, rubbing his arm now, tripping backwards over a chair and kicking the chair across the room, doing up the fly buttons of his jeans as he stumbles out of the room.

Tammy stays on her knees for a moment, listening. As the time passes, she realizes that she is wet between her legs. Looking down at the linoleum between her knees – there's a long, thin isthmus of milk across it, probably spilled when the highchair tipped over – she rubs her hands up and down the material of her white overalls for a few seconds, breathing as smoothly as she can.

The quanitchaq in Luke's house is like a jetway between the outside and the inside of the house, crammed from top to bottom with junk: old worn-out boots, drums of oil, bags of garbage ready to be driven to the dump outside town, a torn parka, plastic toys, frozen carcasses, animal skins. Luke's cleared away a space by shoving some stuff out of the way with his foot; inside, his mom's defrosted some frozen caribou haunches for dinner, and Luke and George have brought it out on paper plates. Luke's mom doesn't understand why they want to eat out here. Both doors to the quanitchaq, the one from the inside and the one to the outside, are shut. They are sitting on the floor.

'So can we get to the computers in the school?' George asks.

Luke nods. 'Yeah, yeah. It's just this new guy – new principal starting out. He's keeping the computer room locked up during the day, when nobody's using it.' He wipes his mouth with a paper napkin. 'But Alice, she's doing some part-time secretarial work in the office, she's gonna get the key for us, and then it'll be OK.'

'How long until your printer's fixed?'

'I don't know. I'll probably get a new printer. I thought you didn't like having hard copies of stuff, anyway.'

George nods and leans back against a pile of coats, closing his eyes. For days now, he hasn't felt right; his guts are jittery, his skin oversensitive to sounds and smells. It's how he used to feel whenever he was off the island, when he was younger, but now he's home and he can't figure out why he still feels it.

'You OK?' says Luke. 'You don't look so good.'

'Headache.'

Luke reaches up a hand to scratch his nose and then keeps eating, finishing off the caribou in a few minutes. 'You know what, Alice is sweet. I don't know how come I never noticed her before.' He lifts the paper plate to his face, licks the remaining grease off until it's clean, then wipes his mouth again with the back of his hand, and his hand on his sweat-shirt. 'I just never took a lot of notice of her, I guess. But I tell you what, man –' he glances over at George, whose eyes are still closed '– you find your way into those snowpants, and you got it made.' He laughs, folding the plate in two. 'That's what's good about summer, hey? Not so many layers to get through.' When George shows no sign of response, Luke rubs his left eyebrow with the back of his thumb and leans forwards on his knees, arms crossed.

George opens his eyes, but not to look at Luke. Instead, he is frowning, focused on a spot in the air a few feet in front of him. Luke starts to re-tie the laces on one of his Nike running shoes. He reaches over and picks up a basketball resting against the wall near the inside door.

'So that Tammy,' he says, dribbling the ball on the floor between his bent legs. 'What's she like?'

George turns his head. 'What do you mean?'

'I dunno. I was just wondering what you thought of her.'

'I only saw her a couple times.'

'Really?'

'Yeah.'

Luke shrugs. 'I thought you saw her a lot.'

'No.'

In George's head are strange thoughts about Tammy: her smell; the way she had appeared outside the HTR warehouse that first night, from out of nowhere; the way she'd looked, naked next to him on the sleeping platform. It's almost as if she hadn't been real. Except people keep asking about her.

'How much did you tell her?'

George struggles to focus on Luke again. After a slight pause, he answers. 'We didn't talk about that.'

'So what *did* you talk about?'

George tries to answer, but he is feeling uncomfortable, off-balance. He shakes his head, a small movement. 'Nothing.'

Luke looks at him for a couple of seconds, then picks up his paper plate and stands. 'Yeah, probably better that way. So are you going up to camp tomorrow?'

George looks up at Luke, his face clearing. 'Yeah – you guys coming up? Fish are supposed to be good.'

'Uh – I don't know. I think maybe we can't make it this year. We're going down to Seattle to visit my brother – the whole family. Should be cool – he got me and him some tickets to a Red Hot Chilli Peppers concert.' Luke pauses, his thumbs hooked in the belt loops of his jeans, jiggling his long fingers against the tops of his thighs. 'My mom's really up for it.'

Luke coughs, and the room falls silent.

'Where are you all staying?' George asks, after a little while.

'Mark's girlfriend's, I guess. Her parents' house or something.'

George looks down at the floor. 'Does my dad know you're not coming up to camp?'

Luke picks up the basketball and puts it under one arm. 'Sure. I think my dad told him. Yeah.'

George stands up and zips up the fleece he's wearing. 'So you guys planning on eating ready meals all winter?'

Luke, who's turned to go back inside the house, turns back. 'What?'

George stares back at him, chin jutting out slightly. 'You know, if you're serious about this stuff, you got to be committed.'

Luke raises his eyebrows, his mouth falling open. 'What? Give me a break! Huh? We're going to visit my *brother*, ya know? Isn't he one of the tribe?'

George's look doesn't falter. 'If people don't do the things they need to do to get their own food, then they're dependent on the store and the corporation, and they're dependent on oil and government cheques.'

'And you think I don't know that? Man, I just spent the last six months helping you out, haven't I? And you're saying my family don't pull their *weight* round here or something?' Luke lets the question hang in the air. He turns back to the door, muttering. 'You're attacking the wrong guy, man. Look who's been gone for the last six months, if you're gonna start pointing fingers.'

George drops his gaze. He raises his hand and rubs his lower lip.

'I *am* serious,' says Luke, turning back. 'I know I wigged out on you for a while there, but I'm back. But you gotta keep things in balance. You can't get so uptight. Or you're gonna start making mistakes. And you can't make any more mistakes, not with the police involved already.' He takes a breath in and lets it out in a rush, nervously tapping one of his feet at the same time. 'I'll see you later, OK? At the school, about six o'clock. Alice is gonna let us in.' He opens the door to the inside.

George looks up. 'Tell your mom thanks for the food.'

Luke glances at George. 'Yeah, sure.'

Tammy is reading the paper.

'Anything interesting?'

Tammy looks up and the sun is directly behind Mr Dervish's head, so she can't see his face. She folds up her newspaper, and takes a drag from the cigarette that's been perched on the edge of the concrete step. 'Kind of.'

'I hate to say this, but I have to.' Mr Dervish raises his shoulders apologetically. 'You really shouldn't smoke.'

Tammy puts out the cigarette on the concrete. 'You're right.'

'I know what it's like – I tried it a few times when I was a teenager. It can be pretty addictive.'

He isn't holding any shopping bags this time.

'How's Mrs Dervish?' Tammy asks.

'She's OK, thanks. A little hot in this weather, in her condition.'

Tammy nods. 'It's been the hottest summer on record.'

'Is that so? Doesn't surprise me.' He starts to say something else, then appears to change his mind, opening his mouth and shutting it again. 'I was just heading in to get some things for her. Can't seem to get enough fruit!'

Tammy nods again, and Mr Dervish raises a hand, turns to go.

'Can I ask you something?' Tammy says.

He spins round, eager. 'You bet.'

'You know that time you took the class down to that research place? The weather place? I can't remember what it was called.'

Mr Dervish frowns slightly, looking to one side. 'You mean the Centre for Global Change?'

'Yeah. I guess. When we were there, there was a man who took us out into the forest . . .'

'I remember. Dr Heller.'

'Right. He said that the wood and the leaves, all the organic stuff, was decomposing faster in the rising temperatures, so it was releasing carbon faster too.'

Mr Dervish is listening, his eyes slightly squinted. 'Yes. I think that's true.'

'And he said something else – about the rate of release? The rate of carbon release? That it could eventually get faster than the rate of taking in—'

'The rate of absorption—'

'Of absorption, yeah, and then the organic stuff would become a *source* of carbon, instead of a sink.' Tammy stops, her hands resting on her knees, where she has been articulating the words she is carefully choosing with the end of her index fingers.

'Hey . . . A-plus!' says Mr Dervish. 'You remembered a lot.' He removes his glasses and wipes at one eye with the back of his hand. 'I wish you were back in my science class.' He puts his glasses back on and looks at her. 'Did you want to ask something more about that? Not that I'm the world's expert.'

Tammy shakes her head, her lips pressed together. 'No. I just wanted to check it.' She looks down at the concrete between her feet, wishing he would go now. His shadow is stretched out a little way in front of him, so it reaches the first of the steps.

'What makes you so interested in all this stuff?' he says. 'If you don't mind my asking.'

She wipes a corner of her mouth with her thumb. 'I don't know.'

Mr Dervish has his hands stuffed into the pockets of his chino pants. His nose is slightly sunburnt, but the rest of him is looking healthily tanned. Tammy bets he grew up in a big house. He nods his head a couple of times, the silence between them getting more and more uncomfortable. 'So how's your dad?' he asks.

Mr Dervish had met Bill once, when Tammy had to be picked up from school after nicking her finger with a scalpel during a sand-shark dissection in his class. It was a real bleeder, spraying across the black melamine surface of the lab table, across the white lined paper of her lab partner's notebook and the sleeve of her white shirt. After the school nurse had bandaged the wound thickly enough to stop the bleeding, she phoned Tammy's parents to ask them to pick her up and take her to the local emergency room to get it stitched. Tammy hadn't expected to see her father – this was when he was still unemployed and he wasn't usually up much during the day. Standing in the cramped, low-ceilinged nurse's office, he hadn't looked like somebody's dad; he'd looked like one of those washed-up, strung-out Eskimos who slept on the sidewalks around the bus station downtown. Sometimes in the mornings, they find them frozen to death in their damp, urine-soaked sleeping bags.

Mr Dervish had come down to check on Tammy after class was over. He arrived just as Bill was insisting the nurse unwrap the bandage she had prepared, so he could see the wound for himself. When the blood started to come again, he looked queasy and put his arms around Tammy's neck, the weight of his body forcing her to take a step to one side. Mr Dervish had walked them to their truck.

Tammy raises a hand to shade her eyes. 'He's working up in Prudhoe Bay.'

'And how do you feel about *that*?'

'Excuse me?' She's wishing she hadn't wasted a cigarette, only half-smoked.

'Well, there are a lot of mixed feelings about oil drilling in this state and I guess, in the light of your interest in carbon release, I thought you might have a certain stance on it yourself.'

Tammy looks at him. 'Right.'

Mr Dervish studies her for a moment more, then smiles and shrugs.

The sun has moved a little higher in the sky, and his shadow's smaller. Tammy stands up and he takes a step back but shows no sign of leaving. She pulls out her pack of cigarettes from her back pocket and lights another one.

'He's not up in Prudhoe Bay right now, anyway,' she says, exhaling the smoke. 'He had an accident, so he's taking some time off.'

Mr Dervish frowns. 'I'm sorry to hear that. Was it a bad accident?'

'Not really. He had a heart attack.'

'How long will he be off work?'

Tammy shrugs. 'Couple more months, I guess.' She looks up at Dervish. 'It's not *your* problem,' she says, smiling, then takes another drag. The strong blast of nicotine is making her dizzy and her chest hurts. The sun is too hot on her face.

Mr Dervish takes another step away to avoid the smoke. He raises his right hand. 'Well, I should get going, I guess.'

'OK.'

He nods his head a few more times. 'You take care.'

After he's gone, Tammy feels dizzy again and shuts her eyes. When she empties her mind with a conscious effort, the white comes. Blue white. She imagines glaciers, glaciers dripping away into milky lakes, unusual, turquoise lakes. The cold water sinks down, deep and deeper until she can feel it in the pit of her stomach. She stamps out the cigarette she is smoking and stuffs the pack back in her pocket.

THE PERMAFROST

In early September, a man from the Fairbanks Permafrost Technology Foundation turns up at the house with his boring drills in a nylon carrying case and makes two small holes through the floor in the corner of the living room, then two in Bill and Beth's bedroom. He confirms that there is displacement of soil and an increase in the water levels underneath the house. Sitting at the kitchen table, drinking a Coke with ice in it, he talks to the family about the house becoming one of the Foundation's trial houses. He's wearing a navy-blue suit and a striped tie.

'What's going on here is there's a relatively high water content in the active layer of your soil. And that kind of soil has to be kept frozen or you get these creep deformations, leading to differential displacement of the building's foundation, of the kind you're experiencing.' He glances at the little side table with its brick supports. 'Usually, you see,' he says, using his hands to demonstrate, 'a layer of permafrost is the warmest at the bottom, where it's closest to the heat coming from the centre of the earth, but what's happening in Alaska at the moment is that the permafrost is actually coldest in the middle and then gets warmer again towards the surface.'

'Why's that?' says Tammy, who is leaning against the wall by the front door.

The man's eyes flick over to her and away. 'Well, it's because of the climate changes we've been experiencing lately, we think.'

He explains they can sell the house back to the Alaska Housing Finance for a while so that the Permafrost Technology Foundation can lease it themselves while they're exploring how to remedy the subsidence problems. The Ongtowasruks will then have first option on buying it back later, when it's been stabilized, he says, and, in the meantime, get a break from the mortgage.

'And where are we supposed to go while you're working on the house?' asks Beth.

The man pulls his shoulders down as if his suit is uncomfortable, and glances at Bill. 'Are there any relatives you could stay with?'

Beth sniffs. She gets up from the kitchen table and goes over to the stove, where she puts a pan of milk on a burner and lights the gas.

'Or maybe you could rent for a while,' the man suggests, 'with the revenue from the sale.'

Bill leans forward across the table, its downward slant lending an enhanced aggression to his posture. 'Yeah, and don't tell me the mortgage guys are going to sell it back to us for what they bought it for!' he says, stabbing a finger at the guy. 'You go and fix this place up, then we won't afford to buy it *back*!' His voice is raised and he stands up.

The man plucks at the collar of his shirt and glances at Tammy. 'This house is a liability as it is,' he says in a low voice. 'No one should be living here. And you'll have to wait until spring now to start digging.'

Bill tells him to get out and the man leaves in a hurry. Tammy watches him from the porch as he throws his briefcase and his boring drills onto the back seat of his car. His car is so clean, she thinks. He must drive it through a car wash almost every day.

141

It's the middle of the night. When Tammy wakes, she's inside the refrigerated lock-up at Kroger's, slumped against the smooth cold wall between two sets of metal shelving. She can't see anything; it is completely dark except for the glow around a small red light over the door. Heaving herself back into consciousness, she blinks her eyes hard a few times and tries to remember how she got here. She'd been working in the store today; she'd come in here at the end of her shift. She takes in a few deep breaths through her nose and smells the ice, its wet, bad-food odour, the scent of damp cardboard packaging. As her eyes adjust to the darkness, she can make out the angles of the boxes nearest her face. Using the metal racks on either side to pull herself up, she tries to stand and realizes she can't feel her legs. She wiggles her toes, leaning over to massage her feet through her shoes. She rubs her hands up and down her thighs, creating as much friction as possible, then does the same to her arms. Gradually it begins to work and she can feel her limbs again. She pulls herself up and takes a step, sending something small and hard skidding across the metal floor. It crashes against the shelves opposite and the noise startles her. She concentrates on the light above the door and limps towards it, hoping Mr Asawa doesn't lock this refrigerator when he closes up at night. It's very cold. In between steps, she closes her eyes and rests.

She wonders what time it is, how many minutes or hours have passed since she woke up, since she came into the lock-up. As her limbs begin to thaw, the pain is intense and intangible at the same time, blooming inside her muscles like clouds of ink in a vial of water. A few steps away from the door, she begins to sob. It seems like something involuntary, connected to the thawing, to the process of the blood re-circulating around her body. She cries without feeling anything, without making any sound. But there is a greater change occurring inside, as if a piece of her has

142

broken off, like a great chunk of ice from the side of a glacier.

After a while, the crying subsides and she makes it to the door. She leans against it and, using all her weight, pulls at the large latch handle. It moves easily and she falls out into the dimly lit store-room. Everything is still. Boxes huddle on shelves in the quiet dark. The warmth feels dusty and old. She passes between the shelves and out into the front of the store. The night fluorescents are still on and she ducks into an aisle, afraid of being seen. The aisle contains boxes of crackers and flatbreads, breadsticks and bagel rings. She grabs a packet of Ry-Krisps and sits on the floor with her back against the shelf. She feels so hungry.

It still isn't clear to her what has happened.

On the wall above the fresh fish section, which she can see from where she is sitting, the clock reads 3.15. The store will open again at 6 a.m. She will stay where she is for a while and then go back into the store-room, where there are places she can hide when the morning shift arrives.

Bill stares down at the cube of dirt he's dug out, about three foot square. At one corner, the house is hanging out over empty space now, like the prow of a ship cresting into the air, up over the top of a wave. Do it in sections, his friend Frank had told him, who used to work part-time in construction. Another block every three feet or so. Then you can feed the steel rods down in between. He rests the edge of the spade in the grass, breathing heavily.

Tammy hasn't come home. He checked again five minutes ago, but the bed's empty, as it was at two in the morning when he got in last night.

He'd thought maybe he was going crazy. No sign of Tammy and the house was humming. He'd tried to watch some TV, but he ended up pushing the mute button on the remote so he could hear the humming better. It was a high-pitched vibration, like the hum of a refrigerator, but it didn't stop when Bill shoved the stove a few inches away from the wall and yanked out the refrigerator plug. Wandering into Tammy's room again, in case she'd slipped in without him noticing, he switched on the overhead light; Tammy's bed was unmade. He slid off the chair, went over to the bed and lay down, still half expecting to find Tammy under the covers, gone flat like some kind of magic trick. He pressed his nose into the mattress and felt the weight of the alcohol he'd drunk pulling over the blankets. Next thing he knew, bright sun was shining in through the windows, making long rectangles of light on the grey carpet. Still no Tammy.

'Who unplugged the refrigerator?' Beth asks when he goes in to wash his hands after he's finished digging.

Bill shrugs. 'She never came home.'

Beth looks at him. 'Who?'

'Tammy, that's who. We should call the school.'

'It's Saturday.' Beth rubs her eyes. 'She was working at Kroger's last night. I went in with Jess to get some eggs.'

Bill walks down the hallway and into Tammy's room. He stands in the centre of the room, very still, letting his eyes roam across the surfaces, like he was out on the ice scanning the surface of the water for a seal. Sometimes you see more when you're not looking straight at a thing.

When he met Beth, when they were both on the hotel staff out at Chena Springs Resort, she'd helped him get rid of a lot of the Eskimo baggage. She knew it would only get in his way. Beth taught him how to dress better, how to cut his hair. She helped him with his English, until the number of times he got stopped by the police – for bald tyres on his car, for turning into a middle lane instead of a right or left, for just about any-thing they could think of – was down to three or four a year, instead of twenty, thirty. She had lots of ideas about what they were going to do.

Now he figures he knows pretty well how to get along most anywhere, get along with anybody. But it pisses him off when guys like Stan Ningeulook, last time he was on the island, call him a 'city kid', as if he's forgotten how to butcher a seal. He doesn't forget anything. Not a thing.

On the floor near a leg of Tammy's bed is a small white thread. He narrows his eyes, trying to analyse where it comes from, whether it's wool or cotton, whether it's a fabric he recognizes. Moving slowly, his gaze travels up to the quilt hanging sideways off the bed, then onto the surface of the bed itself. The sheets are stirred up, like waves breaking into a surf on the pillow. He covers the whole area, scanning the rippled surface, until a patch of white beyond the bed catches his eye and he stands still again, a frown cracking through the lines across his forehead.

Over in the far corner of the room, the corner most hidden from view, a small sample pot of white paint has been placed on a few sheets of newspaper, its colour dripping over the edge of the closed lid in two places. Bill walks around the foot of the bed. There is no sign of a paintbrush, but a patch of wall about five inches square, close down to the skirting board where it can't be seen, is painted white. The patch is neat, with straight edges. A couple of coats, it must be, to cover the pale orange wallpaper on the walls. Bill bends over and touches the paint with one finger; it's dry. He sniffs, straightens up and takes a look at Tammy's bed from another angle. Leaning over, he lifts the bit of the quilt that's hanging over that side, then bends down on one knee to look under the bed.

'What is it?' Beth is standing in the doorway, Jess riding on her hip. Jess stares at Bill blankly like she doesn't recognize him.

'I'm gonna drive down to the store,' he says, getting up and walking past them out of the room.

Tammy has never dated anyone.

When she was twelve, a couple of months after Bill lost his job at the university and they moved house, he got brainwashed by a branch of evangelical Christians and he stopped drinking for a while. They used to go along to the meetings every Saturday night – just she and Bill: her mom was pregnant with Jess – in a tin church out on Airport Way. Whoever was preaching had to raise his voice every few minutes when the big planes came over.

One of the evangelists – there was a team of them – had a red-haired son, Tammy's age, who was always there every Saturday, sitting in a chair at the back of the hall, by the door. His job was to hand out Bibles as people arrived, and to hold up the donation plate as people left. He performed these two jobs with a scornful expression on his face, refusing to speak to anyone, which is what first attracted Tammy's interest. Talking to him after the meeting, during the social period when the adults went to the room at the back of the building for non-alcoholic refreshments, she discovered he had an amazing memory. Tammy could open the Bible at any page, start to read, and he would finish it, go on right to the end of the column. He told her this wasn't because he believed in any of it, but he wasn't allowed to go to normal school and so he'd decided to try and improve his brain-power by memorizing the entire Bible. That way, when he finally got away from his parents, he'd be able to make up for all the learning he'd missed at high speed.

'Are you going to get away?' she asked him.

Once he asked her what she was scared of.

'Retribution,' she answered. She didn't even know what the word meant. She'd read it in a hymn sheet.

His eyes narrowed. 'You mean from God?'

She shrugged. Then he leaned over and kissed her, tilting her head to one side and pressing his lips against hers, even slipping his tongue between her teeth. They lay down on the back pew and kept kissing until they heard the adults coming. That weekend Bill went on a bender and they never went back to the church.

Tammy walks out of the front of Kroger's. No one's said anything to her; no one's seen her come out of her hiding place in the back. She tightens the scarf around her neck. It's started to rain. She walks over to the machines, buys her usual newspapers and takes them down to City's Bagels. But it's difficult to read. She can't concentrate on the facts, finds herself staring out of the window instead. More and more cars pull into the parking lot as the day proceeds. She watches as an Eskimo family pile out of a car way too small for them all. She reaches into her coat pocket and pulls out her cigarettes.

'You can't smoke in here,' says the manager behind the counter.

'I know,' she says, and walks out.

As she's passing in front of Kroger's again, heading towards the loading dock, a horn beeps and she turns to find Bill's truck pulled up alongside. Tucking her cigarettes in her back pocket, she approaches the window as he's rolling it down.

'How ya doing?' he says, sitting back and squinting at her.

'OK.'

He rests his elbow on the car door. 'Where you been all night?'

'I got locked in,' she answers, looking him straight in the eye.

Bill stares back, his mouth twitching. 'Locked in?'

Tammy nods. 'In the store.'

After a moment, Bill turns his head and looks straight ahead. He watches a woman passing in front of the truck with an armful of groceries. He lifts his hand and rubs it across his mouth.

'You want to ask my boss?'

Bill turns his head again. 'Your boss?'

'Yeah. Mr Asawa. He's right inside.' Tammy indicates the front entrance of Kroger's with her hand. 'You can ask him.'

She works her tongue between two back teeth, watching her dad.

After a bit, he cocks his head slightly and smiles. 'I don't need to check it.' He leans across and cracks open the passenger door. 'I'll drive you home.'

George switches on the VHF marine radio to channel 72 and turns it up. The kids have started school again and the house seems quiet. A few of the voices on the radio are familiar; there's nothing going on out there yet – it's too early in the season – just a lot of whaling captains sitting on their asses, drinking coffee and eating doughnuts. He picks up a new brass shell casing from the bomb box and packs it with the black powder and wadding, enough explosive to kill the whale quickly, but not so much that the darting gun will pass right through the whale, as George has once seen happen. He wants to finish repacking all the shells by the time Cliff gets back from his trip to Teller. Damp powder in old shells can mean a lost whale, he reckons, but his father thinks he's too fussy about this. If he repacks them all before Cliff gets back, George can avoid seeming like he's questioning his word.

But there are other things causing conflict as well; the largest example is hauled up on the sandy grass out front of the house: an aluminum boat. Cliff has bought the twenty-three-footer second-hand, off the internet. Its last owner was a fisherman in Oregon, who probably used it in the summer for recreational ocean fishing, wearing Bermuda shorts, a cold beer in one hand. Cliff likes to point out its high sides and heavy V-shaped hull that will cut through large waves. To George, it's a southerner's boat.

The growth of waves on an ocean is affected by three things: how hard the wind is blowing, how long it blows, and the fetch: the distance wind or waves can travel without obstruction. George has known this since he went to tribal skills camp in the fourth grade. The greater the distance the ice retreats, the larger the fetch and the more powerful the wave. No one ever wrote this down for him; everything he's learnt about whaling has been learnt by example, by watching and imitating. That's the way to do it. Now his younger brothers get a little whaling booklet, produced by the school district. Whaling captains put ticks in the book by the side of the skill they're meant to have learnt; 'Knows how to determine where the shorefast ice is grounded', tick, 'Is able to describe the eight winds', tick. Then they take it back to school and hand it in. George is sceptical. There's no place for a textbook on a whaleboat. Some guy in Juneau or Anchorage, some guy who's never set foot in a whaling boat probably, decided this is the way Inupiats should learn what they've been learning for hundreds of years without any outside help. This year, the ice extent out there is probably the lowest it's been in fifty years. It's going to be hard to hold onto anything out there. No textbook is going to tell the boys that.

He looks at the phone on the dining table in front of him. On page three of the small memo pad next to it is the number for Uncle Bill's place in Fairbanks, written in Cliff's sprawling handwriting. George glances at the memo pad from time to time, his fingers busy with shell-packing. Igor Tocktoo's voice comes on the VHF, transmitting his daily alcohol-inspired mix of evangelism and local gossip. George smiles; he had forgotten about Igor. Minnie, who is having a nap on the old sofa across the room, shifts and murmurs something in her sleep. George reaches over to the radio and turns the sound down.

Minnie is sleeping with her round face resting on one hand, cheeks criss-crossed by deep wrinkles. Her eyes open and she smiles at George. 'That Igor?' she asks loudly, in Inupiaq.

'Yeah.'

Minnie sits up, steadying herself with one hand, and asks

what time it is. 'Sure gotta get moving,' she says when George tells her. She smooths down her white hair and slips her wide, flat feet into sealskin slippers.

Two weeks later, 10 a.m., 47°, and George is looking out over grey water from the prow of Cliff's new boat. 'Where'd Oliver get the new boat?' he asks.

Cliff looks up from where he's re-coiling the blue hawser. A thermos of hot coffee is sitting with its cap off on the fibreglass deck, steam rising from the top. 'George Hepa loaned it to the Kotzebue crew for the season.' He laughs. 'He's running for re-election.'

'Has he ever been out whaling in it?' asks George.

'I don't think so.'

'Looks like a Japanese whaler.'

Cliff stands, holding onto the side of their boat as it rocks through a series of waves created by the bigger boat's wake. 'You don't like it?' he asks, watching as it passes on through the channel out of the lagoon where they are anchored.

George shrugs. 'It's OK.'

'It's fast – that's for sure.' Cliff sits down again and pours out some coffee into the thermos cup. 'More chance of catching a whale with a fast boat. And stronger for getting it back.'

'Sure,' George says, standing and raising his hand to a man approaching in another boat.

This boat is a strange hybrid, a small aluminum skiff with low gunwales and a high bow built up out of bits of plywood nailed together. Akpayuk, the man inside it, is small and wiry. He cuts his engine and pulls up alongside. He's grinning.

'Hey, George! Good whaler. We sure miss you in the spring. Ice was no good – a lot of shit ice.'

George nods. 'That's what I heard.'

'You still remember everything?'

'Sure.'

'You got your harpoon?'

'Not with you around to do the job.'

Akpayuk shakes his head, but he's smiling. 'Nah. It's your turn todays.' He swivels in the boat and looks out across the water. 'Probably gonna have to anyway drop anchor – looks like fog coming in.'

George and Cliff both turn to look out at the horizon. George waits for the two older men to speak.

'Lotta big breakers out there,' continues Akpayuk. 'Better to stay in. Fog's gonna get worse.'

'You reckon?' says Cliff. 'I was thinking maybe it would lift. There's some light coming off the water out there.' He points to an area to the southwest, but Akpayuk is looking down at something inside his boat. Cliff looks at the outboard motor hanging over the back of it. 'That engine OK? It don't sound too good.'

Akpayuk glances back, his hand resting on the tiller. 'It's a piece of crap.' He bursts out laughing, eyes squinted up into two slits. 'But she does OK. Breaks down all the time.' He's still chortling when they hear the call over the VHF in Cliff's boat: three whales sighted, ten miles northwest. Without a word to Cliff and George, Akpayuk guns his motor and speeds off, his boat cutting a sharp path through the waves. Cliff throws the rest of his coffee overboard while George opens the bomb box, grabs his harpoon and moves forward towards the prow.

The wind is stronger the further they get from shore and George pulls up the hood of his white parka with one hand, the fur trim blowing flat against the side of his face. He can see other boats approaching the area from the north, probably Kivalina crews. Scanning the water, he searches for spouts. The water likes to tease the eyes; it forms and re-forms the backs of surfacing whales, it glitters and slips. George doesn't let these movements distract him. He keeps his thoughts clear of anything else, focused on what he is searching for, as they circle the area where the whales have been reported.

After an hour, with no whales surfacing, Cliff says maybe they should try a little further north.

'You think?' says George, his eyes still scanning the water. 'The waves are getting bigger. Couldn't tow anything back through this anyway.'

'Sure we can. It's not so bad.'

George turns and looks at Cliff. He steps back from the prow and sits down. 'Whatever you think.'

Cliff blinks a few times, the wind blowing at his hair, a faint smile dimpling his cheeks. He pushes back his hood. 'What do *you* think?'

'I think this is bullshit. There's no ice – whale hunting's supposed to happen on ice.'

'We've always hunted in the fall. For years now.'

'Yeah, but not like this.' George slaps the inside of the aluminum boat with the palm of his hand. 'The only reason we get any whales in this is we can outrun them. Otherwise we'd never get them – shit, they can hear us coming a mile away. There's no skill involved. How many whales you get this spring? The old way.'

Cliff is silent.

'You couldn't get close enough, could you? Not without risking all your equipment. And your lives.'

'Things change. Every year is different.'

'This isn't about every year being different, aapa – there was no ice to get you out there. Whole spring, all that soft ice pushing up against the shore – what are you meant to do? May tenth, there was no snow on the ground up here, was there? *No snow.* I heard it on the weather report.' He opens his hands to Cliff, as if he's asking him to verify this.

Cliff looks up to watch a flock of geese crossing over. After a few seconds he opens his mouth to respond, but at the same moment the radio crackles loudly, broadcasting a prayer of

Thanksgiving. It's Harry Toovak's voice, a harpooner from the Kivalina crew. A buzz of other voices immediately crowds onto the airwaves, congratulating the team, cheering and hooting. George and Cliff lean in to listen, their discussion forgotten.

When they reach the site, the successful whaling crew's flag – a white circle in a blue background – is flying from a pole rigged up in the middle of the captain's boat. The dead whale is floating, rolled onto its side, orange inflated cones still attached to the ends of the harpoons bobbing around, bumping up against its black flesh. Up near the head, there's a lot of blood. It took a long time to kill, the story is going round, charging them once before finally giving up. On the whaling captain's boat, standing balanced far forward on the prow, is a boy aged about ten or eleven, wearing a wool hat with the name of a basketball team decaled across it. Written large across his face still is the exhilaration of what he has just experienced.

'Good catch,' Cliff says to him in Inupiaq as they pass by, and the boy smiles, nods.

Akpayuk is already there, supervising the tying of the towropes to his home-made boat. 'Want some chocolate?' he says to George after the ropes are attached, pulling out a crumpled square of tinfoil from inside his parka and handing it across the water.

'Were you here for the kill?' George asks him.

'Nah. Burt Edwardsen done it. First whale he's got in two years.'

George looks over to the first boat in the tow. He can't tell which of the men is Edwardsen.

Akpayuk sits down to wait while Cliff manoeuvres their boat up to the central hawser, uncoiling the blue ropes that will connect to bow and stern. He turns to George. 'So where were you?'

George looks up. Akpayuk is grinning at him, chewing on something. 'Nome. I went to Nome.'

Akpayuk laughs. 'Not so far.' A couple of seconds later, he asks why.

153

'Excuse me?'

'Why'd you go to Nome?' He's still grinning, his eyes two dark slits slanting upwards.

George takes some time to think about it. 'So I could come back, I guess.'

The two of them break into raucous laughter, so much that Cliff looks back at them, pitching forward against the side of the boat when a wave slams into starboard. George goes to fetch the rope for the bow end. The air is full of moisture; Akpayuk had been right, a fog is coming in. The ropes are slippery with it, and George takes off his gloves so he can make a good knot. For a moment, he's distracted by the surface of the water; it's pitching and swelling without an obvious pattern, white surf appearing in sudden streaks and swirls.

George starts to sweat suddenly, and feels a little nauseous. 'This is gonna be a hard tow,' he shouts over to Cliff, and Cliff nods.

In the last few moments, the mood of all the men has changed. It's decided that Cliff and George's boat will be the last one to join the tow and the other boats head back to the mainland to prepare the landing site, where there will already be people gathering by the metal runway used for fall whaling. At the last minute, a few of the men from the Kivalina crew jump into Akpayuk's boat, on his invitation. Everyone likes to be part of the successful returning crew.

Rounding the coast by Sheshalik, the boats at the front of the line make a right turn to get a little further off from the shore, since the waves are pretty high by now. As they turn, a large wave hits Akpayuk's boat and crests right onto his bow-line, swamping the bow end of the boat with water and pulling it under. Suddenly the bowline snaps and the tension of the sternline still attached to the central tow spins the boat backwards. It crashes against the wash of the next wave and flips over.

Immediately, Cliff grabs an oar and levers their boat

154

alongside the upturned vessel, while George starts hauling men up out of the freezing water. The word passes up the boats in seconds and the column stops, everyone standing in the bellies of their boats looking back. Five minutes after the boat has flipped over, every man is out of the water except Akpayuk, who hasn't surfaced. George watches the tipping surface of the water, his wet arms white with cold. Ten minutes later, Akpayuk is still trapped under the boat and they pull his body out with a gaff. There's no way to revive him.

THE ALBEDO EFFECT

The first snow of the year in Fairbanks is gone within a few days, under the wheels of cars, down the culverts and drainpipes. Tammy stands in the yard looking at the holes Bill has dug around the lower end of the house. There are six of them now, three feet deep and three feet wide, with a gap between each one. At the bottom of each a little pool of water has collected, formed from the melted snow.

She goes inside and lies down on her bed. She rolls onto her side and stares at the white patch she's painted on the wall. Since her night in Kroger's, she has been thinking about heat.

Albedo is a measure of the reflectivity of any surface. An ideal white surface reflects back all of the heat that shines on it, whereas an ideal black surface absorbs it all. The white surface has an albedo of one, the black, zero. In the Arctic, when the sea ice is covered with bright, white snow, 80 per cent of the solar radiation hitting the earth gets bounced back. Very fresh snow reflects back 90 per cent. But take the snow and ice away and there's the open water – lowest albedo level of anything on earth. The more ocean water exposed, the more heat being absorbed by the earth. There is no way to stop this.

Tammy, her hands over her eyes, presses the balls of her hands against her forehead until the strain starts to give her a headache. She thinks that she has been concentrating on the wrong things. Cold-blooded animals inevitably take on the temperature of their surroundings. Warm-blooded creatures try to keep the inside of their bodies at a constant temperature. There is nothing she can do about the heat that is being absorbed; thermo-regulation is the key. She rolls over and gets up.

The kitchen table is still crowded with dishes from breakfast. Beth has taken Jess to the doctor to see about an infected mosquito bite she's got on her leg. Tammy walks over to the thermostat by the front door and turns it up two notches. Any more will be too noticeable. She hears the clumping of boots on the porch steps and backs away from the door.

'Figure I'll need to get one of those little cement mixers, keep it going all the time in the yard,' Bill is saying as he enters, the door sticking in its frame so he has to wrench it open with both hands on the doorknob. He walks past Tammy without saying anything, goes over to the fridge and gets out a beer. 'You can hire those suckers, right?'

Bill's friend Frank is with him, and Ricky, who'd been at the beach in Nome, and a small Italian-looking guy called Googie. Tammy's met him a couple of times before.

'What about the ground?' Googie asks, standing near the door. He's growing a beard, fuzzy and dark with two bare patches in the middle of it, same place on either cheek. He talks in stops and starts. 'Isn't it gonna . . . get too hard to dig soon?'

'I'm done digging, mostly,' says Bill, swallowing as he lowers his beer.

Tammy starts to head towards her bedroom and Bill turns his head. 'What are you doing?' he asks.

She stops. 'Nothing.'

He grabs a hotdog bun out of a plastic bag sitting on the counter and eats it, plain. 'Why don't you stick around?'

Ricky pulls out a chair at the kitchen table and sits, spreading his legs wide. 'Let's see about this, man,' he says, picking an orange out of the fruit bowl, holding it at one end of the table and then letting it go.

Tammy can't help watching it roll; the orange falls off the table halfway down. He's rolled it too hard.

'Yup,' says Ricky, grinning, a pimple near his mouth turning white. 'This house has got a problem!'

All four men start to laugh and Bill cracks open another beer. 'I tell you, I got it made with this NANA money. It's all there for the taking – any house improvements you want, man. Beth filled out the forms for me. It's no problem.'

'Hell, I'm gonna get *my* house to go slanted!' says Googie. He looks like a cartoon character; everything about him is slightly smudged. His mouth forms an open crescent when he smiles, and his hair looks like a solid block of colour with a jagged silhouette.

Through the window over the kitchen sink, Tammy can see the men's pickups lined up in the driveway, like big boys' Tonka trucks. They all stay in the kitchen for a while and then wander into the living room and the TV is switched on. Tammy walks back to her bedroom. A few minutes later, the phone rings. She hears her father pick it up and say 'hello' two or three times but that's it. About three hours later, the trucks fire up, one after another, spraying gravel as they back out of the driveway and tear down the road. She has been sleeping. The house is getting warmer.

Tammy listens for the sound of the television. Moving quietly, she passes through the kitchen, where a couple of empty beer cans and plates with the remnants of sandwiches are piled up in the sink. At the entrance to the living room, she stops and listens again. The room's empty, but the imprint left by her dad's body is still visible in the worn-out leather of his chair, as if a part of him was sitting there, watching her. The phone rings again, but she doesn't answer it.

The cemetery at the top of the ridge is usually a quiet place but today it's been disturbed, left dirty like a kitchen sink full of coffee grounds after the water's run away. George watches Joe

Schroeder's pickup driving down the hill, muddy shovels piled up in the back. The sky is clouding over, threatening snow, long overdue. He stands near the edge of the graves. The crosses are crowding around like children on a school trip, each one constructed with the same uniform design: two flat pieces of whitewashed wood nailed together at right angles, with a small placard in the centre where the person's name has been burned into the wood. Some crosses are bigger than others.

'Akpayuk always listened to real cheesy music, you know that?' Cliff is talking, bending over to pick up a scarf that must have been dropped by a child. 'He liked – who's that lady singer, from Canada? – Ann Murray, that was it. He used to listen to Ann Murray, and Kristy, his little granddaughter, used to go into the shed with him, sing along all day. He could butcher an animal faster than any guy I ever seen. All the time with Kristy sitting on the floor, drawing pictures and Akpayuk singing Ann Murray songs.'

George turns his hands over and looks at the mud on his palms. His father's voice is irritating him. He wipes his hands on his pants, which are covered with mud too; he slipped when they were lowering the coffin into the grave. At least the ground had been less frozen than usual, so it was easier to dig a hole.

'He would have been happy with that whale, huh?' Cliff continues. 'That's sure the biggest whale we've called in for years. If there was any whale gonna take him—'

'The whale didn't take him.'

Cliff turns towards his son. He wipes under his nose with two fingers, leaving some mud in his moustache. 'What d'you say?'

'The whale didn't take him. It was the weather.'

Cliff waits a few seconds. 'Sure. In a way.' He walks over to a cross about ten feet away, and kneels down to wipe some sand off an old pair of snowshoes stuck vertically into the ground in front of the cross, like two saplings planted there, waiting to grow.

George follows him over and stands next to him on the clumps of long grass. 'Do you believe people come back?' he asks. 'In a different form?'

Cliff stays kneeling in silence with his head bowed for several minutes, before answering the question. He stands again, leaning on one knee to help himself up. 'Yes.'

'So why did we give her a church funeral?'

Cliff waits a while again before answering. ' 'Cause I believe in that too. And your ahna wanted it that way.'

'What about Mom?'

'Her too.'

Cliff starts to walk down the hillside into town. A crowd of people can be seen, milling around outside the square wooden church with the single spire.

'Basement's gonna be bursting, with all these folks from Kivalina,' says Cliff, as George catches him up. 'They should have held it in the gymnasium. You going back to the house first? Stacey and the boys went ahead with Minnie.'

'I'll go back to the house.'

George sets a fast pace, his mouth fixed in a straight, hard line. Cliff adjusts his walking to keep alongside.

'You angry about something?'

'We shouldn't have been out there in the first place,' George mutters.

'You mean the whale hunt?' Cliff flips over the shovel he's carrying into a more comfortable position. 'Well, it sure wasn't ideal, but lots of times we've been out like that and nothing happens. Akpayuk wouldn't have been out if he thought it was too dangerous. It was just bad luck.'

George stops, turns towards Cliff. 'You're wrong.'

Cliff stops too and backs away a step from George, stumbling, as if George has drawn a concealed weapon.

'It wasn't bad luck,' says George. 'Nothing that's happening is bad luck. Akpayuk made a bad decision. He couldn't judge the weather because nobody can any more. He couldn't read the signs because the signs have all changed. That's not bad luck. Mom didn't get cancer because of bad luck. She got cancer because that's what we get now, along with tuberculosis, and heart attacks, and Aids, and diabetes, and every other modern disease you can think of.'

'Inupiats have always got sick,' says Cliff, quietly.

'Not like now. You know what the major cause of death is today, for Inupiats? Cancer. You know what we're getting arrested for? Number one: assaulting one another. Number two: driving drunk. Number three: sexual abuse of our own kids. You want me to go on?'

He turns away from Cliff and looks back at the graveyard, running a hand through his hair.

'You know, when I was away in Nome, I missed it here. I missed it a lot. But now I'm back, it's clearer than ever that what I missed doesn't exist. It's some place I've read about, been told about, all those summers in tribal skills camp, something you all talk about in Elder meetings because you can remember it, but we young people, we don't remember it because we've never *had* it. Not really. And we never will. Unless we take it on ourselves to do something about it.' He turns back to Cliff. 'You want me to act a certain way, like an Inupiat – and I want to, but it's not possible any more.'

'It's possible,' says Cliff. He smiles, gently. 'Lots of people do it.'

'Well, they won't be able to for much longer.'

'Why?'

'Because they won't be able to survive. You know it. You've seen it. You know what I mean.'

The smile has faded from Cliff's face and he shifts his weight, standing more erect. 'There are problems, sure. But it's possible to find a balance.'

'No! That's what they tell you, but it's not. The things we

161

need, to continue living the way we always have, are being destroyed. Day by day, systematically.'

Cliff puts his hand on George's shoulder. 'You have to find a way to work with things the way they are.'

George shakes his head. 'Why? It doesn't always work, striking a deal. It isn't always right.'

The two of them face each other for a few minutes, and then Cliff takes his hand off George's shoulder. 'Maybe.' He resumes walking. 'I don't know.'

Outside the front door of the house, Pete is in a huddle with a group of his friends. A few of the boys look up as George and Cliff approach.

'Hey, boys,' says Cliff, raising one hand.

George follows Cliff into the house without acknowledging the boys. From the living room comes the sound of a sporting event on the TV. George glances into the room and sees Mikey slumped on the sofa in front of it. Cliff pulls off his boots and heads into the kitchen. The kitchen table is empty, except for a few crumbs and a crumpled piece of Saran wrap.

'Minnie must have taken the food over already,' says Cliff. He switches on the coffee machine and turns to face George, leaning back against the counter, his hands by his hips. 'Will you tell me? Before you leave again?'

George looks up. After a few seconds, he nods.

'OK,' says Cliff.

When George comes to Fairbanks, the snow comes at the same time. He walks from the bus station, and by the time he is in the car park at Kroger's the sky is getting dark and the lights have come on. Tammy watches him walking across the dark asphalt, cutting through empty spaces, across the white lines. The snow is falling but none of it is sticking yet; it melts as soon it hits the tarmac. She watches for as long as she can from the window in City's Bagels, then gets up and goes outside.

George has stopped in front of Kroger's, near the pumpkin display. He is wearing jeans and a wool duffel coat, with a hooded sweatshirt underneath.

'George?' she says, when she is close enough.

He turns round, pulling back his hood, and she draws in a quick breath. All his hair has been cut: cut short, close to the scalp.

'Your hair,' she says, as he walks towards her.

George lifts a hand to his head.

They stand still, looking at each other, and then Tammy takes his hand and leads him round to the side of the building, near her loading-dock steps.

'Here,' she says, handing him the green apron she is carrying. 'Put this on.'

George doesn't ask any questions. He strips off his coat and ties on the apron, stopping only to check if he should take off his sweatshirt too.

Tammy shakes her head. 'It's OK,' she says.

She walks George into the store, his coat hanging open so the green apron is visible. A girl called Penny working the checkout looks over as they come in, eyes round and blank like the eyes of an overworked horse. As they carry on down the household products aisle, people seem to draw aside, allowing them to pass. Tammy keeps her eyes on the floor. She hasn't looked back at George once, but he is holding tightly to her hand. She lifts her gaze to waist level. All the boxes and bottles blur into a stream of brand names, smiling faces, familiar logos. At one point, she sees coming towards her a pair of workpants like the ones her father wears, and she falters; her fingers loosen, dropping George's hand, and she turns into a shelf stacked with washing detergents. The workpants pass and she feels George pick up her hand again. By the time they reach the refrigerated lock-up the only thing she's feeling is the coolness of his palm in hers.

Inside, sitting cross-legged on the floor between the shelves, her hand against his cheek, head resting on his collar-bone, 'This isn't the answer,' she tells him.

'What?' he says, pulling her towards him and kissing her lips, the insides of her palms.

'In here, the cold.'

George studies her face, framed in his two hands. 'What do you mean?'

She kisses his cheek and puts her arms inside his coat, lacing them around his back and drawing him in until they form a tight round ball on the floor. 'I mean we can't stay here for ever.'

George digs his chin into her left shoulder, until it's almost painful. She strokes his back, softly, underneath the coat.

George moves in on the east side of town, in a second-floor apartment with a guy called Fred. They never hear any noise from the apartment downstairs or see any sign of inhabitants. Fred is extremely pale with a few large freckles like the brown speckles on hens' eggs spaced wide apart across his flat, broad nose. He's got the facial features of a black man, yet his hair is carrot red, or the bits of it are that can be seen escaping round the edges of a blue wool skullcap he always wears. Tammy never sees him take it off; she wonders if he is going bald underneath. Even his eyebrows are red, pale, almost invisible against his white skin. Fred hardly speaks to Tammy; he nods at her when they pass each other going in or coming out, but even that is inconsistent. She senses a wariness coming off him, like an animal expecting an attack.

On a mattress, in a small back room off the kitchen, George and Tammy fuck with the window open at their heads, the sound of the traffic on the Steese Expressway coming in with the damp, cool air. They make up for lost time. The hesitancy of their love-making in the igloo has been replaced by a thoroughness, a stringent, detailed exploration of each other's body, so complete that should either one be asked to identify the other's body, in the dark, using only their fingertips, lips, nostrils, tongues, they would find it possible.

'Where have you gone this time?' she asks him. 'What did you tell Cliff?'

George turns his head on the pillow. 'I told him I was going.' His eyes are wide open.

'Did he know you were coming to Fairbanks?'

George shakes his head, his gaze travelling around Tammy's face.

Next door to the apartment building, across a narrow side street, is a graveyard and when Tammy gets herself a glass of water at the sink in the kitchen, in the early evening before she has to go home, she sometimes sees people walking around in it, stopping by graves with flowers on them. She stands there, watching.

Fred sleeps in another room off the kitchen. He's usually in there. Tammy can hear the tapping of his keyboard, and the strange electronic music he plays. One day Tammy finds a laminated ID card in a wooden bowl with a bunch of odds and ends, pushed to the back of the kitchen counter. She turns the card over and there's a picture of Fred on it, his hair uncovered, brushed down flat. It identifies him as an employee of the Arctic Geology Survey, dated 2003. From one spot in the kitchen, through the crack between the door and the wall, she can glimpse his hands, his forearms, typing. Though his hands are occupied, Tammy imagines that if she opened the door she would find his head was actually facing her way, listening for the creak of her footsteps across the kitchen floor. When she asks George how they met, he says he met Fred online, doing an accommodation search. He's a map-maker, George tells her.

George doesn't come by the store again. Though Bill seemed to believe her when she told him she'd been locked in Kroger's all night, Tammy can feel that he is watching her close. It's too much of a risk to have George visiting her at work. Sometimes Tammy skips work and in the day they go to the movies, where it is dark and no one will see them. All kinds of movies; they hardly look at the titles. Once the show has started, they sink down in their seats and turn their heads to each other, using their fingers to trace cheekbones, eye sockets, the bulges of eyeballs under closed lids. George speaks to Tammy in Inupiaq, then translates.

'How's school?' Beth asks one morning, when Tammy's about to leave the house.

Tammy pauses, her coat half buttoned. 'It's OK.'

'Don't you have some tests or anything? Where are your books?' She is going through a big pile of junk mail, sitting at the kitchen table with a tall glass of diet Pepsi next to her hand.

'I left them at school.'

Beth looks up from a leaflet advertising house painting at competitive rates. 'You think you could get off early today?'

Tammy buttons another button of her coat. 'How early?'

Her mother takes a sip of her Pepsi. 'Maybe skip a class at the end of the day. You know? Jess needs somebody to sit with her – there's a union meeting at work, everybody's s'posed to go. Your dad says he's busy with the house.'

'I was meant to work at Kroger's . . .'

Tammy notices a letter from the School Board pushed to one side of the pile of junk mail. She can't tell if it's been opened. Since George came, she's forgotten to check the mail, almost forgotten she was ever meant to be in school. She glances at Beth, who is tearing open an envelope. After a few seconds, Beth raises her head. 'Yeah?' she says. 'What?'

'OK,' says Tammy. 'I could probably skip the last class. I've got a study period anyway, after that. What time do you have to be there?'

'Two o'clock,' says Beth.

Tammy gets herself a glass of water. She hasn't planned on eating anything, but she fixes herself a bowl of cornflakes, setting the bowl down a few inches away from the School

Board letter. The letter looks crumpled, as if it could have been opened, but this might easily be because it's been sitting around for a while. Beth looks at the mail only once a week or so, if she can face it or if she knows some bills are due.

'Maybe I won't go to school at all,' Tammy says, after she's finished eating.

'OK,' says Beth, and with a big sigh she sweeps up all the rest of the mail and carries it over to the garbage can by the sink.

Tammy watches the letters tumbling into the black plastic liner, just as Jess wanders into the kitchen and stops when she sees Tammy still there.

'Nice to see you again.'

Tammy looks up. 'Hi, Mr Dervish.'

He's carrying a leather briefcase and a rucksack. He coughs into his free hand. 'I haven't seen you in a while,' he says, smiling. 'I thought maybe you'd got another job.'

Tammy shakes her head. 'I've been kinda busy.'

Mr Dervish looks away, back towards the car park for a moment, then looks at Tammy again. 'Getting sort of cold to sit out now, huh?'

She looks around and shrugs. 'I like the cold.'

'You're not even wearing a coat.'

She jerks her head towards the store. 'I left it inside.'

'Well, I just stopped in on my way home for a couple of things. I've been taking the bus to work, in case Helen needs the car. The baby's due in a couple weeks.'

'You only got one car?'

'Yeah. That's right.' Mr Dervish smiles, nodding. 'How's school going for you?'

'Fine.'

'Hey,' says Mr Dervish, 'Helen and I were wondering if you wanted to come over to dinner some time. You packed some groceries for her the other day, ya know.' He laughs. 'She didn't want to introduce herself 'cause you were busy, but she knew it was you—'

'How did she know?'

Mr Dervish frowns slightly, looking a little embarrassed. 'I guess I've told her about you.'

'Why?'

Mr Dervish looks uncomfortable. He laughs and rotates his shoulders, as if the briefcase and rucksack he's carrying are too heavy.

'Because you were one of my best students when you were at Lathrop – I used to mention you. And then when I started running into you here, Helen wanted to meet you. It's no big deal – just a little dinner or something, before the baby arrives. We're scoping out babysitters, if you want the truth. But bring your mom and dad, too – if you want. Bring the whole family.'

Tammy has looked away. 'What time is it?' she asks, turning back.

Mr Dervish checks his watch.

'Can I bring a friend?' she asks, after he's told her the time.

Bill goes hunting every fall. Hasn't been a year except for 1997 – when he broke his foot – that he's come back without a moose or a bear. Sometimes he thinks it's the best part of him, out there in the woods with his gun. All the other guys envy his record; they try to figure how he does it, but they can't. With nothing else getting in the way this year, he reckons he'll go as much as he wants, anytime he wants: beat the holiday periods when every Tom, Dick and Harry is roaming around the woods in their stupid orange jackets. Once he's done with the house, he'll get out there.

He tips the spade at an angle, using the weight of his body to lever free a hunk of soil. The ground is freezing up; it feels too hard already. After pumping the blade backwards and forwards a few times, the bit he's working away at breaks loose and falls forward, into the hole. Shit. He'll have to get down in there and shovel it back out.

Bill always holds a barbecue out in the backyard when he gets back from hunting, no matter the weather. Invites some of the neighbours round, like he used to all the time at the old house, and they stand around in the snow, eating burgers and steaks off the coals, fresh as you can get them. It will be good this year. He can show them all what he's doing on the house. By then, the rods should be in; maybe the concrete too.

He puts down his spade and walks over to a hole he finished a couple of days ago. There's a pool of water at the bottom. That's probably not good. He hears the phone ringing inside the house. Someone picks it up, or maybe it just stops ringing by itself; he can't remember if anybody's home. Is it morning still? Or afternoon? Tammy was around a while ago, must have been after school, he saw Mrs Kokeok dropping off Jess. They're probably both inside. He goes round to the front of the house. Beth's car isn't in the driveway. Maybe Tammy needs some help with Jess. He takes his gloves off, stuffs them in the pocket of his coat and goes inside.

Tammy is on the phone. 'How's school?' she asks.

Bill picks up the hunting rifle he left on the kitchen table this morning. 'Who is it?' he asks.

She covers the phone with one hand. 'Stacey,' she replies.

He starts looking for some rags, opening drawers and the cupboard doors under the sink, where he finds them. He sits down at the table, breaks the rifle in two and dips the end of the rag into a bottle of solvent. A half-drunk mug of coffee is sitting on the table and some kind of insurance form from the hospital where Beth works, with a brown ring on it.

'What's she want? Her brother run off again?'

Tammy shakes her head at Bill, frowning.

Bill tugs the wet rag through the barrel, checks its colour and sniffs at it after it comes through, then picks up another rag and repeats the process.

'Yeah,' says Tammy, into the phone.

'Yeah,' Bill mimics, then he sighs, looking down at the gun. 'Got to get a bunch of clean patches. This ain't working shit.'

'I don't know,' says Tammy.

'You don't know what?' says Bill. 'You don't know how to clean a gun, that's what. You don't know how to shoot straight. I should have had a boy.'

Tammy stares at her father. 'How's Cliff?' she says into the phone.

Bill stands up, still holding the rifle in one hand. Brown solvent is dripping from the barrel onto the floor. He grabs the phone. 'Who's this? Stacey? Where's Cliff? Huh? He know you two are yakking long distance?'

Without waiting for an answer, he passes the phone back to Tammy and holds a hand up close to her face, opening and shutting his fingers and thumb together to indicate a chatterbox. 'I'm going down to the gun shop,' he says, stepping through the spilled solvent and leaving a track of bootprints across the floor. The door slams.

Tammy waits until his truck has pulled out of the driveway. 'He's gone.'

She walks over to the entrance to the living room, pulling the phone line taut, and looks round the wall to see if Jess is OK. It's caught her off guard, Stacey calling her. It's not something they've ever done much, talk on the phone. And they haven't communicated since Tammy left Shishmaref. So far, Stacey hasn't asked anything about George, but Tammy has a feeling it's coming.

'Hello? You still there?'

'Yeah,' says Stacey, her voice uncharacteristically flat and quiet. 'Connie Stenek's pregnant,' she says, after a pause.

'Who?'

'Connie Stenek. Luke's girlfriend – remember I told you about her?'

Tammy doesn't really remember. 'What are they going to do?'

'I don't know. Connie wants to have it.'

Tammy peers round the wall again: Jess is playing with some plastic blocks, putting them in a red plastic bucket and tipping them out again. 'Have you talked to that guy lately?' she asks.

'What guy?' Stacey sounds irritated.

'That guy in Anchorage you were emailing.'

'Oh.' She waits. 'Yeah. He says I should definitely come out.'

Tammy hears someone yelling in the background at Stacey's end; it sounds like Mikey. She imagines where Stacey is sitting, near the dining table or on the sofa.

'Go away!' Stacey says, raising her voice.

'Was that Mikey?'

'Yeah.' There's something to the pause before her next words, some kind of tension translatable down a phone wire, that makes Tammy prepare herself. 'I moved into George's room,' Stacey says.

'Oh yeah?'

There's an even longer pause before Stacey speaks again. Tammy holds the phone slightly away from her ear, her gaze shifting from spot to spot as she listens to the silence. 'Yeah,' says Stacey at last. 'I figured you'd know about it.'

'What do you mean?'

Stacey cuts her off. 'It's OK. I don't want to know. I don't really care what he does.'

Tammy doesn't say anything.

'But you should be careful. I don't think you know what you're getting into.'

A little while later, she hangs up, without saying anything more. Tammy goes into the living room and sits down on the couch; her hands are shaking.

The map takes a long time to emerge from the printer – both of them sitting there watching it judder out. Fred complains as usual about the type of machines they have to use. This is the closest scale of the images he's managed to get so far. It's

171

almost possible to tell the makes of the vehicles, thanks to computer enhancement of the original satellite picture. Other photographic images they've found straight off the web – a diary for the tourists, day in the life of an Arco employee, heavily edited, presumably by the company PR.

George gets up and runs himself a glass of water from the kitchen tap.

'When's your friend coming?' asks Fred. He hasn't been eating a lot, George has noticed. His face is looking thin and there are dark circles under his eyes.

'Couple of weeks. He's supposed to be going to a basketball championship, the Intercollegiate.'

'Basketball,' says Fred, shaking his head.

George looks up from the picture he's been studying. 'Yeah? What about it?'

Fred shrugs.

With a final rushing sound, the printer pushes out the map.

'Here,' says Fred, picking it up and handing it to George. 'Came out pretty good, considering. I can try again and get the shift schedule. Problem is they're cutting back on the amount of information publicly available – this sort of stuff used to be posted on the internet for free. I can try hacking into the AGS information, but it's risky.'

'So this one's already up and running?'

Fred nods. 'Far as I know – sort of exploration for exploration.'

George leans towards the map, his eyes narrowing slightly. 'Looks like all the equipment's on site anyway.' He stands up and goes over to a large office planner tacked to the wall. 'Where are we? First week of October. We don't want it to be completely dark. That's not a lot of time if we're going to do it this year.'

Fred turns to his computer and types a few words on the keyboard, waiting for an image to appear on the screen. 'November 25. Sun down for good.'

George puts his finger on the planner. 'So maybe we should aim for the end of this month.'

Fred turns to look at him.

'Or maybe it's too soon.'

Fred picks up a pencil and starts drumming the side of his desk with it. 'I dunno. No time like the present, if you think about it.'

George rubs the side of his face. He comes back to the desk and bends over the map, pulling out some other images from underneath.

Fred leans back in his chair, tipping it back slightly, watching George. 'What about your girlfriend?'

George keeps studying the images.

'She's not coming too, is she?'

George holds up one hand as if he's following a train of thought and doesn't want to be interrupted, then, after a while, he shakes his head. 'No.'

THE METHANE

The dogs' enclosure in the Dervishes' backyard is big, seventy-five-foot square, the ground covered with a layer of fine sand and wood chips. Each dog has its own plywood house, raised a few feet off the ground on wooden stilts. A security beam switches on as George and Tammy walk round the side of the house, giving the whole area a sort of glow and shining onto the coats of the dogs, who are running around in the cold air, excited by the arrival of spectators, tussling with one another, each encounter punctuated by muffled yips and barks. George stops and stands by the wire fence surrounding the yard to watch them play.

'You keep dogs?' Mr Dervish asks him.

'I used to,' he replies.

Dead centre in the yard sits a small dog, staring intently at Tammy. Its face is pale white, with black fur along the top and round the sides like the ruff of a parka, and more black inside both pointed ears. The expression in its tawny eyes is neutral, neither friendly nor hostile, and its jaw is hanging open, long tongue lolling wet and pink. Every time Tammy looks, the dog is still staring at her, though the other dogs are crowding up to the fence as Mr Dervish walks along it, metal bowls of food in his hands.

'What's that one called?' Tammy asks, pointing.

Mr Dervish opens the gate. 'That's Dersha,' he says. 'Anybody new always gets the same treatment. She takes a while to trust people.' He puts down the bowls, spacing them around the yard. He looks up at the sky. 'Might be some more snow tonight.'

'What do you feed them?' George asks.

'Combination fresh meat and the dried stuff we get from the vets. We give them zinc supplements too, to keep their feet healthy.'

Parked in front of the two-door garage is a dog sled, hitched up to Mr Dervish's snowmobile. Tammy walks over and runs her hand down one of the varnished wooden struts.

'Got that a few months ago,' says Mr Dervish, coming out of the yard and locking the gate. 'It's a great sled – better for rough terrain than my old one. Look at the runners – they've got fibreglass reinforcers – really strong. Haven't really been able to use it yet, 'course. I've got a converted golf cart, three-wheeler, I take them out in that this time of year. Well, not this time of the year usually – what happens to dogs in warm weather where you come from?'

After a few long seconds, George answers. 'They get a rest.'

Mr Dervish laughs. 'Fair enough. Come on. Let's go inside. I want you to meet Helen.'

The first thing Tammy notices is the evenness of the floor. The ground is so level beneath her feet. It feels unnatural. Everything is laid out in straight lines; the long kitchen counters meet in perfectly joined right angles; on the wall behind a purple sofa, framed photos hang in neat rectangular groupings; on the floor, brightly coloured rugs divide the uncluttered expanse of the floor. The windows are square and clean with no coverings. The house is laid out open-plan, with a kitchen to the right of the door and a large living space, under an A-frame roof. In the far corner of the living room sits a wood-burning stove. On a round pine table, four place settings are laid for the next meal. The house smells like wood polish. This is how these kind of people live, she thinks.

Tammy glances over at George.

'So have y'all made friends?' asks Mrs Dervish, standing by a kitchen counter. She has curly brown hair and a round, chubby face. She's heavily pregnant, clothed in a navy-blue dress, its material straining in the middle where her belly is extended. She speaks with a Southern accent.

'George used to keep dogs,' says Mr Dervish. 'Probably knows a lot more about it than I do.'

'Probably he does,' repeats Helen, smiling at George.

To Tammy's surprise, George smiles back.

George is wearing a pair of black wool trousers and a dark-blue shirt. Tammy has never seen him in clothes like this. She would have been less surprised if he'd turned up in full Native gear.

'Who are these people?' he'd asked, when she'd invited him to come along.

'He was my science teacher.'

George asked what kind of science.

'High-school science,' she answered. 'What do you mean? He teaches ninth-graders.'

Helen and Mr Dervish are asking George questions. The way their voices bob along at an elevated pitch makes it some-times difficult for Tammy to follow, as though they're speaking a foreign language. They talk non-stop, and fast, like the people on TV.

'That's great,' says Mrs Dervish.

'Come and sit down, Tammy,' says Mr Dervish, motioning towards the sofa and disappearing down a hallway to the left. Tammy looks down at her boots. She notices Helen is wearing purple bedroom slippers on her feet, but Mr Dervish is still in his outside boots and they are leaving dirt from the yard on the wood floor. She steps onto the rug that runs down the vertical space leading from the kitchen area to the living room.

'Would you mind slipping off your boots, Tammy?' asks Helen. 'Dave always forgets, and this floor picks up so much dust.' She comes out of the kitchen, wiping her hands on a cloth. 'So, did you grow up around dogs too?'

'No,' Tammy replies, bending down to untie her laces. 'I grew up in Fairbanks. And my mom doesn't like pets.'

Helen nods, twisting a ring on her finger so the jewel is in front. 'Animals are a lot of extra work, that's for sure. I grew up with animals. But I had no idea before we got the dogs. Don't get me wrong, though, I love them. And they're Dave's obsession. I swear, first thing he's going to do when the baby comes is take it out for a ride on the sled.'

Mrs Dervish has that healthy, well-fed look, smooth hair and pink cheeks. Her dark hair, pulled back in a ponytail, shines. Even with the curls. She apologizes for her appearance, gesturing down towards her swollen belly. 'There's not a whole lot of clothes left that fit me,' she says, laughing and moving carefully across the room to sit down in an armchair by the wood stove.

Tammy realizes she should sit too.

'What can I get people to drink?' asks Mr Dervish, coming back into the room. He is wearing jeans and a flannel shirt. He never looked this way in the classroom; he looks younger, and for the first time Tammy wonders how old he is. 'Can I get you a soda?' he asks, looking at Tammy. 'And what about George? Are you old enough for a beer? Or maybe you'd prefer a glass of wine?'

'No, thanks,' says George. 'Water's fine.'

'Perrier?'

George shakes his head. 'Just tap.'

For a moment, Mr Dervish looks a little worried, as if he's said something wrong, and then he goes into the kitchen.

'So how do you two know each other?' asks Helen.

Tammy turns her head towards Helen. 'We're cousins.'

'Oh, you're *cousins*. Did you grow up together, then?'

177

'No. I grew up in Fairbanks.'

'Where did you grow up, George?'

George takes a step towards them. 'On an island off the west coast.'

'In a Native village?'

He nods.

'You'll probably think this is a typically touristy thing to say, but I've always thought that is the way to grow up, the way people live in Native villages. They seem like real communities – everyone helps everyone else . . .' She glances at Tammy, blushing a little. 'At least, that's what I've read. I saw an article recently, about the code of ethics the Inupiats live by?' She lets the question float, looking from George to Tammy.

'The Ilitqusiat,' says George, finally.

'That's right! That's what it was called.' She laughs, lifting a plump hand with clean nails to stroke her hair. 'I wasn't sure how to pronounce it. I used to work with teenagers, down in the States, before I met Dave, and I was reading an article about how they're trying to help Native kids who are in trouble, using this code. Do you both speak Inupiaq?'

'Could I use the bathroom, please?' asks Tammy.

In the Dervishes' bathroom there are some bottles and jars in a wicker tray on the counter next to the basin – hand cream, face cream, lip gloss, body lotion, antibacterial soap in a pump dispenser. Tammy twists off the lid of the face cream and smells it – it smells like oranges – then takes a little bit and rubs it into her face while she inspects herself in the mirror. Her eyebrows look thick and dark; they seem ridiculous to her, like the plastic eyebrows people wear at Hallowe'en. She replaces the lid on the face cream and very quietly opens the long cupboard just inside the bathroom door. On the lower shelves, piles of towels are stacked, and there's a foot spa, boxed up, next to what looks like a face steamer. On the upper shelves sit more bottles and boxes, fluid for contact lenses, Mr Dervish's razors, shaving cream, boxes of tampons, cold remedies, aspirins, a basket containing a jumble of Mrs Dervish's hair accessories, some strands of her dark curly hair tangled up in them. Tammy closes the cupboard door and walks over to the toilet, unzipping her pants. Around the base of the toilet is a light-blue fuzzy mat; it looks brand new, as if no one's ever stepped on it.

When she goes back into the main room, Mrs Dervish is in the kitchen, with Mr Dervish helping her, and George is examining the family photos along one wall. Tammy joins him. The photos are in small groups, framed in identical wooden frames: Mr and Mrs Dervish on a ski slope, in red and blue ski pants, smiling brightly behind mirrored sunglasses; a wedding shot in a warm climate, posed in front of a black iron trellis, leafy vines with purple flowers criss-crossing through it and spiralling down all around the couple; a group shot with Mrs Dervish in the middle of a long line of women in shorts and T-shirts like hers, out in somebody's backyard. In Eskimo houses, there are family photos too, but not like these ones. Eskimo photos come in gold-plated frames, or wooden, or plastic, or no frames at all, pasted or hung in no particular order onto every inch of wall in the house. Year after year of school photos, hunting and fishing shots, a grainy black-and-white photo of a relative when she was a young woman, dressed in her reindeer parka, standing by a sled, taken by a white man in 1953. To Grandma Minnie, this wall would be confessing a pitiable lack of family.

They gather round the table to eat. Tammy sits with her body straight against the high back of the wooden chair. As the meal progresses, she becomes more and more unsure of herself, of her existence in the room. The situation seems implausible, as if she is dreaming this odd combination of people and setting. In contrast, George appears to be completely at ease, and the more he engages with the Dervishes, the more Tammy fades away. It's like the three of them have entered another dimension and though she is able to see and hear them, even talk to them occasionally, she herself is very hazy, not quite translatable. She imagines herself like a sort of hologram, broadcast from a much dirtier, older world, a world of three colours, white and brown and grey. She looks at Mr and Mrs Dervish, their clothes, the way they eat their food. These are the people, she thinks, who will somehow adapt themselves, whatever happens; these are the people who will survive what's coming, if anyone does. They will manage to invent something at the last minute, at two seconds to midnight, something that will preserve their calm, flat spaces and they will endure in these spaces, being kind to one another, never raising their voices or their fists, feeling faintly guilty about their good fortune, while everybody and everything else in the world outside their large triple-glazed windows withers and burns.

Tammy looks around the room again while Mr Dervish is getting the dessert. She imagines this house: aluminum foil-covered cardboard over the windows, to reflect the heat back outside; heavy draperies on the inside; the heating vents in the floorboards switched off, closed. Their unborn child will be most at risk, since children under five are least able to control their own body temperatures. They may not be able to invent anything to save it. She sees the whole family in lightweight, loose-fitting clothes, covering up as much skin as possible. Mrs Dervish will wear a wide-brimmed hat at all times. Mr Dervish will have created a greenhouse garden inside the house, so they can still have green vegetables. They will play a lot of board games.

Dave puts down a bowl on Tammy's place mat. In the centre is a mass of white meringue, with what looks like vanilla ice cream leaking out around the sides.

'We couldn't resist,' he says.

'Baked Alaska,' says Helen. 'I've actually *always* liked it, ever since I was a little girl.'

Tammy stares down at her bowl.

'You can tell we're still newcomers,' says Dave. 'Still crazy about this place – can't believe we're here, some days.' He puts a hand on Mrs Dervish's shoulder.

Tammy lifts her spoon. 'Thank you,' she says.

Turning her head to look through the window near the back door, she can see two dogs outside in the backyard lying down on the light flurry of snow that's fallen in the last half-hour and seems to be sticking. They bob their heads, lifting their noses to an occasional snowflake.

Mr Dervish insists on driving them both home, and Tammy gets him to drop her off at George's, though she can sense some uncertainty on his part. She pulls out a pack of cigarettes as soon as the car drives away. Before she can light one, George kisses her, pulling her round the side of the house, where there are no street lights shining down on them.

'Where were you?' he asks, drawing back from the kiss.

'When?'

'Back there – the whole night. You went somewhere.'

Tammy lights the cigarette she is holding in her right hand, pushing him away. 'That's how I usually am.' She takes a drag and looks up at him. 'How come you can talk to them so easy?'

George kisses her again, on the neck. 'They were OK. I was practising. He takes good care of his dogs.'

'Practising what?'

George shrugs and a car passes, distracting him for a moment. When he turns back, Tammy is looking down. 'What?' he says. 'You have to be able to talk to people.'

She is shaking her head. 'They don't have a clue.'

George backs away from her. He turns and leans back against the weathered planking of the house. 'Who says they don't have a clue? What do you want them to do?'

She throws down her smoked cigarette. 'I better get home, before my dad notices.'

Tammy gets under the covers still dressed. Sleep comes more easily than she expected and she dozes for a few hours, every so often pulled back to consciousness by sounds: a glass clinking against the side of the sink, the front door slamming, the sound of truck wheels on the gravel outside. It is always dark, each time she wakes. She dreams she is digging outside the house, alongside Bill. Sweat starts to drip down the side of her face and the wooden handle of the spade stings when it rubs sweat across her calloused palms.

She dreams about the end of the world. It happens all at once. Everything tips, north to south; hot is cold and cold gets very hot. In accelerated motion, the ice sinks and the seas boil over. Tammy is standing in the kitchen of her house, listening to weather reports on the radio. In her mind, eyes moving under her closed lids, she sees red arrows surging across a map like battle stratagems, tornadoes and hurricanes, malaria and dengue fever. On the bed, she coughs in her sleep; she dreams she is suffocating from carbon dioxide, water vapour, methane. She is walking down an aisle at Kroger's, and she sees Mr Asawa at the other end. 'What are you doing here?' he asks her. 'Go home.' She walks to the exit and sees, hovering low over the car park, a yellow cloud, poisonous. Someone pushes her out of the door.

When she wakes up, she is too hot, sweating into her sheets. For a moment, she can't remember where she is, if she is still with George. She turns and looks at the clock on the floor by her bed. The red numbers are glowing; it's 6.15. She hears something moving in the corner of the room and sits up in bed, her heart pounding. Jess, a small dark shape, is pulling something, a book, off the shelf below her desk.

'Jess,' she says, and her sister turns. 'No. Don't do that.'

Jess stays still for a moment, facing Tammy, then turns to consider the book again, halfway extracted. She reaches her hand towards it.

'Jess! Stop.'

She gets out of bed.

182

In the kitchen, Bill and Beth are sitting at the table. Beth is in her dressing gown and Bill is fully dressed. He looks up as Tammy comes in, with Jess in her arms. His eyes are hooded, bleary; he probably hasn't been to bed yet. He sways a little as he looks up. Tammy notices a bottle of gin open on the counter by the sink and a glass in Beth's hand.

'What is it?' says Tammy.

Beth's eyes are swollen. She turns her head slowly.

'Your grandma's dead,' says Bill, slurring the words.

'Minnie?'

Beth snorts. She's drunk too. 'Not Minnie. She isn't even your grandma. She was Ginny's mom, your Aunt Ginny's. She isn't your grandma.' She takes a long drink from the glass of gin she is holding. 'No. *My* mom. She had a heart attack. Last night, in her sleep.'

Tammy shifts Jess to the other hip. 'So are we going down there?'

Beth nods. 'I'll have to get some days off work.'

'What about Grandad?'

'He's in a home. He's been in a home for two years. I'll have to clear out the house.'

'I'll come with you,' says Bill. He's slumped forward, his head lying on his elbows.

Beth looks over at him, and in a matter of seconds seems to sober up. 'I'll go on my own,' she says, closing her eyes.

'You don't want her to see me!' says Bill, raising his head and stabbing a finger at Beth.

'She's not gonna see you anyway, is she?' Beth yells. 'What in the hell are you talking about?' Finishing off her drink, she gets up, goes to the sink and rinses the glass out. 'I'm going back to bed.'

Tammy takes a step forward. 'Should I look after Jess?'

Beth turns, scowling. 'What?' She looks down at Jess, and her eyes fill with tears. 'Whatever,' she says.

'What about when you go to Nevada? I can get off school.'

Beth turns back at the door. 'Why?'

'To take care of Jess—'

'I'll take Jess with me.' She leaves the room, bumping against the door frame. 'Mom never got to see her.'

Tammy turns her head and looks at a photograph pinned to the wall of Beth and Bill at a rock concert in Griffin Park, before she was born.

'Why is it so *fucking* hot in here?' says her dad, letting his head fall onto the table.

'Look at this.'

As Fred comes into the kitchen, Tammy is showing George a photograph, ripped out of a magazine. They're making an early lunch. George is standing by the white enamelled stove-top frying some eggs. He turns to look at the photograph and Fred walks past, getting a pan off the stove and filling it with water.

'What is it?' George asks Tammy.

She glances over at Fred and sticks a hand in the pocket of her jeans. 'It's a methane plume. Coming up through an ice sheet.'

Fred starts to whistle a tune.

'What causes it?'

'Methane hydrate deposits in the ice suddenly getting released when the pressure on the ice is reduced, because it's getting warmer. Oil drilling can cause it too.'

'You making eggs?' Fred asks, walking back to the stove with his pan of water. He turns on the gas.

George turns. 'Yeah – want some?'

Fred shrugs. 'OK.' He glances at the photograph. 'There was a theory going round, a couple of years ago, that the ships disappearing in the Bermuda Triangle were getting engulfed in methane releases like that. They reduced the buoyancy of the water and made the boats sink.' He looks at Tammy. 'But then, for that to be true, they'd have to have been happening for a while, fifty years back or so, when the water wasn't really warming up yet.' He turns back to the stove. 'Science – it's pretty inexact.'

'There's a lot of methane under the permafrost round here,' says Tammy. 'If you think about how much permafrost there is across the Arctic, if that should all start to melt . . .'

'Whoopee,' says Fred, a drop of condensation falling off the wool rim of his cap back into the pan.

George brings the eggs over to the table and divides them onto three plates. Fred pours some hot water into a mug and sticks a teabag in it.

'So, George,' he says, coming over to the table and sitting down opposite Tammy, 'when are we gonna head out?'

George's fork hesitates, halfway to his mouth.

'Tonight?' Fred continues. 'Or early in the morning?'

Tammy starts to eat. Fred sits there, looking at George. When he doesn't answer, Fred smiles and turns to Tammy. 'How come you're not in school?' he asks.

Slowly Tammy raises her head. 'It seems irrelevant.'

Fred laughs. 'Irrelevant! Big word.'

Tammy stands up and carries her plate over to the sink, eggs half-eaten, and Fred turns to watch her. 'How old are you?' he asks.

'Fred.' George puts a hand on the table next to Fred's plate.

'Fourteen,' says Tammy, turning from the sink and meeting Fred's eye.

'So what are you doing?' he asks. 'Besides hanging out with your boyfriend, of course.'

'I'm getting information.'

Fred tilts his head to one side. 'Getting information?'

Tammy nods. 'Yeah. Like you.'

Fred shakes his head, turning back to his eggs. 'Is that what you think we're doing? Is that what he's told you?' He stands, tipping back the chair he's been sitting on so it falls over. 'You should be in school,' he says and walks into his bedroom, shutting the door behind him.

George is looking down at the table. From Fred's room, the sound of music starts, the clicking of his keyboard. Tammy walks into George's bedroom and a few moments later he follows. She reaches for her coat on the floor.

'Don't let him get to you,' says George.

'No big deal,' she says, putting on her coat.

'Where are you going?'

She turns to face him. 'I was going to ask you that. Tonight? Early in the morning?'

'We're going up north for a couple of days. Just a couple of days and then I'll be back.'

'If you don't want to tell me things, then don't. I don't care.'

George takes hold of her arm.

'We're going to look at a drilling site.'

'You better not tell me.'

'Have you ever heard of Area 1002?'

Tammy pulls her arm away and sits down on the unmade bed. She runs a finger along a stripe in the rug they've been using as a bedcover. 'It's the part of the ANWR the oil companies are fighting over,' she replies.

George nods.

They hear the door to Fred's room open. He is whistling and there's a clink as he puts something in the sink. A few seconds later, the front door slams, hard.

Tammy looks at George. 'Who is he?'

'Fred?'

'Yeah. You knew him before, didn't you? Before you came here.'

George hesitates. 'I hadn't met him. But I'd been in contact with him. He's a map-maker. He used to work for the government.'

Tammy stretches out on the bed, stomach-down, and

186

through the window at the foot of the bed watches a red pickup coming off the exit ramp. It's a lot like her dad's truck, except for some rainbow decals on the back window of the cab.

'I read about him on the internet, when I was in Nome. Then we hooked up by email when I got back to Shishmaref.'

Tammy runs her finger along the window frame, lifts it to look at the dirt she's picked up. 'What do you mean, you read about him?'

'He got fired by the Arctic Geology Survey because he made a map, about the caribou calving territories in Area 1002, in the ANWR.' George sits down on the bed and rests a hand on Tammy's leg. 'He was helping a friend out with a grant application. He didn't even think about it. But when he posted the map on the internet, it was when all the shit was hitting the fan in Washington about oil drilling in Area 1002, and the big guys, the secretary of the interior, the executives running the oil companies – shit, probably even Bush – blew their tops and wanted to know who the hell this guy was, working for their own geologists, getting payrolled by the government and releasing stuff like this. Fred turned up for work on the following Monday and his supervisor told him to clear his desk. He asked for a chance to give a written explanation of what he'd done, but they wouldn't accept it, so he posted his explanation on the internet. And that's when everything went global, and he became this green icon. He wasn't trying to be one. It was forced on him.'

Tammy turns round to face George, drawing her leg away from his hand. 'Did they arrest him?'

George shakes his head. 'He didn't do anything illegal. But they tried to make out he was some sort of troublemaker, doing things he shouldn't have been doing. And that the map was wrong.'

'Was it?'

'That's what's funny. It *was* wrong. Right after it happened,

Fred did some more research, working with a scientist who knew more about the caribou, and actually the hot-spot area for calving is a much larger territory than Fred had mapped out, which would have been better news for the oil companies if he'd got it right first time. But it was too late by then. And if he wasn't a troublemaker before, he is now. He can't get a job anywhere.'

'So he's working for you?'

George hesitates. 'In a way.'

Tammy doesn't ask anything more. After a while, she puts her head back on the pillow.

George comes over and lies down next to her. 'What are you thinking?' he asks.

'My grandma died yesterday.'

George leans up on one elbow.

'She lived in Nevada – my mom's flying down tomorrow morning. With Jess.'

'Not you?'

Tammy shakes her head.

'What about your dad?'

'He's staying here too.' She laughs. 'The black sheep.'

George reaches over and strokes Tammy's forehead with his hand. 'Do you want to come with us?'

She raises her eyebrows, turning her head. 'What? With you and Fred?'

George nods.

Tammy looks at him for a few moments, then turns away. 'My dad.'

Tammy walks out of the front of Kroger's. She is carrying a large cardboard box, almost too big for her arms to get round. She puts it on top of another one that's already sitting on the sidewalk, near the display of firewood, where logs are tied in net bags and stacked up in two large wire crates. Printed on the outside of both boxes is a picture of a pineapple and the words

Del Monte. She looks to the left, then the right, as if she's waiting for someone.

Her mom had left that morning, the taxi rolling up at 5 a.m. While Beth was doing her last-minute packing, Tammy tried to wake Bill, but he was comatose, lying face-down on the sofa in the living room. Her mom put the time and date of her return flight on the fridge under the fridge magnet. 'In case anybody feels like picking us up,' she said, before walking out of the door.

Now she is alone. Tammy looks down at her feet on the wet pavement, biting the skin around her fingernails, one finger at a time.

'Waiting for someone?' Mr Asawa is walking up to the store. He's just coming on shift. He smiles at her, looking good in a new light-blue coat, spotless. His glasses are slightly fogged up.

'Customer pickup,' Tammy says.

Mr Asawa nods his head and stands beside her, looking out across the parking lot. 'Everything OK?' he asks.

Tammy looks at him. 'Yeah,' she says, as if there couldn't be any other answer.

A blue Honda drives up and the driver rolls down his window.

'This is my guy,' Tammy says, and Mr Asawa does a little bow, then walks into the store.

Mr Dervish is leaning out of the car window. 'Hey, Tammy!' he says.

Tammy raises one hand, staying near the boxes.

'I wanted to tell you. Helen had the baby!' It's starting to rain, and he draws his head back inside the car.

'Great,' Tammy calls over, pulling up her hood.

'It's fantastic! A little girl, eight pounds, five ounces!'

'You must be happy.' Because of the distance between them, she has to say it in a loud voice and she looks around to see if anybody is listening.

189

'We're over the moon!' The rain is dripping into his open car window. He wipes away water on the window frame with his sleeve. 'You and George should come out and visit sometime.'

Tammy places a hand on the top box. 'Sure.'

'Hold on.' Mr Dervish glances in his rear-view mirror, and then turns off the car and gets out, rolling up the window before he shuts the door. He walks over to Tammy, zipping up his coat, and pulling up the hood. 'I was wondering if George might like to exercise the dogs for me one of these days. I'm gonna be a little busy helping Helen and I don't really know anybody else who doesn't have their own dogs to think about.' He coughs into his hand. ' I know he's got the experience – I'd pay him. In fact, now I mention it, we're going away in a couple weeks, down to see Helen's mom, with the baby. Her mom can't travel. Maybe George would consider keeping an eye on the dogs for us while we're gone – what do you think? Would you ask him for me?'

'OK.'

Mr Dervish runs back to the car and pulls out a little pad and a pen from the glove compartment. He writes something down, kneeling on the front seat, using the steering wheel as a surface. 'Here,' he says, handing her the piece of paper. 'Here's our number. In case you lost it. Tell him to give me a call. I'd really appreciate it.'

'He's gone away for a couple of days.'

'No problem. When he gets back.' Mr Dervish looks at the boxes next to Tammy. 'Do you need a hand?'

Tammy shakes her head. 'It's OK. I'm just waiting for a customer pickup. Here they are now,' she says, pointing to a canary-yellow Volvo that's pulling up behind Mr Dervish's car.

He looks at the car. 'Right . . . don't want to keep you from your job. Take care. And come and see the baby!'

Tammy nods and picks up the box on top. As soon as Mr

190

Dervish's car has turned onto the main road, she puts it down again and waits for the taxi she's ordered.

Later on, the rain turns to snow. Tammy goes to stand outside on the porch, her head flung back, letting it make her dizzy. As a little girl, she had spent hours this way, trying to identify individual snowflakes as they fell. Somewhere up there, above the white sky, above the snow clouds, the sun is still shining. She can't imagine what it will be like to live in a hot climate all year round, to never experience this reprieve. All her life, these have been the colours around her: snow that's fresh, almost pink-white in its newness, especially at certain times of the day, snow that's grey, icy over the ground, one day old and in only one day fallen, compressed, weighed down by its water content. Snow that's stippled through with tiny veins of exhaust; snow along roadsides soiled by mud splashed up from the tyres rushing by; snow that's sallow, unaffectionate. Pale blue snow, icy on top. Golden snow, warm, shimmering, not to be looked at straight on, blinding in the sunshine. Black snow, quiet, in the night hours.

She tries to look through the falling snow, between the flakes, to the sky above it, but it's impossible – she's tried it before. Everything slows down until the flakes seem to hang in the air, turning on the spot. It's only when she lets her gaze drop a little, just as far as the tree line, that she can see the white moving against the dark green, and everything else speeds up too.

A door opens behind her.

'What are you doing?' Bill says, and she grabs onto the porch railing to keep herself from falling down the steps. Her bare hand sinks into the new snow on it, cold and wet.

'Nothing.'

Bill's holding a snow shovel. 'Good. You can come and help me.'

'What are you doing?'

191

'What do you think?' He looks down at her feet. 'Get your boots on.'

She goes inside, drinks a glass of milk and eats a doughnut from a packet on the counter. By the time she goes out, the snow is falling harder. All the tree branches are coated and the tracks her mom's taxi had left have disappeared. She expects her father to be shovelling out the driveway, but he's not there. Round the top end of the house, near the bushes by her bedroom windows, she finds him, digging. A small mound of snow is piled up next to the house, and as she approaches she sees an area of brown earth where he's scraped away all the snow, down to the frozen grass. Without looking up, he hands her his shovel and tells her to start clearing away more of the snow. He picks up a pickaxe and begins to hack at the frozen earth.

Halfheartedly, Tammy begins to shovel snow. 'Why are we doing this?'

Bill grunts as he plunges the pick into the frozen ground. 'I think you were right, what you said.'

Tammy straightens for a moment to ease her back, aching already from the weight of the wet snow. Snow is falling on her face, coating her eyelashes and the front section of her hair not covered by her hood. She frowns at her dad. 'What did I say?'

'You said the other side of the house would need to be lowered. That if we got up one side, we'd need to lower the other.'

Tammy stares at Bill. 'I was kidding.'

Bill doesn't stop hacking.

'It makes no sense.'

Bill kicks at the earth he's broken up with his pick. 'Too frozen,' he mutters.

'Yeah, it will be. Why don't we go inside?'

Bill lowers his axe and looks up at her, a sneer on his face. 'You. You've got no fucking guts. Complain, complain, all the

192

time. All you do is sit around, reading, sleeping, packing other folk's groceries – don't got any *fight* in you.'

Through the window in front of her, Tammy can see her bed with the covers pulled back. It feels like she is seeing it as an outsider, like it's somebody else's room. It's true, she doesn't know what she is doing. She doesn't have a clue. There's no way out of it. 'I'm not going to help you dig more holes,' she says, putting down her shovel. 'The house will fall down by itself. We don't have to do anything.'

Bill stares at her. He looks disgusted.

'I'm getting a hair dryer.'

He needs to feed the extension cord through Tammy's window. When he goes into her room, she's just sitting on the bed, staring into space. She looks like some sort of zombie. The more he thinks about it, the more he's sure there's something going on with her. He's thinking about calling Cliff today, just to make sure George hasn't flown the coop or something. Earlier today, he'd seen Tammy talking to some guy in a blue car, in front of Kroger's. It wasn't George – this was an older guy, white – but it looked like they had more to say to each other than you'd say to just any customer, and he hadn't taken any groceries from her either. Then she'd got into a taxi.

Now there are two cardboard boxes in her room. Bill glances at them as he passes, then pours himself a shot on the way back through the kitchen just to keep himself warm. The house is hot as fuck – next thing he'll do, after getting the house pinned, is check out the heating. When he gets round to the window outside, Tammy is walking out of the room inside. She's changed clothes, into shorts and a T-shirt. He points the hair dryer at the ground and switches it on, putting a hand in front of it to test the heat. He's left his gloves inside. After a couple of minutes, he tries the ground with the shovel again. It's not so bad, he thinks, clearing a shallow patch. He

193

needs more heat, to cover a wider area. He puts down the shovel, and pushes up Tammy's bedroom window and climbs through.

There's no sign of her in the kitchen or the living room. The house is creaking bad as he moves from room to room. He hasn't noticed that sound before today. 'Tammy?' he calls.

He finds her in his bedroom, sitting on the floor, next to a garment bag. 'Going somewhere?'

'Mom must have pulled it out, decided not to use it. Look at this dress.' She pulls open the zip of the bag. Inside is a silk dress with black and white squiggly shapes all over it. He vaguely remembers it, from a long time ago, before the kids came along.

'Yeah – so?' He moves across the room and yanks out the plug of the electric blanket on their bed.

'She probably needed something black,' Tammy says.

Bill, stripping back the sheets on the bed so he can get at the electric blanket, doesn't comment. Tammy wanders out of the room. Rolling up the blanket and heading back down the hallway, he sees her in Jess's room, standing by Jess's cot. There's a white smear in the middle of the blue rug. 'House needs cleaning,' Bill says as he passes.

In Tammy's room, he plugs in the blanket and shoves it through the window. Laying it out flat on a section of snow, he picks up the hair dryer and works with that as well. The snow is falling onto the blanket, but after a while it starts to melt as soon as it lands. Timing the process by his watch, every ten minutes he stops, pulls back the blanket and drapes it over the window frame, digs out a bit more, then puts it back over the place he's dug out. He's not sure whether it's the heat having an effect, but the closer he gets to the side of the house, the muddier things get. He can see damp patches rising up the cement base below Tammy's window. He puts his hand out and touches the cement. It feels warmer than he'd expected.

'Tammy,' he shouts through the open window. There's no answer. 'What's the thermostat say? Feels like it's about up to eighty!' He sighs and leans his shovel against the wall, lays out the blanket and climbs through the window. 'Tammy?'

The bathroom door is shut.

'Tammy?' He knocks. 'What are you doing?' He hears the sound of water moving around in the tub. 'You in the bath?'

'Yes.'

He stands there, looking at the door a few inches from his face. Quietly he tries the doorknob but she's locked it. She's not making a sound. He frowns and puts his fist against the door, gently. 'I'm gonna make a call.'

When he gets to the kitchen, he makes himself a rum and Coke and a ham sandwich. He's forgotten about the electric blanket. He takes the phone off the wall and rings a long-distance number. Grandma Minnie answers and she hands the phone to Cliff.

When Tammy gets out of the bath, Bill is still in the kitchen, phone in his hand. She's got back into her T-shirt and shorts, and the heat of the bath is making her skin pulse. Standing in front of Bill, she notices a cold draught coming up the hallway from her room. The light is starting to fade outside. She switches on the lights in the kitchen.

'Hey,' he says, taking his time to look up.

Right away, she can see something nasty brewing in his eyes. She thinks about where she can go, in the snow-storm, what excuse she can use to get out of the house. Bill is looking overheated. His face is red and there's sweat on his neck. She wonders how heat affects people with weak hearts.

'Who were you talking to?' she asks.

A smile floats up on his face. 'No one. One of the guys. They're going hunting. Wanted to know if I wanna come too.'

Tammy looks out at the weather. 'When?'

Bill nods, as if she's asked a different question. 'They got a cabin hired for the weekend.'

Tammy wipes the back of her thigh where a drop of sweat is dripping down. 'You think you should drive in this?'

Bill stands up, walks over to the sink and pours himself another drink.

Even from three feet away, she can smell the alcohol rising off his skin. 'So we're going tonight?'

Bill, who's been staring out of the window, turns to face Tammy. 'Oh. It's a guys-only thing, honey. Sorry.'

Tammy studies Bill's face.

'You'll be all right for a couple of nights, huh?' he says. 'I'll be back in a couple days.' He smiles and walks over to her, puts a hand gently against her ass and pulls her slightly towards him.

Tammy looks at the floor, holding still. 'I'll be fine, sure.' She starts walking down the hallway to her bedroom, just as the lights go out.

George is standing by the window in her room. He lifts his arm and wipes at the condensation on the glass. 'That's the hole?'

Tammy nods. 'He was trying to thaw the ground with an electric blanket. It shorted all the electricity.'

George turns his head. 'Shit. Could have started a fire.'

Tammy nods. 'And then he just left, once he'd got them back on.'

George is holding a pencil. He kneels down and lets it go, watching as it rolls across the floor.

Since Bill left, a day ago, Tammy has been busy. There is nothing in her room any more except a bed, the two cardboard boxes, and the wardrobe by the door, which Tammy had been unable to shift on her own. She has pulled up the carpet, hacking it into strips with an exacto knife and taking the rolls out to the woods, near to the place where she tacked the tape measure to the tree. Only one piece remains, beneath the empty wardrobe. Underneath the window, lined up near the skirting board, is a small orange, a tennis ball and another pencil. On the bed, the pillowcases she has chosen have cartoon pictures of Snoopy on them.

'Where are all your clothes?' George asks, opening the wardrobe doors.

'I took them down to the Salvation Army yesterday.'

He looks at her. 'What are you doing?'

'I can't stay here any more. I'm going to leave.'

George sits down in a cross-legged position on the cement floor by the cardboard boxes. He pulls open the flaps of one of them as Tammy sits down near by, on the bed. Slowly, George pulls out the papers inside the box, most of it newsprint, with some magazine cuttings as well, and a few small spiral notebooks. He puts a pile on his lap and reads. After about fifteen minutes, he lifts his head. 'What is all this?'

Tammy is sitting with her legs together, her hands pressed between them. She is naked except for her underwear. 'It's all the stuff I know.'

George looks down again.

'About what's happening. What's going to happen.'

'And you've been collecting it for a long time?'

Tammy nods her head. 'I was doing experiments. The things I read, I measured for myself, the angle of the house, the ice melt, plant growth, the temperatures. In there,' she adds, pointing to one of the spiral notebooks. 'The results.'

George opens one of the notebooks, reads for a few minutes, then looks up. 'Why are you showing it to me now?'

Tammy comes over and crouches on the floor next to him, between the boxes. 'I want to come with you,' she says, her expression hard. 'Whatever you're doing.' She touches the pile of papers. 'This is the proof, that I deserve to. Not because we

197

sleep together. Because it's my thing too. And it was before I knew you.'

George looks at her. Tammy doesn't know why he looks so sad. He looks away. 'You don't understand.'

Tammy gets up and tries to close the bedroom door but it's no longer hanging straight and it won't close any more. She pushes it shut as far as it will go, walks back to George, and sits down on the floor again, next to him.

It's the wind – howling around the house as if they were a hundred feet up – that wakes Tammy. But there has been something else too that has woken her, another sound, she is sure. She turns to George, who is asleep, flat on his back, the sheet pulled halfway down his body, his hands folded across his chest giving him a corpse-like look. She slides her legs off the bed. As she is reaching for some clothes, she hears a sort of thump outside the window, a muffled clump like snow falling onto snow off the roof.

From closer to, the sound is repetitive. She lifts a hand to her mouth. When a beam from a flashlight suddenly darts across the blind, she ducks and crawls back across the floor until she reaches the bed. 'George.'

George wakes at once, eyes open as if she has turned on a switch, but he doesn't move. 'What is it?' he asks.

'You need to go.'

He doesn't ask why but Tammy sees him raise his head and look towards the window, from where the clumping sound is now coming, more obvious and more rhythmic than it was at first. He comes and crouches next to Tammy on the floor, leaning in close so that the top of his head is touching hers. 'Is it Bill?'

'I think so.'

'What is he doing?'

'Digging.'

George puts his arms around her, the muscles of his arms

tensing against her shoulders. Tammy shakes him off.

'Why is it so hot?'

George looks at her. 'You turned up the heat again, remember?' He reaches for his clothes and pulls them on, lacing his boots as he sits beside her.

Tammy watches him. The heat is having an effect. She lists the symptoms in her head: insufficient blood flow to the brain; painful muscle spasms; rapid, strong pulse; dizziness; nausea; confusion.

'Tammy?' George touches her arm. 'Are you OK?' When she nods, he stands up.

'What are you going to do?' she whispers.

'Go.'

'What about my dad?'

'He won't hear me.'

'How will you get home?'

'I'll walk.'

George tilts his head and listens again; the sound has stopped momentarily but soon recommences, the same steady fall and cut.

'What if he sees you?'

'He won't. He won't be thinking about it.'

'Because he's drunk, you mean?'

George doesn't say anything for a few seconds. 'That's not what I meant. But I guess that might be true.'

The sound is becoming clearer by the second, as if someone were tuning in a radio. They can hear each fall of the shovel followed by a grunt and then the fall of earth upon earth. Tammy stares at the blind drawn down over the window and imagines it suddenly spinning up of its own accord.

'Wait,' she says to George, reaching out her hand.

He leans towards her. 'What?'

'You're right. You don't have to go. He doesn't know where he is. He'll keep digging until he passes out.'

'If he passes out, he'll freeze,' says George.

199

Tammy looks at George, but doesn't say anything. She stands up and trips over a stack of newspaper cuttings, tipping over a coffee cup left on the floor the night before. The cold liquid runs across her bare foot, making her flinch. When she reaches George, she pulls his face towards her and begins to kiss him. George doesn't stop her. She draws him back to the bed, until they are lying sideways across it.

'We'll hear if the digging stops,' she whispers.

'Are you sure?'

She nods.

George lifts her T-shirt and turns his cheek to place it against her breast, kissing the skin above her right nipple. She lies back, one hand holding his head. She tries to take deep breaths, imagines the air is cold, dry. All the time, the sound of the digging – the fall of the shovel, the slice, the grunt – marks time in the back of her consciousness and she has no idea how long they have been lying there when it stops. George slides up so his face is close to hers and kisses her. She can feel a pulse beating in his forehead where it presses against her. He turns his head towards the window, the sweat making his skin slide. He has kept his shirt on and it is wet against the small of his back when she reaches around to place her hands there.

Together, they listen as the front door to the house is yanked open and then slammed.

George speaks into Tammy's ear. 'Will he go to bed?'

Tammy nods her head up and down against him. She realizes she has been holding her breath.

For a little while, a series of crashes and bangs come from the kitchen, then they die down and everything is silent. Tammy feels the muscles in George's body relaxing. The silence lasts for almost five minutes, and George raises the top part of his body on his elbows, either side of Tammy. He is just about to get up, when they hear a clink and the sound of a bottle rolling, followed by smashing glass.

'Shit,' Bill says, and the voice sounds so near, as if it is in the same room, or just outside the door. Without being able to explain it, Tammy knows that Bill has made his decision. He's going to come to her tonight. She grabs George's head and pulls his ear close against her mouth.

'He's coming in here. Go into the space over there, between the wardrobe and the door. He won't see you.'

The bedroom door is pushed slowly open, sticking a little, just as George reaches the spot. Bill switches on the overhead light, plunging the room into bright electric light. Tammy has taken the shade off the lightbulb.

Bill stumbles back, shading his eyes. 'What the fuck?' he says. 'Jesus.' He squints towards the bed. 'Tam?' he calls. 'What you do in here?' He peeks down at the cement floor, the weight of his head pulling his body over with it. 'Where's the fucking carpet?'

Tammy fights the urge to open her eyes and check where George is. In the second before her father came in, she has pulled the sheet up over her body. She can tell by the change in the light through her eyelids when he switches off the light again. She waits for the weight of his body on the bed. If he chooses this side of the bed, he will be closer to George but he will be facing in her direction.

The bed sags. Tammy's hands grip the bottom sheet to stop herself from rolling towards him.

'Tam,' he whispers, his breath floating towards her. 'You up? It's so fucking hot in here. You got some extra heaters on or something?'

When he puts his hand on her hair, she rolls over. 'Dad?' she murmurs. 'What is it?'

He lowers his head carefully onto the pillows next to her, as if it's an egg that might break, the bed quivering with the effort it costs him. 'Hey there, Tam,' he says, sounding sentimental. 'How you doing?'

'Why are you back?' she asks. 'What happened to the hunting?'

Bill rolls onto his back. His voice suddenly changes tone. 'You had anybody here while I been gone, Tam?'

Tammy freezes. 'What do you mean?'

He sighs. 'I called Cliff. George's taken off again. You been seeing him?'

'No.'

Bill doesn't say anything for a while, so long that Tammy wonders if he's fallen asleep. She turns onto her side.

'Where's your mom?' His voice sounds sleepy, out of focus.

'She's at the funeral, Dad. Remember? Down south.'

Bill's hand lands on her arm and he pulls her towards him, her back against his front. 'Oh yeah.' His hand comes to rest on her hipbone.

The wool collar of the shirt he's wearing is slightly damp, rough with what feels like dried dirt. She thinks about the dark space next to the wardrobe. Bill has left the door open and a little light from the hallway is spilling into the room. George must be able to see the bed. As her father begins to put his hands up her T-shirt, his fingers hot and puffy, she draws her head back slightly. Bill starts to play with her nipples. He picks up her hand and places it where he needs it to go. At some point, he has unzipped his pants and it is not difficult to slip her small hand down the front of his underwear.

'Good,' he murmurs, kissing the back of her neck. 'That's so good.'

He reaches down between Tammy's legs, rubbing through the underwear. Slowly, he begins to push his erection against the side of her hip.

'Dad,' she says, trying to keep any emotion out of her voice. 'Dad,' she says again.

Twisting her body around, she can see George standing quietly in the dark, close to the bed. The shock makes her lift her arms, as if she were trying to hide her face, and her elbow smashes into Bill's nose.

'Shit!' he cries out, cupping one hand around it. 'What the hell?'

Before she knows it, Bill hits her across the face. He is straddling her, pinning her arms to her side, when the overhead light is switched on.

For a second, Bill squints, confused, releasing Tammy's arms and twisting round to stare up at the naked bulb hanging from the ceiling. Then he sees George.

'Get the *fuck* out of my house!' he bellows, jumping off the bed, doing up his pants. He stabs a finger into the air, towards George, stumbling. Tammy's not sure if he knows who he is. 'You want me to kill you? I'll *kill* you!'

George doesn't say anything. His expression remains completely blank. It reminds Tammy of the night she had met him, when they had walked around in the snow and whenever she spoke, he had scanned her face dispassionately, like he was looking at a series of data. This is how he is looking at Bill now. He walks over to the bed and helps Tammy to sit up, straightening her T-shirt.

'Get away from her!' Bill screams.

George ignores him and goes over to where Tammy's boots are lying on the floor, one tipped over next to the other. He brings them back to the bed. 'Can you put your boots on?' he says, placing them on the floor in front of Tammy. Then he looks over at Bill and, as if the spell that has kept him fixed to the same spot until now has suddenly been lifted, Bill strides out of the room.

Tammy doesn't look at George. The place where Bill has hit her is red and feels like it's starting to swell up. George kneels down and helps her put on the boots. She jumps as a door slams at the other end of the house. She reaches down to put a finger into the back of her boot where the heel is sticking. 'We need to get out.'

George nods and Tammy stands up just as her father comes back into her bedroom with a shotgun and a box of bullets.

There is something comical about him as he takes his time loading the bullets and even drops one and has to scrabble for it on the floor. George stands very still, and Tammy takes a step towards him. When Bill has loaded the chambers, he clicks the cylinder back into place, straightens up and looks at them both, then raises his gun and points it straight at George's chest.

'Are you going to shoot me, Uncle Bill?'

The gun wavers a little. Bill's eyes widen and he stares at George. His eyes flick over to Tammy and she looks away.

'Oh, I get it,' he says.

He readjusts his aim and pulls the trigger. The bullet explodes through the ceiling above George's head. Tammy finds she is now in the corner of the room, pressed against the wall, on the far side of the wardrobe. She looks over at George; he hasn't moved.

'Akkaga—' George says.

Bill pulls the trigger again, and George moves his head a small amount. A bullet hole appears in the wall behind the bed.

'Don't you fucking *uncle* me! Talk fucking *English*! You're not supposed to talk that shit! Don't you know that, you *fucking Eskimo shit-loser? Nobody wants to know!*'

As if this outburst has tired him, Bill starts to move towards the bed, the gun still raised and pointed at the centre of George's chest, shaking a little. George counters him, so that he is moving nearer to the door while Bill is reaching the end of the bed. George glances over at Tammy for a moment and gestures to her to leave the room, his eyes still on Bill.

Bill swivels and points the gun at Tammy. His eyes squint, his face alternately screwing up and then stretching out, as if he's having trouble seeing her. Sweat is running down his face. Tammy stares at her father's hands. She is watching the finger curled around the trigger, like it's at the end of a magnifying glass: the creases at the side of its knuckles, the hair follicles. She looks at the end of the barrel. The bullet is waiting at the other end, nestled in there, ready to be expelled. The sweat on the inside of her bare legs where her thighs are locked together is starting to sting. There's a sort of groaning, creaking noise building in her brain, like a table-top straining under the pressure of too much weight. She looks up from the gun barrel into her father's eyes; she knows just what she is going to say to him at the last moment. And that is when the floor begins to tip.

PART THREE

THE OIL

Tammy re-enters the cold, hard as candy. The dogs pull across the uneven terrain. But the top layer of snow is burnt by cold, and icy, and in the forest when the sled tips sideways, tumbling over a tree root, she worries about her father's body coming off it belly-over onto the snow. Under a nylon tarpaulin, the shape of his foot draws her eye, sticking up like the flag on a mailbox; she can't look away for long. She wonders if the toes have turned blue, if they could be snapped off like breadsticks, and thrown to the dogs.

Every half-hour, George stops for a rest and some water. Tammy stumbles off the sled and tries to get the blood moving in her cramped legs. She is riding nearest the driver's end, forced to curl up into the small space left above her father's head. The forest around is very quiet. Underneath the cold, smells that keep themselves for night-time – musky, sour smells – gather round whenever they stop.

'OK?'

George says just a few words each time as if conversation were oxygen and he is trying to preserve it. An electric torch on a band around his head shines straight into Tammy's eyes.

'Not so far now,' he says at nine-thirty in the morning. The sky is still dark. He walks forward to the dog at lead position, only a few yards in front, but he might as well be walking into another world.

Since they left Fairbanks, Tammy can only focus on things very close by. The cold makes her want to whimper. Whenever she closes her eyes – which George has warned her not to do – she sees Bill's face: its look of dumb confusion when the floor of her bedroom started to split beneath him, and the walls coming away, and the whole room cracking apart as if it were lifted up by a giant and split open over his knee. It had been laughable, his expression. Like a still from a *Road Runner* cartoon. It had almost made her laugh. To see his bewilderment as the bed he was holding onto for balance – gun still gripped in his other hand – slid down the sloping floor and crashed against the end wall of the house, splitting the glass of a window. She hadn't heard the gun discharge, one last time. By then, she and George had crawled into opposite corners; they braced their legs and clung on to whatever they could, a shelf on the wall, the bottom of the tipped-over wardrobe. It was only when things stopped moving – the sound of running water from somewhere, cold air rushing in and settling on the new surfaces, steam rising, it could have been an hour or a second that had passed – that she saw the blood spreading across one of her Snoopy pillowcases.

George had spoken first. 'Is he hurt?

With effort, she yanked her gaze away from the stained pillow to her father's quiet body, spread stomach-down across the sheets, looking almost comfortable.

Once George and she managed to find a safe way out of the room, which was like climbing through a cabin hatch in a sinking ship and up the gangway to the upper decks, they hadn't called for help. They'd stood in the dark kitchen, breathing, staring at the linoleum floor under their feet as if it too might shift any minute, marvelling at how ordinary the kitchen table looked, how nothing was very different in this room. The entire upper end of the house had snapped off clean, from the

210

dividing wall between the kitchen and Tammy's room, taking the front door with it, as well as most of the porch. Through the opening where the door had been, the red glint of Bill's truck in the driveway was faintly visible, reflecting off the street lights.

George and Tammy listened for noises from the bedroom. Under the table, shards of glass from a broken bottle of whisky lay in a pool of liquid like sharks in a lagoon.

Now the trees are rushing by on either side of the sled, which is travelling in a tunnel cut through the forest by its runners, like a boring machine pushing through a sea bed. The dogs at the back of the line lean their heads together, their noses almost touching. When the sled emerges from the north end of the woods hours later, the black sky opening up above it like a deep breath is filled with a bright green swathe of light. At the top the light is wide, twisting down and in towards the line of the earth, a celestial tornado. It glows and shifts, disappearing and reappearing as the sled moves along, a trick postcard.

Tammy turns her head towards George behind her, wondering if he sees it too. He nods, his face barely visible within the layers of clothing he is wearing. She can't tell if he knows why she has turned. When she looks ahead again, the green light has faded.

She is so tired. She closes her eyes for a second and at once sleep pounces upon her, a ton of sleep; she opens her eyes as wide as she can, letting the cold air blast into their corners. Her head falls back against the frame of the sled. She opens her eyes even wider and the green light throbs, brighter than ever, a hallucination.

At sunrise, mid-morning, they reach a large, open field and George stops to feed and water the dogs. The sun is invisible, low slung behind the tree line.

'You OK?' he says, handing her a paper bag. In it there are about fifty different food bars – power bars, chocolate bars, cereal bars. 'Eat a couple,' he tells her. 'How's your nose?'

She puts a gloved hand on it. 'I can still feel it.'

211

The cold will kill you, he's told her. She thinks about a pair of students from the university she read about, used to walk around campus barefoot, wearing light cotton clothing, whatever the weather. A scientist had seen them strolling across the snowy lawn outside his office window, and had asked them to come in for some tests. He got them to study for him, clad in their usual light clothing, in a room cooled to about 32°, while he measured the temperatures of their fingers, their toes and chest. They sat and studied for an hour and didn't even begin to shiver until fifty minutes had passed. A US Air Force soldier, whom the scientist asked to undergo the same test, was shaking so violently after thirty minutes that the scientist terminated the experiment.

George and Tammy stand in the pale grey light, eating the bars and watching the steam rising from the dogs' piles of meat, dumped directly onto the snow.

'Drink some water too,' he tells her, handing her a bottle from between the rugs that are stowed underneath her father's body. 'I'm going to make a fire.'

'A fire? Why?'

At one end of the field of snow there's a broken line of birch trees; at the other, the land rises, forming a spiny ridge with a few rocks exposed where the snow has failed to stick. The musky smell that was with them in the forest is fainter here, unclenched by the fresh air.

'What time is it?' Tammy asks.

'About eleven, I think.'

'When did we leave Fairbanks?'

'I don't know. Four? Five?'

Tammy hadn't gone back into the house. She'd watched the beam of George's flashlight passing through the rooms. He'd found some rope in the back of Bill's truck and tied up the body in a nylon tarpaulin, having rolled him up in the bloody sheets first. There was nothing to do about the stains on the mattress. The easiest way out had been through the smashed bedroom window, pushing the body onto the snow near the hole that Bill had been digging an hour before.

Tammy looks down at the snow in this field. It seems different stuff out here. Every crystal is lying exactly as it fell.

'We need to burn the body,' says George. He looks over at Tammy, and after a little while he adds, 'I think that's probably the best thing to do.'

One of the dogs lifts up his head and whimpers at something, a scent. Tammy looks up too, but there's nothing. The sun has finally appeared low on the horizon, where it will stay for a few hours before the sky starts to get dark again.

'Is this a good place?' she asks.

'I think so. We're going to run into a road soon, and we can't take it to where we're going.' He pauses. 'I didn't want to start a fire in the forest – too dangerous, even with the snow.'

George stands there for a few moments, looking at Tammy, then he unhitches the dog's lead line from the sled, attaches the line to a snow hook and plunges it into the ground, before pulling the sled and its cargo about a hundred feet across the field. Most of the dogs are resting. They've curled up in compact circles of fur, tails tucked round their bodies, the white flecks of ice in their fur shimmering when the sunlight catches them. Tammy turns to watch just as George is tipping over the sled, and the body slides off. It lies there in its orange tarpaulin like a discarded carpet roll. She imagines it moving, unrolling, an arm slowly extending to seize the wrist of the arm George is using to empty a drum of gasoline over it. When George steps to one side, she is looking at her father's face – the head protruding from the tarpaulin – nose-down in the snow, one cheek and one eye pressed close against the ground and one naked ear thrust up into the cold air. His hair looks black and greasy, still alive. They should have put a hat on it. Tammy looks away and a few minutes later she hears the quiet plumpf of an explosion and the light from the burning fire appears reflected on the snow around her. The dogs lift

213

their heads and a few spring to their feet; some of them bark.

'At least there's no wind,' says George, back beside her.

Ten minutes later, the fire has settled down into steady, blue flames and is sending up a plume of black smoke. Tammy turns her head, glancing back at it, and George looks too, one hand shading his eyes. Tammy is shaking. George walks over to a dog, takes the bootie off one of its paws, lifts the leg and checks the under surface of the paw.

'Thought he was limping. Looks OK now.'

Before they leave, he walks across the field one more time. Tammy can't help looking. Standing near the fire's edge, looking down, his body is a dark silhouette. When he bends over, it looks as if he's becoming a part of the fire, like he's leaning right into the centre of it. There is an odour floating across the field now that even the smell of the dogs and the fresh snow can't disguise. It's the odour that has haunted her all along on this trip, but now it is everywhere, the top layer in the chemical stratification of the air. She turns away and puts her gloves up to her nostrils, breathes deeply, filling them with the damp odour of the fur, until the freezing air makes her cough.

She's able to stretch out on the sled now. George puts the blankets over her and ties down the rest of the gear. After a final check of the dogs, he walks a few paces away from the sled, bends over and vomits in the snow. He remains bent over, wiping at his mouth, still turned away. The dogs stand silent in their harness. They look to George then back to Tammy, heads turning, there and back.

'George?'

He straightens up, coughs and walks back. 'Smell,' he mutters, stepping onto the runners and picking up the leads.

Limping from the pain in her frozen toes, Tammy climbs up the wooden porch steps and yanks open the front door of the cabin. She follows the sound of amplified reggae music, round the L-shaped entrance hall packed with equipment to where the room opens up into a larger space, lined on either side by bunk-beds built into the wall. Standing in the centre of the room is a white guy, medium-sized, young, couldn't be much older than George, but his skin has the look of money on it even though he's wearing a frayed T-shirt and stained, wide-cut judo pants. His face is tanned – there's red, peeling skin on his nose, and his cheekbones are tight with sunburn too. He lifts a hand in greeting and then with two fingers rubs along his hair-line, back and forth a few times. His hair is short, dirty and blond. On a wooden table nearby is a chopping board and some cut-up greens; a bottle of water and a carton of soy milk; a sharp hunting knife and the kind of wide fork used to barbecue meat; and a neat stack of dollar bills.

'Where should I put these?' Tammy asks George, who is standing next to the guy. She is carrying the rolled-up sleeping bags from the sled.

The cabin is more like a real house than any cabin she's seen. It's not large, but it's well maintained – she's used to cabins patched together out of scrap plywood and canvas, the holes in the seams sealed up with sod, if anything at all. She feels unnerved by the yellow shine of this place's varnished planks, the glass windows, the brown curtains, the small framed photograph of a mountain range on the wall. It's a white person's cabin, a Lower 48-er rental. There's a wood stove in the corner and a small refrigerator with bowls and mugs on top of it.

'Put them anywhere you like,' the guy answers. 'Those bunks over there are empty – I'm sleeping on the other side.'

'Thanks,' Tammy mumbles and limps over.

George pulls back a chair from the table and sits down.

'Rough night?' the blond guy asks him.

'Long ride.'

'You came by dog sled? No shit?'

George nods.

The other guy shakes his head, picking up a knife from the table. 'Shit. I admire you guys, I really do.'

'How's everything up here?'

'Good. Fred's up in Coldfoot – he radioed in. Weather's been fine – no problems. They're coming back tonight.'

Tammy unlaces her boots and sits on the side of a bunk to take them off, rubbing one foot, then the other. She closes her eyes and imagines hot suns, warm sand, sizzling asphalt. She tries to visualize this warmth, place it inside her feet.

George stands again, zipping up his parka. 'I'm going to take care of the dogs.'

'Whose dogs you got?' asks the guy.

'A friend's.'

George looks over at Tammy then walks out of the room, his boots making a lot of noise on the floor. A few seconds later, Tammy hears the sound of the cabin door being opened and shut. Outside, one of the dogs barks.

'Your feet warming up?' says the guy, looking up from the table where he's cutting onions. 'Shit – all the way from Fairbanks. I can't believe it.'

The music on the tape player finishes and, wiping his hands on his apron, he walks over, ejects the tape and gets another one out of a plastic bag next to his bunk. He turns up the new music a little louder, goes back to the table.

'I'm Matt, by the way. You sure you don't need anything? A drink or something?'

Tammy shakes her head. 'I'm OK.'

'Looks like you came off the sled.' He points at the side of her face, still swollen where Bill had hit it.

Tammy puts a hand up to feel the place. 'Yeah.' She watches him in small glances as he goes over to the stove, lights the gas, then fills up a large pan with water and puts it over the flame. He seems comfortable in the cabin, like he's been here a while. 'Is this your place?' she asks.

'Mine? No. It belongs to my uncle.' He goes over to the

216

corner of the room, roots around in a few sacks lying on the floor, picks out some potatoes from one, carrots from the other.

'Do you live here?'

Matt turns his head, crouched back on his heels, down by the sacks. He's smiling. 'You're the curious type. I got here a couple weeks ago.'

'Can I do something?' she asks.

'Do you cook?'

'A little.'

'You can help cook, then, sure, if you want.'

Tammy stands up – her feet feel like the ends of two baseball bats. 'What are you making?'

'Soup.' Matt hands her a knife. 'Watch out, it's sharp.' He scoops up the neat pile of dollars and stuffs them in his back pocket. Tammy slides into a chair and begins to chop carrots. 'So how long are you staying?'

The knife slips, narrowly missing Tammy's little finger. 'I don't know.'

'Do you live in Fairbanks?'

Tammy nods.

'How'd you meet George?'

Tammy concentrates on cutting the carrots into pieces exactly the same size. 'He's my cousin.'

'Your cousin?'

Tammy glances over at Matt – he's walked to his bunk and is sitting on the edge of the mattress, holding a lighter to the pipe on a small bong. He takes the bong away from his mouth. 'Do you mind?' he says, smoke falling from his mouth in a clump of dense, white cloud.

Tammy shakes her head, looking away. Carrots done, she scrapes them to one side of the chopping board and starts on the potatoes.

'Cousins, huh?' says Matt. 'I didn't know that. Not that it's any of my business.' He takes another drag off the bong,

217

pressing the plastic top of the funnel over his mouth. 'Makes sense, though.'

A few minutes later, George comes back inside, smelling of dog food. His skin looks pallid in the afternoon light, slightly puffy.

'Dogs OK?' Matt asks.

'Yes. I took them off the leads for a while.' He drops into a chair at the opposite end of the table to Tammy and rests his head in his hands. 'I'm tired.'

'Yeah,' says Matt, releasing a small amount of smoke from between his teeth. 'Not surprising, really.'

Tammy and George finally sleep at about four o'clock in the afternoon, when the sun has gone down and Matt's doing some errands in Livengood. They lie next to each other on one single bunk, eyes open, staring up at the bed above. A spider's web, its strands thickened by dust, is spread across a section of the wire springs, and Tammy watches an ant making its way up one of the wooden legs of the bed.

'I didn't say anything to Matt,' George says.

Something creaks in the corner of the cabin, by the wood stove. George has stuffed the stove full of logs in preparation for the night and the cabin's starting to warm up.

'Do you think anyone will come looking for us?' Tammy asks.

George shifts his position, bringing his arms down by his side. 'I don't know. Not right away.' He rolls onto his side to face her. He pulls a strand of hair off her forehead, looking into her eyes, but not as if he's seeing her. 'Your dad . . .'

Tammy turns her head slightly and stares at the pillowcase beneath her head. 'Yeah?'

He pauses, mouth half-open. 'Did that kind of thing happen a lot?'

'A couple times.'

Tammy waits for a moment then glances at George. His eyes

218

blink. Two times. Three. Tammy starts to count and after a little while the lids are moving in slow motion. She is noticing every detail – the tiny pores on the surface of the lids, a few uneven lashes like witches' broom-ends, red veins on the whites of his eyes.

George starts to ask something, but Tammy interrupts. 'There are more important things to think about.'

George doesn't say anything for a few minutes and then he nods. 'OK.' He turns onto his back again. 'You never talked about Mr Dervish to anyone, did you? To your mom?'

'No. But he might go to her if he finds the dogs are missing. All he'd have to do is contact the school to get my address.'

'We'll get the dogs and the sled back. Luke can drive them down tomorrow.'

Tammy looks up. 'Luke?'

'He's coming tomorrow. He's been up north with Fred.'

A half-hour later, George is asleep, deeply, as if a hospital orderly has crept in and given him an injection. When Tammy hears his breath coming out in long, steady rhythms, she edges herself off the mattress and climbs the wooden ladder to the upper bunk. There's an old *Fairbanks Daily News* lying on top of the rumpled green wool blanket; the headline story is about a lawsuit against BP, who have pleaded guilty to illegal waste disposal off Alaska's North Slope. The newspaper is faded, discoloured in one corner; it's got a little crescent of paper ripped off one corner, like someone needed to write down a phone number. Tammy falls asleep finally a few hours later, returning to a vista of unending sled rides through dark forests, bonfires in snowy fields.

In the morning, stumbling around outside in the half-light with a flashlight, Tammy trips over a dog's curled-up body and lands face-down on the stiff burlap bags George has put out for them to sleep on. The dog raises its head and stares at her. She gets to her feet and continues trudging through the snow to the outhouse, where she finds a round hole in a wooden seat, and wood chips in a pail beside it. On the back of the door someone has carved out a motto: *Visualize industrial collapse.* There's a mild feeling of cramp in her belly; her period is due. She runs her fingers along the platform she is seated upon; the wood is splintered and rough at the edges. She hears a few dogs stirring outside, the rattle of their leads, and then a loud knock on the door that makes her jump.

'Tammy?' It is George's voice.

'Yes?'

'You OK?'

'Yes.' She raises a hand to her mouth and runs her teeth along a thumbnail, waiting for him to speak again but he doesn't.

When she goes back inside, George is sitting at the table, writing in a spiral notebook, a kerosene lamp giving him light in the dark room. He's changed into traditional Eskimo clothes: caribou-skin pants and a dark-blue aktikluq. In his bunk, Matt stirs in the sleeping bag. He must have returned late last night. She wonders if he'd looked at them both while they slept, shining a flashlight across their faces. He groans a little and turns onto his back, pulling the sleeping bag over his face. George has stoked up the fire but it's cold inside the cabin. With her parka still on, Tammy pulls up a chair next to George.

'When's Luke coming?'

George keeps writing. 'They should be here today.'

'Wouldn't it be better for you to return the dogs?'

George looks at her. 'I don't think so.' Suddenly, he leans over and kisses her.

Tammy breathes in through her nose, closing her eyes. She puts her hands either side of his face, and he leans his nose against her cheek after their lips part.

A few minutes later, Matt sits up in his sleeping bag. 'Hey,' he says, wiping his face, voice husky, 'Tom here yet?'

George shakes his head and Matt extracts himself from the bag, putting his feet on the floor. He is wearing thick wool socks. 'Tom the truck!' he exclaims, raising one fist in the air. 'Our Dalton highwayman. Our man on the inside.'

George looks up from his writing and explains to Tammy. 'Tom works in Prudhoe Bay.'

'He works for us,' says Matt.

Slipping a grey hooded sweatshirt over his long-sleeved T-shirt, he walks over to the table and looks down at what George has been writing. Tammy notices the stubble on his cheek grows out much darker than the hair on his head.

'Tom's had to put up with a *lot* of bullshit, that's no lie.'

George is quiet. He turns and looks at Matt.

'What?' says Matt. 'Don't give me that voodoo stare, trying to psych me out. She's here now, isn't she? You planning to try and keep everything secret?' He fetches his boots from where he's left them by the wood stove, gaping open like two long-tongued mouths eating the heat, and tramps out into the yard.

George gets up, searches through some brown-paper bags in the corner of the room and comes back to the table with two shrink-wrapped packets of beef jerky. 'Want some?'

'Sure.'

'You don't have to be part of this, you know. You could stay here in the cabin for a while—'

'Here?'

George nods. 'No one will trace you here. There's enough food, enough wood.'

Tammy looks around. 'And when would you be back?'

'Two days. Possibly three.'

The logs in the wood stove shift, collapsing against each other.

'I can't go back to Fairbanks,' she says.

George is chewing his jerky; his jaw stops moving, and he swallows. 'No.'

After a little while, Tammy speaks again. 'I wouldn't want to stay here by myself.'

The room falls silent again until they hear the sound of the front door. Matt walks back into the room, humming a tune. 'Pretty overcast out there. I need some coffee,' he says, fetching a pot from the top of the fridge. 'Anybody else?'

Tammy spends most of the day sleeping. When Luke and Fred arrive, mid-afternoon, in a green Mitsubishi truck spattered with mud, it's Luke's voice that wakes her. She turns her head on the pillow and sees him, his scalp showing through the crewcut he's been given. He is wearing a black hooded sweatshirt and he's standing with his back to her, telling Matt how they'd been delayed by high winds going over the pass and ended up staying the night in Coldfoot. On his feet is the same pair of boots he'd worn out on the ice the day he took her for a ride; there are doodles all over them in green ballpoint. Fred sees Tammy over Luke's shoulder and nods.

Luke turns round. For a second, there is something in his eyes, a nervous, cornered look. 'Hey,' he says, a grin forcing his mouth into a tight, flat line.

Tammy sits up in bed. 'I came with George.'

Luke flinches slightly.

'Yeah. I heard.'

At dusk, the rumble of a large vehicle coming up the road through the woods starts the dogs barking. Tammy jerks upright in bed.

'Tom,' says Matt, looking up.

George goes to check. A few minutes later, voices sound in the hallway and he walks back into the room with a big Eskimo, wearing a grey synthetic parka over green overalls. The new guy says a few words to Matt as he stands by the wood stove, warming his hands, then climbs up fully clothed

222

into an upper bunk, pulls the blankets over himself and turns his back.

At six o'clock that evening, they all gather in the L-shaped front section of the cabin. Boxes of tinned goods and other domestic supplies crowd the area, lining the walls; they're so tightly packed that they should provide some insulation, yet everyone's breath is coming out in a fog. In the centre of the space, in little piles like junk campfires, Matt has laid out an assortment of equipment: socket wrenches, crescent wrenches, plastic gallon jugs filled with sand and grit, cans of spray lubricant, plastic funnels, cloth gloves, spools of black electrical tape, military surplus angle-head flashlights, six of everything, brand new and clean. Tammy stands closest to the front door, her hands in her pockets.

Big Tom is leaning against the opposite wall, broad shoulders, muscular forearms holding a chipped mug with coffee in it. He's frowning, tongue running over his teeth, staring at a space in the air right in front of him. Fred sits cross-legged on the floor, a grey laptop open in front of him, and Luke's opposite, with his back against a wall, legs sprawled, a can of Coke in his hand. He's wearing a floppy leather hat. Tammy remembers what Stacey has told her about Connie Stenek's baby. She wonders if Connie knows where Luke is.

Luke reaches over to one of Matt's carefully sorted piles of tools and picks up a can with a funnel-like lid. 'Pool cleaner? What's that for? We gonna build a pool while we're here?' He giggles, and Tammy realizes that he's nervous.

'No,' Matt says, taking back the can. He looks round at everyone. 'OK? Should we start?' Fred moves his laptop out of the way as Matt unrolls a piece of paper across the floor. The picture on it is difficult to decipher, a satellite image covering a large area from a long distance. 'This here,' Matt says, circling an area with his finger, 'is Area 1002.' He glances at Fred, who nods, a small, single nod. 'As y'all know, the oil companies have already started doing exploratory drilling in there, with the eye to set up permanent sites as soon as they get the green light from Washington. And that is just about to happen. This little spot right here' – Matt draws a circle with a red marker around a tiny dark rectangle – 'is the drilling point we're going for. It's new, just gone operational a few weeks ago.' He looks up at Tom and Tom nods, more slowly than Fred, blowing into his coffee. 'We're hoping to surprise them, going in so soon, and at this time of the year.'

Fred shuts his laptop. 'Hoping is about it,' he mutters. George steps out from where he's been standing behind Matt, and Fred looks up at him. 'I just think we should face facts, you know?'

'Sure. You're right,' says George, after a pause.

Matt looks back and forth between the two and then begins again. 'What we're talking about on this job is basic vehicular sabotage. Obviously it's dangerous up there, with lots of potential to go seriously wrong, but the action is not that complicated, or difficult to actually execute. We just need to be quick and quiet. The short-term effects of the sabotage will cause real headaches, though, and if it goes right, then the idea is, I think,' he glances at George, 'that we'll be planning more. We're for sure thinking of this as a long-term campaign.' He stands up and runs a hand through his dirty hair, leaving it standing up on end, then turns and picks up some papers from the floor behind him and hands out a sheet to each person. Tammy is the last one. 'You'd better familiarize yourself with this, if you're in,' he says to her. 'Do you know much about heavy vehicles?'

'I think the aim,' says George, directing his comment to Fred, 'is to make things as difficult as can be for the oil companies that are going in to explore.'

The paper in Tammy's hand is printed with silhouettes. They are labelled: bulldozer, front loader, grader, tractors, articulated loader, backhoe, power shovel.

'How difficult can we make it, realistically?' Fred answers. 'I'm not saying I don't agree, I – I just think everyone should know we're up against a huge sort of Goliath here.'

'Think you could tell the difference between these in the dark?' Matt says to Tammy.

She studies the paper. Lines show the exact location of engine parts, the oil filters, the radiator caps. 'After a while,' she says. 'Do I get to practise?'

'I think it's possible,' says George, still talking to Fred. 'For them, time is money, lots of money, and every shift they have to cancel loses them thousands, hundreds of thousands. It's worked before.' George looks around at everyone. 'Eventually they just give up.'

Fred looks at the floor, rubs his lips together. 'I used to work for these people, remember. They've got a lot of money to lose.' He looks at the satellite picture. 'I'm not saying don't do it – what choice is there? Just seems like we should be doing more.'

Matt begins to hand out supplies from each pile like he's dealing a poker hand. He checks over each object as he gives it away, handling it delicately. He's changed into a clean, caramel-coloured pair of pants, with large pockets down the side of the legs. The hems are frayed and there are some black stains on the seat, but to Tammy they still look expensive. 'We'll go through the techniques over the next few days. Until you can do them in your sleep. George and I have done them all before – but not exactly in these conditions. We don't have that long, because we don't want to be up there when the sun's set for good. It's the middle of fucking nowhere. How long's it gonna take to get there, Tom?'

Tom crosses his arms. He's still wearing the grey parka he arrived in, an oval decal over his heart that reads *Arco Alaska* in green flowing script. ' 'Bout ten, eleven, hours,' he says. 'You can't go any faster this time of year. And you never know with the weather. Could take longer.'

'How close will you get us?' asks Luke.

'Ten, maybe five, miles out.'

'No closer?'

'Not unless you want everyone knowing you're coming. There's no good reason for me to be out there, 'cept if I were lost, which I wouldn't be.'

'We don't need to get closer,' says George. 'It's safer that way. We mapped all this out already – last trip.'

Luke smiles at George, holding up his hands like he's facing a robber. 'Yeah, OK; don't lose your shirt.'

'What happens afterwards?' Tammy asks.

Everyone except Luke looks round at her.

'What do you mean?' asks George in a quiet voice.

'After we're done. Where do we go?'

Luke chuckles, spinning a crescent wrench on the floor like he's playing Spin the Bottle.

'Everything's on a schedule,' says Matt. 'We've got a pick-up point and arranged time for Tom, the following morning. We'll talk it all through, don't worry. Less paperwork the better, you know?'

Tammy looks at George. 'So we stay the night?'

George shakes his head. 'Not on the site.'

'How do we find the pick-up point?' Luke asks, playing with a twisted bit of pipe cleaner he's pulled out of his pocket.

Matt sighs. 'How do we *find* it? How do you find anything? Compass? Map? It's not like we've never done this before.'

Luke shrugs, his lips shoved forward in a pout. 'Easy to get lost, that's all. All that fucking snow, you know, everything looks the fucking same. *We* almost got lost, didn't we, Fred?' Fred doesn't look up; he's typing something, the computer reopened between his knees. Luke looks at Matt again. 'Just because it's all in *your* head.' He turns to George. 'What if you go AWOL on us again?' He laughs, nervously.

'You leave an object near the pick-up point,' says George, addressing everyone. 'Something to identify the spot. Something we all know about.'

'Like what?' asks Fred, still typing.

'We haven't decided yet.'

'So Tom,' says Luke, standing up, 'all those guys working up there, on the oil fields, they think you're just another good ol' boy? Nobody gets suspicious?'

Tom tips back his cup, drinking the last of the coffee. 'Why would they get suspicious? Eskimos don't give 'em hassles – it's the white guys who complain.' His slow gaze rambles around the room. 'Most Eskimos are totally behind this shit, right?'

'Right,' says George.

'We're pretty much the outsiders.'

Luke laughs his nervous laugh again, taking a step towards Tom and wagging a finger at him. Tammy doesn't remember him being this jumpy back on Shishmaref. 'That's *true*! I know that's true back home where *I* live – where *we* live,' he adds, nodding towards George. 'Hell, I didn't used to think there was anything wrong with it myself . . .' He pauses, and frowns as if something internal is giving him pain and has stopped him. Then he laughs again, still pointing at Tom. 'Hey! Maybe you're a double agent – did you ever think that, George? Tom here could be a double agent.' He spins round in the centre of the room. 'Then again, maybe we're *all* double agents!'

Fred has stopped typing and is staring up at Luke, his mouth open. George walks over and shepherds Luke into one corner of the room, putting an arm over one shoulder. He says a few words in Inupiaq that Tammy can't understand. She turns away and looks out of the window by the front door. Outside, a small black bird with a yellow beak is balanced on a bush, trilling a bright, repetitive call. The call goes on and on and the bird is hopping about nervously from branch to branch. Tammy moves to the other side of the window, trying to see what is bothering it.

Fred shuts his laptop and stands up. 'Can I say something?' His face looks slightly yellow in the wash of the overhead light. 'Everything I've ever read about this – and I've read a lot in the

227

last month, believe me – says most Inupiats want more drilling in the ANWR. That way, there are more jobs, more money coming their way. There's no way you can go back to how things were before. You can't ask people who've had running water and heating for the first time in their lives to go back to peat fires, or whatever. And the thing that pays for all these amenities is oil, right? So why not get more of it?' He pauses, swallowing before going on. 'People don't care about long-term, in general. If they can have heat and gas for a couple more months, that's what's important, that's the pressing need.' Tom yawns and Fred starts to speak more quickly. 'I guess I'm questioning what's in this for any of you.' Fred looks at Luke. 'Don't you like modern conveniences?' He looks at Tammy. 'Central heating?' He turns his head to George. 'I'm just saying.'

'He's got a point,' says Luke, laughing again. George drops the arm from Luke's shoulder.

Matt is shaking his head. 'No. It can't last, that's the point. The whole planet's going under. That's what we're trying to save – what I'm trying to save, anyway.'

Fred turns to face him. 'You're trying to save the whole planet? Wow.'

Tom pushes himself with one foot off the wall and walks out of the room. While Fred watches him go, George moves to the centre of the room and starts to roll up the satellite image.

'Look,' he says.

Tammy turns away from the black bird, which is still sounding its alarm.

'Everyone is nervous. Now that we're here. It's natural.' He straightens up, the satellite picture rolled under his arm, and speaks again, more quietly. 'And any one of you can leave too, anytime, if you want to.' He looks at Fred. 'OK?'

Fred pulls off his wool cap and sits down again, near the pile of supplies Matt has given him. George walks over to Tammy. He looks at Luke, now leaning against the wall in the spot where Tom had been standing, then at Matt, and nods his head.

'Right. I think we should divide the work up into elements,' says Matt. 'Into methods of attacks – so that each one of us only has to worry about one kind of method, one action on each vehicle, if you get what I mean.' He looks at Tammy. 'You're definitely in on this?'

'Yes.'

'You sure?'

She nods.

He twists his lips to one side, biting the inside of one cheek. 'I thought you could deal with sand. You know how to find the oil filter in an engine?'

Late that night, Luke finds Tammy smoking by the side of the latrine, the glow of her cigarette flaring in the dark. She's been listening to the sounds of Luke and George loading the dogs, and thinking about Mr Dervish. The top layer of the snow has turned icy and when she reaches out a hand to steady herself her fingers slide across the frost-coated boards of the latrine walls. As night comes on and the temperatures drop, she is feeling more and more awake, like she is descending inch by inch into a plunge pool.

'How'd you get away from your dad?' asks Luke, making her jump.

'Fuck.' She pulls the hood of her parka forward.

'Sorry,' he says. 'Didn't mean to scare you.' He is staring at the bruise on her face. One section of her hair has escaped from inside her hood and is curling round the edge and along the shoulder. Tammy runs her hand down and tucks it back inside. 'So what did you tell your folks?' Luke asks.

Tammy crouches down and extinguishes her cigarette in the snow. 'Are the dogs loaded?'

Luke nods. 'Sure.' Tammy's hands are shaking a little. 'You OK?' he asks.

For the first time since he's arrived, she looks straight at him. 'Sure.'

'I won't take the dogs back, if you don't want me to.'

Tammy frowns. 'I want you to take them back.'

Luke nods his head up and down a few times, fast. 'Good. That's cool. I thought maybe . . .' He looks round, back towards the cabin. 'This is crazy, huh? Pretty extreme. I thought you weren't part of it.' He looks at her. 'How did he get you to do it?'

'He didn't.'

'Sure, sure, I know. But he's pretty good at convincing people.'

'It was my decision.' Tammy looks up at the sky. 'Cold.'

Luke looks up too. 'Be a lot colder where we're going.'

Tammy puts her hands in her pockets.

'It's going to be intense,' he adds. 'I'm just warning you.'

Tammy nods her head and walks past him into the yard.

George is standing by the Mitsubishi with its engine running, the headlights spilling light across the banks of snow on either side of the driveway. In the front passenger seat, a dog sits, staring ahead. George turns towards Tammy as she approaches. She reaches a hand up to pet the dog when it sticks its nose through a crack in the window.

'You told Luke how to get there?' she asks.

George nods. He smiles. 'Fred printed out a street map.'

'What about the key?'

'He knows where to leave it.'

'Is he going to be OK?'

After a moment, he nods again.

The yellow eyes of the dog turn towards Tammy. When Luke drives away a few minutes later, she catches a last glimpse of the animal in the front seat, in the glow of the cabin's interior light. The tyre treads on the driveway have iced up into hard little ruts like a ploughed field, and the truck bumps from side to side.

THE MIGRATION TIMES

From the top of the ridge, the ground falls away sharply and George can see a long way to the north. A few miles off, there are signs of a public campground, a dark ribbon of a road leading to it, cleared of the fresh snowfall. A few people are walking along the road, like tiny birds of paradise in their brightly coloured parkas. As he watches, they climb over the bank of snow on the road's edge and cross a field towards a place where steam is rising off a dark pool of water. Hot springs. He looks down at the snowshoes on his feet and lifts one, jiggling his foot to dislodge some wet snow. He is wearing a white parka, the one he uses for hunting. Tammy has told him that white is a colour that will protect them, because white is the colour that reflects the heat instead of absorbing it. When Tammy talks about the ice and snow melting, it is in these terms, dark and light, as if one were good and the other evil. For George, it is a question of allowing a life to continue. And the life he wants depends on its climate. But Tammy's way of talking has got under his skin and he finds himself lately thinking about the darkness in people. Perhaps the two are not disconnected.

When he gets back to the cabin, Tom is asleep and Matt is sitting at the table with Tammy, looking over a diagram of engine parts. She is holding the housing of an oil filter in her hand.

231

'Getting quicker,' says Matt, without looking up.

George sits down at the table and strips off his wet socks. In his bare feet, he walks over to the fridge and leans over to look inside. 'How much longer?'

'A few more days. Depends,' says Matt. 'I don't know about the others.'

'Where's Fred?'

'He went for a walk.'

'Luke should be back tomorrow. We can start doing some group drills. At night.'

'In the dark?'

George comes back to the table with a pineapple. 'It will be dark when we do it.'

He finds a knife and begins chopping up the pineapple. Tammy reaches forward and with one finger stops a little stream of juice from running over the edge of the table, rubbing the liquid into the wood. Matt shunts his pieces of paper away from the chopping board, gathering them into a thin pile on his lap. The top paper is a printout of an Arco employee time-sheet.

'Wanna play a game?' says George, when he's finished and all the slices of pineapple are on a plate.

'I don't want to play any fucking *Eskimo* games, that's for sure,' says Matt. 'They're designed to humiliate white people. Last time I almost dislocated my hip.'

Tammy drums her fingers on the table, a faint smile appearing. 'I don't know any Eskimo games.'

'I meant a board game,' says George. 'Didn't I see some somewhere?'

Matt points to a cupboard cut into the wood panelling across the room. 'In there. They're pretty old, though. I used to play them when I was a kid.'

Three hours later, they're playing the second game of Monopoly. Tom wakes up and makes a supper of rice and beans for everybody, then joins the game. Occasionally

George gets up to put some more wood into the stove. He watches Tammy throwing the dice whenever they are handed to her.

In the middle of the night, she lowers herself down to George's bunk and finds him awake. As soon as he feels the weight of her foot on the mattress, he sits up, pulls her down towards him, and begins undoing the buttons and ties of her clothing. For the first time since leaving Tammy's house, they fuck; only ten minutes and it is done. The action is violent and cleansing, like the beating of rugs.

A little while later, George says in a low voice, 'We'll have to go somewhere afterwards.'

'What do you mean?' Her lips move against the vertebrae at the base of George's neck, as if being able to read their movements will compensate for how softly she is speaking. Over in the corner of the room, George can see the dark shape of Fred's sleeping bag with Fred inside it. He turns around and Tammy settles in his arms.

'Matt's offered to fly us to the States for a while.'

Tammy is silent.

'That's where he's going. He's hired a pilot he knows to pick us up from an old airstrip. We'll fly to Anchorage and then out from there. His family have a house outside Chicago – we can stay there for a while. His grandparents don't use it, he says. Nobody's ever there.' He looks down at her face.

'Is that what you want to do?' she asks. 'Go to this house?'

'Just for a while. Have you got a passport?'

Tammy shakes her head. 'What about later?' she asks. 'After a while. Where will you go then?'

'Depends what happens. I've got some friends up in Nuiqsuit. We could stay with them.'

Tammy closes her eyes, squeezing them tight as if something is making them sting. Across the room, Tom begins to snore.

'Everyone will know by now,' she says.

George's hand, moving back and forth across the softness of her lower back, stops.

'Do you think my mom would call Cliff?'

He spreads his hand across her back, extending the fingers. 'Probably. Eventually.'

Tammy turns onto her back, head slipping off George's pillow. She reaches for her clothes, which are lying in crumpled heaps at their feet beneath the covers, and starts to put them on. George puts a hand on her shoulder. She goes back to the upper bunk.

On the fourth day in the cabin, Matt surprises Tammy by asking if she'll drive into Livengood with him. He's shaved, and is wearing a pair of clean, pressed chino trousers with a white plain T-shirt and a green V-neck sweater. It's as if he's magicked these clothes out of thin air; there seems no corner of the dirty cabin from which they could have emerged so pristine. His hair has been wetted and given a side parting.

'You look like a college student,' Tammy comments.

Matt snorts, looking down at himself. 'Oh yeah? I need to buy some things; it pays not to stick out.' He jiggles the car keys in his hand. 'And it would be useful to have someone else besides me buy certain objects. A girl.' He looks down at Tammy's clothes, the same clothes she's worn since she arrived. 'Do you need some new clothes?'

They drive to Livengood in a light-blue Honda that has been parked all this time in a broken-down shed next to the latrine. Inside this building is a whole range of junk: piles of newspapers, tins of paint, oil, lighter fluid, a kid's bike, a collection of old skis and bent poles leaning against the walls, a broken tennis racket. Tammy trips over a soccer ball, halfway deflated. In the back far corner, dimly lit by the weak sunshine that fills the place when Matt drags open the double doors, a rusty orange barbecue sits open-mouthed. Matt bangs his hands against the thin wooden walls as he squeezes forward to the car door.

'I think there's something living in here,' he says.

'Were you trying to hide this?' Tammy asks, making her way to the passenger door.

'What – the car? Yeah, well, it could look wrong, brand-new rental car sitting outside an old place like this. Just in case the wrong person drives by. You never know.'

Matt drives cautiously, obeying all the speed limits, and it takes about an hour and a half to journey the fifty miles to Livengood. When they reach the main road to Eureka, the surface has been snowploughed and de-iced, though there are fresh snow flurries starting to come down, re-coating the road like a sieving of icing sugar. Black spruce line the northern edge of the road. Matt turns on the radio and after listening to the news he finds a university radio station from Fairbanks. They drive in silence. Tammy glances down at Matt's hand on the gear lever. It looks softer and cleaner than she would have expected, fingernails white and evenly cut.

He catches her looking. 'Hands can give you away,' he says, returning his eyes to the road. 'First rule of sabotage. Keep it clean.'

It's cold in the car even with the heating on and Tammy brings her knees up, pulling the hood of her parka forward.

When the pipeline came, Livengood was transformed from an isolated end-of-the-road community into a million-dollar construction camp. It's slid back some since the work was completed, but enough people have stayed on and now it's one of the final stock-up places for adventure-seekers heading up the Dalton Highway. Matt stops at a bank in the centre of town. He tells Tammy to wait in the car and when he comes back he's carrying a thick white envelope. They drive to a large shopping mall on the eastern outskirts of town. She follows Matt into Meyer's department store and he heads for the ladies' clothes section. Pulling out two hundred dollars, he tells her to buy herself some clothes. 'Keep it Republican.'

After Tammy's made her choices, Matt tells her to go and change. 'I need you to buy a couple things from the drugstore. It's better if you blend in. You better try and wash a little, too.'

In the ladies, Tammy washes her face and hands. She runs wet fingers through her hair, trying to flatten it down. She rips the tags off a new pair of pants and shirt. The material feels stiff and cool against her bare legs. It smells slightly sour. She's forgotten to buy some clean socks, and her old boots are stained with salt. She stuffs the clothes she was wearing before in the trash and goes out.

Matt is leaning against the wall opposite the toilets. He looks her up and down, nods, and hands her a list. 'Is there anything you don't understand?'

Tammy scans the piece of paper, torn from a ringed note-book. ' "A couple of rags"?'

'Yeah. Dish towels, anything cheap, doesn't matter.'

'Does it have to be Score hair cream?'

Matt nods. 'I know they got it.'

'What colour nail polish?'

'Clear.'

After she's made the purchases, they go to a Mexican place in the Food Court. Tammy watches the people milling around. A couple of big Eskimo women are sitting eating enchiladas, with bags of shopping spread out around them. At the next table sits a thin white lady in a childish dress, angrily stabbing at a salad. Occasionally, she talks to herself, in brief outbursts. Everything about this place – the orange trays, the pink neon signs in swirly lettering, the pimply white teenager walking by in his Mexican poncho uniform – makes Tammy feel like she is invisible.

'Two more stops,' Matt says walking back to the car.

Back in the centre of town, he parks in a diagonal bay on Main Street and they walk down to a gem store on the corner of a small side street. It's the kind of shop you see everywhere in Alaska: a little bit of everything inside. Caribou-skin lampshades, plastic tool boxes for fishing lures, mini Alaska licence plates, Eskimo soapstone pottery, salt-water taffy, thousands of miles from salt water. About half of this place is dedicated to rock collecting, with little woven baskets of sample stones, agates roughly polished, quartzes, fool's gold, turquoise, lined up on the shelves low enough for kids to get their grubby hands on.

Before they go in, Matt looks Tammy up and down again. 'You could have sisters, right?' he says. 'Or little brothers?' He smiles and says hi to a family – mom, dad and two boys – going past them into the store. 'Or maybe you're into rock collecting yourself. What we need is silicon carbide.' He makes Tammy repeat the words. 'It's the stuff they put in rock tumblers to polish the stones. Tell the guy you've got a Krelling tumbler, Model 240, and you need the silicon for it because it's run out. Or maybe you've just got the tumbler as a present and you haven't used it yet – yeah, that's better.'

Tammy pauses, hand on the doorknob. 'What are you going to do?'

'I'm coming in too.'

The man behind the counter is bald, wearing a black, shiny waistcoat, with a gold watch chain rising out of its pocket, over a red and white checked shirt. 'Hello, miss,' he says to Tammy, smiling to reveal crooked teeth. 'What can I do for you?'

When Tammy says what she needs, he bends down behind the counter and brings up a large box from the under-counter display. Tammy realizes Matt hasn't told her what quantity of silicon carbide he wants.

'Is this the kind of tumbler you have?' the man asks, putting down the box in front of Tammy. Tammy looks at the photograph on the side of the box. It's a green plastic machine with a round central base and a funnel coming out of the top.

'Yes, that's it.'

'OK, well, you don't want silicon carbide for this one,

sweetheart. Just ordinary grit'll do – it comes with its own product, made up by the manufacturers.'

Tammy looks down at the list in her hand. She squints and licks her lips, reading the words 'Sport Wash', one of the things she'd bought at the drugstore, which she'd eventually found not with the clothes detergents but in the hunting section. 'I'm sure it said silicon carbide.' She wonders if Matt is listening. 'Maybe that's not my machine.'

The man behind the counter frowns. 'You sure? Silicon carbide's pretty strong stuff. Most tumblers like this one use a softer equivalent.'

'I definitely remember the words silicon carbide.' She raises her head and looks at the man. 'My mom's a gem-stone collector. She makes jewellery – sells it at the Native Store in Nenana. She told me what to get.'

'Your mom with you?'

Tammy shakes her head. 'No. She's at work.'

After accepting this explanation, the shopkeeper bends down again, brings up a small box and opens it briefly to check the contents. 'This is the stuff.' He hands it over, smiling affably. 'Thirty-two dollars.'

For a moment Tammy panics; she can't remember Matt giving her any money. But when she looks down, she finds five twenty-dollar bills scrunched up in her left hand. She hands two to the man.

'Thank you kindly,' he says, cranking down the handle of a manual cash register. Tammy stares at the handle while he gets her change, wondering if he uses this cash register for effect and has an electronic one in a back room somewhere.

Outside, it's starting to get dark already and they make only one more stop, at a hardware store, where Tammy buys some canvas gloves in her size and three bags of sand. Matt seems energized by the completion of these purchases and they make the return trip in a lot less time. It's stopped snowing and the sky is clearer, sun turning the roadway dark with slush. When they turn into the cabin yard, Luke's Mitsubishi is back, spun round in an arc and skidded to a stop, judging from the tracks.

The best way to paralyse heavy equipment is to introduce some sort of abrasive into the lubricating system. This can be sand, but silicon carbide is easier to transport and use. It's extremely fine, pours well and, best of all, enough of it to destroy a large engine can be carried in a pants pocket. They use the sand Tammy has bought for practising. Matt concentrates on teaching them all – except for Tom, who won't be going to the site – to identify as quickly as possible the oil-filler caps on different types of engines. In case the oil-filler caps have been padlocked, he also explains how to gain access to the oil-filter system in other ways and Tammy spends a few hours each day with a socket wrench, taking apart different kinds of systems, removing the filter, and filling the housing with sand before putting the whole thing back together. Matt times her with a stop-watch. When she gets frustrated and asks Matt if he needs to practise, he just smiles at her.

Even though it's George and Tom who best understand the landscape they are going to and how to survive in it, it is Matt who takes over the next few days as the leader of technical sabotage training. One day, Matt and Luke come back with a Caterpillar bulldozer engine in the back of the Mitsubishi and it's hoisted onto a table concocted of two sawhorses and a piece of ply.

George wants them to practise as much as possible out in the open, and at night when the conditions are as similar as they can be. 'There should be more starlight up there,' he says.

Tom is standing on the porch steps, in the dark. 'If the weather's good,' he adds, sounding like that's unlikely.

During the day, while the others do their training, Tom has been making pemmican out of venison and melted suet mixed with dried berries and nuts, great slabs of the stuff that he cuts into bars after it's hardened. Every day he takes his gun out into the woods, and on Friday morning he comes back with a dead hare. 'Road kill,' he mutters, sitting down on the porch steps and skinning it in fifteen minutes with a large knife.

For three nights running, they rehearse the actions they'll need to accomplish at the site. They work in silence. Strapped to their heads are military-surplus angle-head flashlights, with red gels covering the lenses.

To Tammy, it feels like they are a bunch of kids sneaking out of the house to play pranks. She asks questions when she and George go to bed. 'Will there be someone there? A security guard?'

'Hopefully not. Tom says there's a gap between when the crew leave and the night security come on, because they're coming from another site.'

'How big a gap?'

'Three hours.'

George carefully considers all of Tammy's questions, as if she is a detective trying to corner him into a mistake.

'The first time I came to see you – in Nome with Luke, and you weren't there – were you out on a hit?'

George turns his head. It is a different sort of question. 'Yes,' he says.

'Where?'

He hesitates. 'The less you know, the better.'

'Better for who?'

'You.'

During the day, in the three or four hours of light, they prepare the kit, like soldiers, wrapping all the tools in black electrical tape to camouflage them. One afternoon, George gets Tammy to sew canvas covers for everyone's boots, to prevent identifiable tracks in the snow. He sits at the table across the room, filling zip-loc baggies with silicon carbide. The others are out snowshoeing, except for Tom, who's gone out to a bar in town.

Tammy notices on the table near George's arm the Score hair cream she bought at the drugstore. 'What's that hair cream for?'

George looks at the plastic bottle and frowns. He puts down the funnel he's using to pour out the silicon and picks up the hair cream. 'Where did it come from?' he asks, eventually.

'I bought it for Matt, when we went into Livengood—' Tammy swears as the big needle slips through the thin canvas and into her fingers. 'Couldn't we just use elastic bands?'

George puts down the hair cream and walks over to her. He holds up one of the booties she's made already and tries it on over his boot. 'Good. We'd have to get rid of the elastic if we used bands. There needs to be as little as possible to get rid of afterwards.' He walks back to the table. 'I don't know what it's for,' he adds, meaning the hair cream.

After a solo practice session on snowshoes the next day, as she's taking off her gear in the L-shaped hallway Tammy over-hears Matt and Fred talking.

'And she's about fourteen or something, isn't she?'

'They're cousins,' says Matt.

'I know. So? She's a baby.'

'So she won't want to turn in family. She knows his dad, his sister. Eskimos stay tight.'

Fred laughs. 'Who told you that? Tight drunk maybe.'

Tammy stands very still, holding her wet boots.

'Number-one rule in the book, as far as I've read: *Don't do it with your girlfriends.* Right? What if they split up and she decides she wants to get back at him?'

There's no answer for a while, then after a clank that sounds like a wrench being dropped, Matt says there's nothing they can do about it now anyway.

Fred coughs. 'And what's the deal with the other one? Luke. What kind of drugs is he on?'

'Huh?' asks Matt, sounding like he doesn't want to talk about it.

'That time with me? Pulling up the road stakes, when he said we got lost? *I* wasn't lost. He wasn't making any sense, thrashing around in the trees. Then as soon as we get back to the campground, he goes into the bathroom and comes out all hunky-dory again a few minutes later.'

There's a long silence.

'George?' Matt calls out. A few seconds later, he pokes his head round the corner.

'It's me,' says Tammy.

Matt smiles. 'Oh. Hey.'

Alone in her top bunk, she wakes up in a cold sweat one night, from a dream in which she's back in her bedroom, searching among the rubble, searching for a notebook or a cup or something – it keeps changing – and she comes across George's discarded clothing.

'What is it?' says George. He's climbing up into the bunk.

Tammy opens her eyes. It's dark. She sits up on her elbows; her heart is pounding and she feels sick.

In the top bunk on the opposite side of the room, Tom switches on a flashlight and shines it their way.

'You were yelling,' says George. He's rubbing his eyes. 'It's OK,' he calls over to Tom in a whisper and the light goes out.

Tammy lies back, putting her hands over her face. 'Your clothes,' she says, through her fingers. 'Did you leave your clothes in the room?'

George pulls Tammy's hands away from her face. 'What room?'

After a few moments, he lies down next to her and puts his mouth close to her ear. 'I put my clothes back on – remember? Before he came into the room. I was dressed already.'

Tammy nods her head. George puts an arm across her chest and pulls her towards him. He leans in to kiss her, but she

242

turns her head to the wall, then turns back again, searching for his mouth with hers.

It's nearly noon when Tammy wakes up. The temperature inside the cabin is warmer than it has been since she arrived, which may be the reason she has slept so long. Even without a window to look out of, she can sense that the sun is shining outside and the grey cloud cover of the last week has cleared away. No one is around. She lowers herself down from the bunk and heads over to the corner where the food is stored, finds half a loaf of bread, cuts off a slice and eats it plain.

This is the first time she's been inside the cabin alone. On the floor by Fred's sleeping bag is the small, old-fashioned suitcase he's brought with him. She turns her head and listens, then kneels down and snaps open the suitcase's two silver catches. Inside is a tangled swirl of clothes including a large red sweater that Tammy has never seen him wear and which is shedding fuzz onto the other things. She moves aside a pair of pants and uncovers a black-and-white photograph, slightly curled at the edges and creased in the middle. It's a landscape, dark mountain ridges across a grey sky. In one corner of the frame the figure of a man is standing, facing the other way. Tammy stares at the photo. She feels around in the bottom of the suitcase. When she hears the sound of boots on the porch, she closes the suitcase quickly and backs away from it.

'I gotta get out of here,' says Matt, striding in, two cans of Calor gas tucked under each arm. Tammy is standing by her bunk, with one hand on the cross-beam. 'Look who's up,' says Matt, dumping the cans with a clank onto the floor. He turns back to the others filing in behind him. 'Let's go down to the roadhouse for lunch – what do you say? School trip.'

They all go, piled into Matt's rented Honda, with Tammy sitting between George and Tom in the back seat, Fred in the front seat and Luke on his own, driving the Mitsubishi.

'Shit. Does this mean I can't drink?' says Matt, rolling down the window and waving on a four-wheeler that's been hovering on their ass since they turned onto the main road. The vehicle cruises past; it's nothing more than a souped-up dune buggy, driven by a man dressed in leather from top to toe.

Fred turns his head to watch it pass. 'Real tough guy, huh?' He turns to face the front again. 'This is some other world.' More than a minute later, as if Matt has just asked the question, he says, 'Sure you can drink, Matt. Tammy will drive us all back, won't you? She's too young to drink anyway.'

Outside the Manley Springs roadhouse, three pickups are parked, red, yellow and forest green, along with the souped-up four-wheeler that passed them on the road.

'Looking forward to talking to *this* guy,' says Fred, patting its fender.

Luke pulls up in the Mitsubishi and gets out, grinning and slamming the door behind him. George goes over and shakes his hand, as if they haven't seen each other in a long time. 'OK?' he says.

'Yeah, sure,' says Luke, shrugging George's hand off his shoulder.

Two men near the bar look up as the group enters. Both are dressed for hunting, fluorescent orange vests over flannel shirts. There's no sign of the man in leather. The room is more like the foyer to an old-fashioned country inn than a road-house. Sunlight is flooding through the front windows, which are framed by curtains made out of a violet, flowery material and drawn back on either side. A Budweiser sign fits exactly in the small glass pane over the front door. On the walls hang framed pictures of snowy Eskimo scenes, of white settlers with long moustaches and even longer rifles. A stuffed king salmon is displayed over the hallway leading to the toilets.

Big Tom goes straight to the bar, orders himself a drink and throws himself down on a low-slung, worn-out sofa. A middle-aged white guy wearing a denim shirt, pleasant-looking, with blond hair going thin on top, is bartending. While he talks to the two hunting guys, he keeps an eye on Fred, who is taking a slow tour of the room, peering at the things on the walls, picking up knick-knacks and turning them over in his hands. He hasn't shaved in a couple of days and his wool hat has collected bits of wood shavings and an oil stain on the back, near the brim.

Luke comes back from using the facilities and walks over to Tammy, who is still lingering by the door. 'Buy you a beer?'

'No thanks,' she says.

Luke spreads his arms open. ' "No thanks"?' He's wearing a long-sleeved blue T-shirt with *No excuse* in white lettering scrawled across the front. His face has a weird sheen across it, like oil on a road. 'What – I can't even buy you a beer now?'

'I'm not old enough. I shouldn't even be in here probably.'

' "Not old enough"?' Luke says this in a loud voice and the bartender looks over. Luke calls to him, pointing at Tammy. 'Can she be in here?'

The bartender smiles. 'I don't have a problem with it. Long as she doesn't bust up the place.'

Luke turns back to Tammy. 'See there? No problem. This is a family place.'

'A family place,' says Fred, appearing beside them. 'Perfect for you guys.'

Luke frowns at Fred. 'What do you mean?'

Fred raises his eyebrows and looks back and forth between Tammy and Luke. 'Aren't you two related too?'

'Me and her?' Luke shakes his head. 'No. It's just her and George are cousins.'

Fred smiles a tight little smile. 'Oh, yeah. I forgot. Her and George are cousins.' He laughs.

Luke stares at him for a second, then laughs too and pretends to punch him on the shoulder.

Tammy walks over to the bar and orders an orange juice.

While the bartender is getting it, Fred comes over and leans on the bar next to where she is standing. 'She won't drink,' he tells the bartender. He extends an arm in Tammy's direction, as if he's formally introducing her. 'This girl will not drink. She does a *lot* of things,' he continues, in a singsong voice, 'but *drinking*'s not one of them.'

Tammy can feel the two hunters by the bar watching them.

'*I* might have something, though,' Fred says, pointing a thumb at his chest. 'Something *alcoholic*.'

'Drinking age is twenty-one,' says the bartender, plainly.

Fred stares at him. 'What? You don't think I'm twenty-one?'

'I don't know. You could be. Hard to tell sometimes. If you can give me an ID . . .'

Fred pulls out his wallet and extracts the same work ID that Tammy had seen in the apartment in Fairbanks. 'There's my birth date, there,' he says, shoving the card a few inches away from the bartender's eyes. 'I'm fucking thirty-eight.'

The bartender draws back his head and nods.

Fred puts the wallet away and leans his elbows on the bar again, looking over the display of bottles. 'I don't drink much usually,' he says in a low voice. He shifts his attention to the shiny keg pumps at bar-level. 'I could have a beer, I guess.'

One of the guys along the bar turns away, lifting his glass to his mouth.

'What about wine? Do you have wine?'

The bartender nods and Tammy picks up her drink and walks to the other side of the room. She leans against the window frame and looks out. There are a couple of guys talking by one of the pickup trucks. They've got rifles in their hands and a dog circling around by their legs. One of the men reminds her of the father of a girl she'd been friendly with in grade school: Carrie Downs. Tammy had spent a night at Carrie's house once, when she was nine, and Carrie's father had come into the bedroom just after they'd turned out the

246

lights. Tammy froze on her mattress next to Carrie's bed and wondered whether Mr Downs knew that she was there. All he did was give Carrie a good-night kiss and leave, the warm light from the hallway spilling into the room and then the door shutting.

After a while, she wanders over to the table where everyone is sitting. Matt has his feet up and he's leaning back on his chair with his arms behind his head. She stands between Matt's chair and George's end of the sofa, holding her empty glass.

'People will start coming over from Russia, and Asia,' Matt is saying. 'When the seas up here are clear of ice, there'll be no stopping them. People will see it as another way into the US.'

'Who wants to go to the US?' says Tom.

'A lot of people. But the US will be fucked by then, too. Half of the big cities under water. Millions of urban junkies having to move in with Uncle Jay-Bob in Kansas, and they never saw it coming, not with three-quarters of the scientists in the world telling them? Oh boy, that's gonna be fun. Fucking politicians.'

Fred is sitting on a bar stool he's dragged over. He stares down into a glass of red wine. 'That's only one way it could go,' he says, in a slightly nasal voice. 'Could be another ice age.'

Tom shifts in his seat, sitting up and rolling his shoulders to stretch his back. 'Some of the guys I work with up in Prudhoe Bay, the ones that come up from the States? They've been stock-piling shit for years. They're counting on something happening.'

'What?' says George. 'What are they counting on happening?'

Tom shrugs. 'Whatever. End of the world. They don't care.'

George puts his empty beer bottle on the table. 'And they want it to happen.'

Tom nods his head. 'Sure. They like it – gets 'em excited. One guy keeps talking about this big meteor that's gonna come

247

and collide with Earth.' He takes a swig of his beer. 'I figure it gives them something to do. Getting ready all the time.'

Fred looks up, with a blank expression, stares at a space on the floor in front of him. 'Some people don't like the world much, do they? They're fine about it ending.'

'Some people are stupid,' says Tom.

Matt gets up and goes to the bar.

Tammy is watching Luke. He's sitting on a narrow wooden chair, a little way from the group, scratching his forearm and looking around the room nervously, head jerking like a small bird. He meets her eye and smiles, a few moments later turning to George and stretching a leg out to kick him in the shin. George turns his head.

'Hey,' says Luke. 'Remember all those stories Minnie used to tell, about Maniilaq?'

George nods.

'Didn't he say it was gonna snow until the snow was as high as the treetops?' Luke's leg is jiggling. 'Didn't he say that white people were gonna come and make a big city somewhere, where they'd find something everybody wanted, and then everybody would come?'

'Ambler,' George replies. 'He said Ambler was going to become a big city, because of something valuable in the mountains behind.'

'What are you talking about?' Fred asks, lifting his head, with what seems like effort.

Luke laughs.

'Maniilaq,' George explains. 'He was an Inupiat – sort of a religious figure. He lived in the nineteenth century.'

Luke leans towards Fred, almost coming off his chair, spit gathering on the sides of his mouth, and whispers: 'He told folk that white people would be coming in vehicles that flew through the air, and that there would be boats that people didn't have to row, they'd just sit in them and go.' He sits up again, stroking his hands along his legs and speaking in a normal voice. 'Maybe he just got the location a little wrong, with the big city thing. Maybe he was talking about Prudhoe Bay. That would count as a lot of people.'

George stands up, thrusts his hands in his pocket. 'He also said a great whale would surface in the river near Ambler, and after that had happened the world would come to an end.' He looks at Tom. 'So there's something else for you to warn the guys at work about. Look out for a big whale.'

Tom grunts, then leans his head back on the sofa and shuts his eyes. 'I got two kids at home,' he says. 'I got plenty to worry about.'

'You got kids?' says Luke, turning his head.

Tom keeps his eyes shut. 'Yup.'

Luke looks around at everyone else, his eyebrows raised.

'Did he actually say the world would come to an end?' Tammy asks George.

George turns to her. 'He said he didn't know what would happen after the whale came. But the story goes he always looked sad when he said it, as if he knew something that he didn't want to say.'

'Bullshit,' says Fred. He gets up and goes down the hallway to the toilets.

Luke laughs, watching him go. He turns back to the group. 'He's a funny guy.'

'Should we get something to eat?' George says, after a silence, turning towards the bar.

It's dark by the time they leave, a single street light outside the roadhouse shining down on their two vehicles. At the last minute, Fred decides he's going to ride back with Luke in the truck. Instead of eating, he's had four more glasses of wine and he shuffles across the pavement to the Mitsubishi, walking as if he's afraid to lift his feet any distance off the ground.

'You sure?' George calls.

'Sure,' says Fred, waving a hand without looking back. 'It's me who's drunk.'

The ride back in the Honda is silent. At one point, George leans forward to Matt in the driver's seat and asks if he thinks they're ready to go. Tammy doesn't know what he means at first, then she realizes he means up to Prudhoe Bay. Matt drives on in silence for a while before he says yes. George sits back, taking Tammy's hand. She turns and looks through the rear window at the green Mitsubishi following them, with Fred and Luke inside.

THE HEAT

Early next morning after the midnight drill, a large fire is lit half a mile away from the house. Matt and George put into the flames all their paperwork, all the notebooks they've been scribbling into, all the receipts, lists, maps, diagrams, Bureau of Land Management documents, Arco time-sheets and employee lists – everything gets burnt.

'Did we forget anything?' Matt asks George, standing by the fire. George is watching the smoke rising, his eyes following any sparks that are blowing into the trees. Tammy watches him, thinking about the last fire he'd built and wondering if he is remembering it too.

By noon, when the fire is starting to burn down, they go back and douse it with buckets of water, and then bury the ashes, packing it all down afterwards so it looks as if nothing is there.

'Meant to snow tonight,' says Matt.

'Good,' says George.

Around seven, Tom returns from Fairbanks, where he's spent the day picking up his shipment for the oil company. He backs the truck into the driveway and they load it up with their possessions, leaving no sign of their presence in the cabin. The truck is full of large machine parts, but towards the front, well hidden, Tom has left a space about four feet square where all the equipment for the hit is stored.

'We riding in back?' asks Luke.

Tom shakes his head, banging shut one of the doors. 'Too cold.'

Earlier in the day, George has walked out into the woods and come back with a small spruce tree, just a sapling, about four feet tall. He leans it against the open truck doors. 'The marker. For the pick-up point.'

Everyone stares at the little tree.

'Won't it be hard to tell it from any other tree?' Tammy asks.

'There won't be any other trees,' says George. 'No trees up there.'

'Hold on,' says Matt and goes back inside the shed. He comes out a few moments later with a length of red tinsel.

'What's that?' Fred asks.

'Christmas decoration.' He strings it around the tree. 'That will make it stand out.'

'Yeah. Like a sore thumb. Whose is it meant to be? The polar bears'?'

Matt, smiling, adjusts the top of the tree until it's standing straight. 'Some workers could have put it there – some crazy workers. What d'you think, Tom?'

Tom looks at the little tree. 'People do stuff like that. Specially round Christmas.' He starts locking up the back of the truck. 'Don't think they'd blow it up or anything.'

No one says anything for a moment, and then Luke laughs, slightly crouched over and rubbing his hands together. 'I like it.'

George looks at the tree and nods. 'OK,' he says.

After stopping at a dump outside Livengood to get rid of stuff they've accumulated that wouldn't burn – the practice engine parts, extra clothes and food – Matt has to drop the Honda at the rental place, so they follow him there as the light's fading, and Fred leaves the Mitsubishi in a vacant lot by the side of a meat-packing factory. George tells everyone they should try to get some sleep on the drive up. They take turns on Tom's bunk inside the cab of the truck, behind a blue curtain that pulls across.

'You guys go first,' says Fred, looking at George and Tammy and Luke. 'Matt and I'll start in front.'

'That OK?' asks Luke, looking at George.

As soon as they're on the Dalton Highway, Tom turns on the CB radio. The CB picks up police radios too, and sometimes the angry buzz of a police code startles Tammy, jolting her out of dozing sleep and making her heart race. Luke is lying head to their feet, the furthest in with George in the middle. She hears him turn over a few times and wonders if he's sleeping. It's hot and there's no air. She shuts her eyes, then opens them again after what seems like hours, but nothing has changed.

When they stop in Coldfoot to refuel, Luke climbs over Tammy and George to take a leak outside the truck.

'I want to teach you something,' George says.

'What?'

'There are a lot of things that can happen when you're under stress – tunnel vision, time distortion.'

'Why are you telling me?'

'I want to teach you a breathing exercise. We use it a lot when we're doing this sort of thing – I don't know why I forgot to tell you about it until now.'

George moves his head forward, as if he is going to kiss her, but instead speaks low into her ear. 'Take a deep breath, on a count of five.' She is holding his hand and she counts out the five with her fingers, on the back of his hand. 'Now, hold the breath for another five.' She taps the five out with her fingers in the opposite order. 'Good. Now let the breath out again, on a count of five.'

George nods when she's finished this. 'That's it.' He gets her to do it a few more times. 'Tomorrow, if you feel like you're starting to panic when we're at the site, start to breathe and count it out. Take the time to do it, even if it seems crazy.'

The curtain is pulled back and Matt's head appears. 'My turn,' he says, and climbs over them to take up the space where Luke has been.

'What about Fred?' asks George. 'Does he want to sleep?'

'Says he's OK. He says he'd get claustrophobic back here.'

At one point in the night, Tammy pulls back a bit of the curtain, behind Tom's head, so she can watch the muddy gravel road, gritty with salt, winding in under the truck. She dozes that way, George's arm around her waist, and wakes whenever the truck hits a pothole, to find exactly the same picture in front of her as before. The road enters her dreams and turns into a city road, taking her past familiar places. Climbing over Atigun Pass they run into high winds, which slam into the sides of the truck, and Tammy watches Tom's large hands gripping the wheel. He handles the truck abusively, like a disciplinarian dealing with an out-of-line kid, swearing under his breath as he downgrades gears. Going down the steep curves on the other side of the pass feels even more dangerous to Tammy, but Tom's mood seems to improve, and when another truck passes, heading south, he flashes his lights and picks up the mike on the CB to talk to the driver.

At six in the morning, the truck pulls up in Dead Horse, the last stop before Prudhoe Bay. Tom goes into the store to get some food, leaving the engine running. Tammy climbs over into the front seat and presses her forehead against the cool glass of the window. The truck's headlight beams are shining onto the blue and white sign of the Arctic Caribou Inn. Parked alongside is an Arctic Ocean tour bus. Luke has slid over to Tom's place and he's got his hands on the steering wheel, staring straight ahead. No one is talking.

Tom returns with a brown-paper bag. 'No hot food,' he mutters. 'Something wrong with their microwave. Coffee machine's working, though.' He passes back a large coffee in a Styrofoam cup, and everyone takes a few sips.

'Where's Fred?' asks George.

'Went to the john,' says Tom. 'Anyone else wanna go? Last chance of doing it inside.'

The toilets are inside the Arctic Caribou Inn. Tacked onto the wall by a door is a thermometer. Tammy stops and leans forward, squinting at it. −50° below. The inn is a larger building than Tammy had first thought. She searches for the toilets down a long hallway carpeted in a thin olive-green carpet. There's no one around and no sound but the hum of the fluorescent lights and the building creaking in the cold. Halfway down the hallway, a space opens up to the left, with a few square fold-down tables and a buffet, hooded in plexiglass, the heat lights pointing down onto the absent food.

In the cubicle of the ladies' room, somebody has scratched the following lines on the back of the door: *Fuck you to bitch I will kill you call the cops and those mother fucking dogs.* Tammy looks down at her naked thighs, pressed flat against the toilet seat.

When she gets back to the truck, George is sitting in the front seat next to Tom. He opens the door and pulls her up. Tom puts the truck into gear. They drive a few miles north until they reach the ocean and Tom turns right.

'Better get in back,' he says a few minutes later. He nods his head towards a fence across the road ahead with a small trailer next to the open gate. A light is on in the trailer. 'They're checking. Wasn't sure . . . sometimes they're not manned this time of night.'

Tammy and George climb into the back and the truck is waved through.

'That there was the most dangerous part. Security's increased round here, two hundred per cent since 9/11. And Eskimo drivers get stopped ten times as much as others. Thought they might stop me with the bunk curtain drawn.'

Tammy crouches on the bunk, squeezed between Fred and George. Almost everyone is looking down at their hands, except for Fred, who is staring at the blue curtain, half an inch away from his face, as if he can see through it. She looks at his hands. They are gripping the bed, tight as two claws.

'Fred?' she says in a low voice.

'Yes?' he answers, without turning his head.

'Are you OK?'

A few minutes later, he turns his head. 'I threw my computer into the fire.'

Tammy glances at George, but he has his eyes closed. She leans towards Fred. 'The fire back at the cabin?'

Fred nods his head. 'Later on. I went back.'

'Is that bad?'

He blinks, once. 'Everything's gone.'

George squeezes his finger and thumb around Tammy's ankle, and shushes them both.

When they reach the road to the site, Tom announces it and Tammy feels the truck swing onto a much bumpier surface. Tom turns off the CB. They don't meet any other traffic and after about an hour of driving slowly, Tom pulls over and grinds the truck to a stop. He draws back the curtain.

'Everybody out.'

Inside the trailer, everyone changes clothes in silence. Tom stays up front in the cab, smoking a cigar. The drilling site, about five miles to the east from where they have stopped, will be fully manned now, a few hours into the daytime shift though it is still dark. Another six hours at least before transport ferries bring back all the workers along this road, to the base in Prudhoe Bay. For this leg of the journey, everyone is wearing Native clothes. They allow for quiet movements – no swish of Artex – and if they are seen, there will be a reluctance on the part of any Arco employee to question Natives in the area. Fred pulls on polar-bear leggings and parka; the fur is yellow to the point of luminosity in the light from the hurricane lamps inside the truck. Tammy's parka hood is lined with arctic hare. The burlap bags she sewed slip around everyone's boots to prevent identifiable footprints. In their backpacks, besides the tools they will need, are provisions for two days of meals.

When they have changed, Matt and George go over to the far end of the trailer and throw back a white sheet to reveal three snow machines, parked with their runners pointed towards the doors.

'Tom's got the keys in the glove compartment,' says Matt. He opens the doors and jumps down into the snow.

'I thought we were snowshoeing,' says Tammy, approaching the machines.

George is leaning over a machine, wiping a hand across its seat. 'Later,' he says.

The others stand around until Matt comes back with the keys, then they haul the machines down a ramp onto the ground. Last thing, Matt gets the little spruce tree out of a corner of the truck and plants it in the deep snowbank by the side of the road.

'Reminds me of that fake forest outside Nome,' he says, looking at George. 'Remember?'

George nods. He's staring at the road surface. 'Look at this – gravel road. It's supposed to be ice, but there isn't enough water round here for ice roads. That's what everybody told them.'

After slamming shut the truck doors, George pounds on the side of the trailer. The truck releases a blast from its smoke-stack and starts to rumble away. Gunning over the snow at the edge of the road, the snowmobiles head southeast, Matt riding solo, Tammy and George on one, Luke and Fred on the other. Tammy looks back when they are about fifty feet from the road. She watches the white rectangle of Tom's truck passing the other way along the road, heading back to Prudhoe Bay. At the side of the road, she can just about see the red blur of the tinsel in the spruce tree.

George reads the snow. The drifts are etched diagonally across the tundra, snow flurries blowing northwest. The thick fur of his hat is keeping his head warm but he can't hear much. He feels Tammy shifting her hips on the seat behind him, her thighs pressing against his backside. He increases his speed and squints into the weather.

In George's mind is an odd feeling that he has missed something. He's been disturbed by the quality of his focus during the last days. His thoughts have been out of order, a moth battering against a bright light. In the cabin one night, he had dreamt about his mother and woken with a pain in his chest. Even now, random memories of her are coming at him, thick and fast, like a blizzard, disorienting. If he had a choice, he would call off this hit, but since Bill died – since the night he ran into Tammy outside the HTR warehouse – things have seemed beyond his control, have seemed to have their own momentum. He has made decisions he doesn't understand. He hasn't always recognized himself.

Tammy thumps his back; the thump is hollow against layers of clothing. He turns his head and she leans forward.

'Matt's stopped.'

George turns the snowmobile to circle back. Stopping the machine about fifty feet away, he gets off and walks across to Matt, flinching at the squeaking of his steps on the dry, compacted snow. He's always hated this sound: it's like the rubbing together of Styrofoam packaging. It makes him feel sick, like nails down a blackboard. Halfway over he stops, taking a breath in before continuing.

'What is it?' he asks Matt, who is kneeling down at the back of the machine.

'Something got snagged in the track. I must have hit something – a rock, I don't know, might have been a piece of old antler. Anyway, it got wedged in and next thing I knew there was a big noise like a gunshot. I can't see any sign of it. But the rubber's got a little tear in it, a couple studs have come out.'

'Can you still run?'

'Just about. Maybe. But I don't want to push it, or the whole thing will come off.'

George bends down to look more closely at the track. 'We'll go slow. It will be OK.'

'What about the trip back?'

'I dunno – we can double up somehow. Or I'll stay for another night. Walk out.'

Matt looks up. 'No way. Feds will be all over this place.'

George shrugs. 'We'll figure it out.' He's standing there with Matt when a sudden noise makes him crouch down on the snow, his stomach tensed. The sound is so out of place it takes George a few seconds to realize it is coming from Luke and Fred, sitting on their snowmobile a hundred feet in front. They are singing. Laughing and leaning on each other as if they were drunk in a bar. Luke starts to sing again – the American national anthem – and Fred joins in, their voices sloppy and loud.

Shaking with anger, George sprints to their snowmobile and hauls Luke off the seat, holding him by the shoulders and shaking him hard, then hurling him down onto the snow. Luke is up again a second later and throws a punch that misses when George ducks his head to the left. He throws another punch and George catches his arm and pushes him away with it. Luke turns, and they stand facing each other at a distance of a few feet, their arms held away from their sides. Fred is sitting quietly on the snowmobile, watching the fight.

'You know how far sounds carry, this kind of place?' hisses George. 'Are you *crazy*?'

Luke stares at him, breathing hard, his arms still tensed, then he lifts his hands to his face and wipes down from his hairline to his chin.

'What's wrong with you?' George says, in Inupiaq, still angry. His face is flushed, the black stubble standing out against his reddened skin.

Luke drops his hands and looks at George again. He doesn't answer.

259

'Get back on the machine. We have to get inside.' George waits as Luke passes him, and then walks slowly back to where Tammy is waiting.

When they stop again, Tammy pitches forward against George's back. She lifts her head and looks around. There is nothing. Someone approaches and reaches out a hand. The fur on his sleeve is coated with fresh snow and she slowly realizes that snow is falling everywhere, aggressively, around her in the air. This is the nothing; visibility is gone beyond a few feet. The fur of the person who has reached out his hand is yellowish white; it is Fred in his polar-bear clothing. Another face approaches, thick lips red and familiar.

'Tammy,' George yells into her face. 'Wake up!'

Tammy nods at him and smiles. 'I'm fine.' She feels warm. She turns her head to see a figure to the right melting into the snow. It disappears in front of her eyes and she turns back to see if George has seen it too.

'Come on,' George is saying to her, pulling at her arm.

When she gets off the machine, she notices a low hill of snow, round and gently curved like a breast. The breast is crisscrossed with boxy lines, white against white.

'In there,' says George, pushing her towards a small, square opening, like a fox's hole in the ground. It's the mouth to the igloo's tunnel, heading downwards.

Inside, in the pale light of the army-surplus flashlights hanging round their necks, the others are standing motionless, like cattle caught in a storm. Matt, the tallest, has his head slightly bowed, half an inch from the roof of the dome.

'Come on,' says George, entering behind Tammy.

Fred has his arms wrapped around his chest and he is shivering so much it looks like a grotesque kind of dance. 'What happened out there?' he says. 'Shit.'

'The temperature dropped,' says George. 'It happens.'

260

Tammy stares at Fred. She shuts her eyes and sees a red glow behind her eyelids.

George is busy. He lights a white gas stove in one corner – it pops to life, a low hiss. The igloo is laid out like the one in Nome, except for an added vestibule on one side, where the stove is set under a small hole in the roof above. George is working quickly; he peels off the lid of a white plastic tub, slices off some slabs of its frozen contents and throws them into a saucepan over the flame. All the surfaces are hard and dry; Tammy feels at home. She looks at George and wants to go over and touch him.

Matt and Luke are leaning against the sleeping platform. Matt starts to move next, slowly easing off his pack, fumbling with its clips and reaching inside for chocolate, and the pemmican Tom made back at the cabin. He hands out the pemmican, then drops a bar of chocolate onto the floor and, kneeling down in the snow, tears off the bright orange wrapper. The chocolate is frozen solid. Tammy drops her pemmican onto the snow floor and stamps on it. The little pieces she puts in her mouth have no taste. The smell of seal oil is strong now and George lifts the saucepan off the flame and fills lamps with it. After lighting the wicks, he reaches up and turns off his flashlight, telling everyone else to do the same.

'Strip off anything wet and get into dry clothes,' he says. He goes back to the stove and begins to heat another pan after filling it with bottled water.

Near the stove a drying rack constructed of wooden dowling crudely tied together is set up like a clotheshorse. Everyone changes into fresh clothes from the dry sacs inside their packs, and hangs their wet clothes to dry. As Tammy strips off her last layer of leggings, she notices Fred reaching out two fingers to touch the snow on the sleeping platform. He brings the bare fingers to his face, a few inches from his eyes, and frowns. She glances down at her bare legs. They look strange and soft, not a part of her. They are covered with curious blue flowers and

261

goose-bumps. She closes her eyes again, feels the warmth in her centre blooming like a billowed fire. When she opens them, Luke is watching her. She grabs the dry long underwear out of her sac and pulls it on.

'What time is it?' Matt asks.

George looks at his watch. 'One o'clock.'

Matt nods. He suddenly laughs. 'So what should we do? Watch TV?'

George hands round hot drinks, one for each person. 'Everyone should eat. Luke?'

Luke looks up, the hood of his parka hiding his face. He hasn't moved since he came in, except to accept the food and drink. 'Yeah?' comes a voice from inside the hood.

'Cook. There's some stew inside that larger container. Put it on the heat with a little water from your pack.'

'I want to sleep,' says Fred.

'Not a good idea.'

By five o'clock, the snow has stopped falling. Tammy and George have huddled up in a blanket on the floor of the igloo near the stove, leaving the three others to share the sleeping platform, though Luke has sat up playing cards with himself instead of lying down. He isn't saying much.

'What happens next?' says Tammy, her mouth against George's ear.

'We walk to the site,' he replies, his eyes closed.

'Walk?'

'It's closer than you think – just over a ridge, other side of the igloo.'

Tammy pictures the outside: the three yellow snowmobiles pulled up in the snow, half submerged by now, probably; the quiet mound of the igloo.

George is shaking his head.

'What?' she whispers.

'We shouldn't have taken the body.'

'What body?'

George opens his eyes and turns his face to her.

'What else could we have done?' she asks.

He turns away again, frowning. 'It seemed disrespectful to leave it. But maybe that was wrong. I wasn't thinking clearly. I should have thought it out more.'

'Why are you thinking about it now? It doesn't matter any more.'

He closes his eyes, and two lines appear between his brows, as if he is experiencing pain inside his head.

'You shouldn't be thinking about it now.'

'You're right,' he says, nodding.

Tammy kisses him. 'Feel how warm I am?' she says, taking his hand and putting it between her thighs.

George rolls over towards her and tucks his head against her chest. Tammy looks up and sees that Fred has sat up and is leaning into Luke. They talk in whispers for a while, Fred demonstrating something with his hands and Luke nodding, before they notice her and Luke turns his head. He doesn't smile; he pushes back his hood and looks at her with a vacant expression in his eyes. Fred lies down again.

The first sign of the drilling site is a floodlit area on the horizon, a line of large rectangular boxes, coloured red. Underneath this, Tammy sees as they get closer, is a solid grey line running horizontally, like an electronic flat-line on a white screen: the fence surrounding the site. And sweeping in from the left, a line of reflective sticks – sticking out from the snow at crazy angles like orange toothpicks – mark the road that Tom had driven them in on, though there's no sign of it under the snow. The new snow is a good thing, Matt has said. It will have covered any snowmobile tracks and also make it difficult for anyone to get to the site for a while.

'Maybe they won't even try . . . give the guys a day off.'

'How do we know they got out before it started?' Fred says.

As she walks, Tammy visualizes the oil-filler caps, as Matt has trained her to, sees herself turning them easily, placing the funnel and pouring the sand from each zip-loc bag until all her bags are empty. The vision goes wrong. When she sees herself opening up the filter housing, instead of a clean interior she finds white feathers clogging the canister. She starts to panic. They are sticky, splattered with oil; the shaft ends pierce through her gloves; one falls onto the bulldozer blade. She jerks her head to shake off the vision, and looks up.

'You OK?' says Luke, who is walking beside her.

The next oil canister is full of sand eels. She looks up and there are thousands of birds above her in a slate-grey sky; she lifts the canister up and flocks descend like furies upon it, hungry for food. A light flashes across the snow by her feet. She looks up again to find she is still walking and Luke and the others are far ahead. George has stopped, and it is the light from his flashlight that is shining on the snow by her feet. He waves an arm, gesturing for her to catch up.

Fred reaches the fence first and uses his wire cutters to snip a rectangle large enough to crawl through. As he bends to go through, George stops him. Holding Fred's shoulder with one hand, with the other he pulls back his hood, takes his hat off and listens. Matt sees him and does the same. After a few seconds, George nods and pulls his hood up again.

Once through the fence, only fifty feet or so from the lot, the deep snow tapers down to the tarmac; they remove their snow-shoes and bury them under the snow until only their pointed tips protrude a few inches above the surface. Tammy realizes she is crouching in the security lights, as if that will stop any-one from seeing her. George stops again to listen, and this time Matt grabs him by the arm, shaking his head, then taps his wrist with a finger where a watch would be. Not waiting for George to give the OK, he reaches down and switches on his flashlight, and from that moment on, everything starts to speed up.

Tammy heads to the first vehicle she recognizes, a bulldozer, and whether it's beginner's luck or something else she spots the oil-filler cap as if it were painted for her in fluorescent yellow. It isn't padlocked either: it's just sitting there waiting to be opened, as easily as a jar of mayonnaise. As she lays the cap on the engine, she can feel George inside her head. He is thinking about her right now; he is with her. She's surprised to see her hands are shaking a little as she lifts the zip-loc bag to position it over the funnel. She is not feeling nervous. It's very important not to spill any silicon carbide, she hears Matt's voice saying in her head, because any on the ground around the engine will immediately arouse suspicion when the driver does his oil checks. After replacing the cap, she finds her can of lubricant and sprays the area to get rid of any grit.

The next two engines are just as easy to tackle. Tammy can't say what sort of machines they are; she hardly looks at them. All she does is locate the one part of the engine she's been trained to find and complete her task. She has no idea how much time she spends doing this – could be five minutes, could be half an hour – which is something George has warned her might happen. She is listening while she works and every time someone passes near by she can tell by his steps who it is. She feels very connected to them all. She wonders if this is because of the silence, or the warmth in the air. At the fourth machine, there is no sign of an oil-filler cap. When she directs the beam of her flashlight to the outer body of the machine, which is like looking up at the head of an animal being milked, she slowly understands it is a fork-lift and tries to remember a fork-lift in Matt's study diagrams. The snow on the ground between her boots is blank. She bends down and begins to trace silhouettes in the snow, the silhouettes from Matt's study sheets, which is too difficult to do with her gloves on so she takes one off, letting it drop onto the snow. As it falls, George is there, picking it up again and putting it back onto her hand, shaking his head at her. He looks at the engine in front of them, opens

265

his pack and pulls out the socket wrench; then he bends down to loosen the drain plugs on the oil-filter system hanging downwards like two udders. As soon as he does this, Tammy knows what she is meant to do: she grabs the plastic milk bottle he is holding out to her, with its lid cut off, and places it ready below the drain plugs. The oil oozes out like blood from a wound. Once it has slowed to an intermittent drip, George slips the plugs back on.

Turning away from the machines with the milk bottle full of oil, the wide-open lot is disorienting. Tammy feels dizzy and looks up at the stars. Matt touches her back as he passes and she heads in a straight line towards the bank of deep snow near the wire fence, where she carefully digs a small, deep hole and pours in the oil, careful to keep it away from the sides. George appears beside her again and slowly extracts the dripping oil-filter from the housing over the hole that she has dug. He places the filter in the plastic bag she pulls from her pack.

It is when she is heading back into the yard that she notices Fred. He is standing away from the machines, over by a large truck parked near one of the red trailer boxes. Fred is still wearing his polar-bear coat and at first Tammy thinks she is seeing a wild animal lumbering on the edges of the lot. But the bear is wearing a flashlight around his neck and fiddling with a plastic baggie. As she watches, Luke comes out from underneath the engine of the truck. He is holding something in his hand and both men step away from the truck, looking down at the ground. Fred retreats another step and turns his head, glancing back towards where Tammy is standing exposed in the vacant lot. George emerges from two engines to the left of Tammy and walks briskly over to her. At the same time, Matt comes round the side of a bulldozer and puts his thumb up, nodding to show he is finished.

As George looks around for the others, Fred is kneading the contents of the baggie. Luke nods at him and he kneels down, pitching the baggie under the engine of the truck. George sees them; he is frowning; he suddenly freezes.

Seeing his expression, Matt turns, just as the baggie disappears.

'What was that?' His voice sounds so loud, though he is speaking softly.

Tammy looks at him. 'He threw something under the truck.'

His head snaps round. 'Under that truck?' He starts running towards Fred and Luke. 'Get out of there!' he is yelling as he runs. 'It's gasoline!'

Fred and Luke turn, as if everything's shifted into slow motion, confused expressions on their faces. 'It won't ignite for fifteen minutes . . .' Fred starts to say, sounding like a child.

'It's not diesel, you fuck! That thing drives on gasoline! You'll blow the whole fucking place up!'

As Matt reaches the truck, a small trail of black smoke is floating up the side of the door to the cab. He throws himself onto his knees in the snow and as he reaches under the truck to pull the baggie out, the explosion occurs.

Someone is pulling her up and dragging her away. The person bends down, stumbling as they hit the bank of deep snow, and switches off Tammy's flashlight. On the snow around them lie pieces of burning metal and the light from the fire is creating a strange kind of glow. Tammy isn't sure where they are. She runs, up to her thighs in the snow, her arms rowing through it like oars through deep water. Finally, when it becomes obvious this route is too difficult without snowshoes, she veers left to the orange stakes and onto the road, where the snow is only a foot deep. George follows her. They stop and he looks at her for the first time. She turns back to face the site. To one side is the truck still in flames, a pyre where the cab and engine had been. On the ground near by, Tammy can see a black shape, burning less ostentatiously. She feels George pulling on her hand and they continue, in a rapid walk. Tammy can feel something sticky running down her neck. She looks over at George and sees he has been burnt badly on his left arm. A large patch of his parka sleeve is gone; the remaining edges black and still smoking. She looks ahead down the road and suddenly tugs him off it, dragging him towards a gulley running along underneath a pipe raised off the ground on black legs. They lie in the trench underneath the pipe, staring up at its convex belly glimmering faintly in the reflection of the fire.

After a long time, they speak.

'Someone shot the pipeline a couple of years ago,' George says, putting his hand up to touch the pipe that is above them. His breathing sounds difficult. 'The big one.'

Tammy licks her lips; they're coated with something. The collar of her parka feels damp, and she wonders if it is blood. 'What? With a gun?'

George nods. His cheek has a little blood on it, from a wound that starts to bleed freshly whenever the fur on his hood rubs against it. 'With a rifle. The guy was drunk. Or crazy.' Half of the fur on his hood is singed black.

'What happened to the oil?'

'About a quarter of a million gallons spilled – just north of Fairbanks – Pump Station Seven.' He is talking in short bursts. She puts a hand on his arm, and he turns his head and looks out into the dark across the road. 'It's too far back.'

'To the igloo?' she says, and he nods.

'I can't get there.' Another explosion occurs and George flinches, covering his head. 'But we need to get further away.'

Tammy helps him up and they set out across the flat again, heading north. A wind has come up, thick with oil.

'We can walk along the coast. We should get rid of our tools, through the ice.'

Tammy nods.

A few minutes later, George trips and falls forward into the snow, shouting in pain as he lands on his burnt arm. Tammy bends down to help him and he kicks at the snow, pushing her away. 'Stupid!' He lies with his cheek flat against the ground and kicks again. 'Fuck. I should have seen it coming!'

Tammy crouches next to him. She looks at her hands. Her gloves are perfectly clean, as if they've hardly been used. 'What was it?' she asks quietly.

George turns his head, his lips pressed against the snow. 'An ignition device. Swimming-pool chlorinator, and Score, that hairdressing cream you bought in Livengood for Matt. He uses them sometimes, to burn billboards, shit like that, nothing big. I heard him telling Luke and Fred about it. I should have known.'

'Known what?'

'Known they might use it.'

'Was it meant to explode like that? Was Matt in on it?'

'I don't know. I don't know.' George shakes his head. 'I dunno what happened. They screwed up.'

A line of sweat is running down the side of George's temple. He glances down at the burn on his arm. Tammy reaches out across the snow towards the injury. Carefully pulling taut some of the material near the wound, she can see that the skin from his elbow to his wrist is black and yellow like the patterns of lichen on a rock.

Tammy looks up and George is watching her. He nods, his lips tight.

'Does it hurt?' she asks.

He shakes his head. 'Can't feel a thing,' he says, looking down at the wound and gently rotating his arm. 'Come on. We have to keep moving. It's too cold.'

Taking her hand and using her as leverage, he forces himself to stand. Tammy puts her arms around him and for a second he collapses, leaning all his weight on her.

'It will be all right now,' she says, kissing the side of his mouth.

Very gently, he breaks free of her embrace and starts to walk.

269

Tammy doesn't feel warm any more; she doesn't feel cold. She feels at home. The wall she is leaning on is rough against her back, even through the layers of clothing. A security floodlight that snapped on when they arrived flashes on again, intermittently, whenever she moves an arm or a leg. They've reached the coast, found a sea-water treatment plant. Though there's no way to get inside, the fence was easy to cut through and this side of the building is providing a sort of windbreak. Tammy's taken her parka off to wrap it around George. She knows he's shivering from the shock of his burn as much as the weather, but it would have been better for him if they had found some shelter inside.

She thinks about Luke, his bones black in the middle of that fire. It must have been instantaneous, his loss of consciousness. Matt too, and Fred. She shines the red beam of her flashlight on George's face. He looks very tired, but his eyes are always on her, waiting for her to speak.

'What will we do?' she asks.

As usual, he takes his time to answer. When they come, she can barely hear the words. She has to lean her ear in, right against his mouth.

'No such thing as future tense in Inupiaq,' he says.

She smiles and shifts the leg that is underneath his body. The security light flashes on.

'Why's that?'

Once again, it's hard to hear his answer.

'Present's all that's real.' The effort of speech makes him close his eyes and drop back his head.

Tammy thinks about this, looking out across the dark sea to one side of them; perfectly flat, it skates away to the top of the world and off the edge. 'I guess that's right,' she says. 'I think it is.'

George winces suddenly, squeezing her hand. She is afraid to pull back the cloth of his burnt-away sleeve, though she knows she probably should. His eyes search her face.

'Hold on.' She puts him down gently onto the icy cement. A few yards away, there is a mound of clean snow, cut along one side by the wind like a saw has been at it. She scoops up a dry handful and brings it back to him. 'Here,' she says, kneeling down next to his body. 'Eat some.'

His eyes widen like a horse that is frightened and his lips pull away from the cold. Tammy nods her head, reassuring him. He can't sit up so she pushes a fingerful through his lips. As soon as it is in and he can taste it, he starts to relax. She keeps giving him the snow, in small amounts, two fingers at a time, like feeding a baby. After a while, he pushes away her fingers. She frowns at him, insisting, but he keeps pushing her hand away with his good arm. He is pushing it towards her own mouth.

'Oh. OK.' She eats the snow too, going back to the mound several times for more.

After a while, George stops wanting any and closes his eyes.

'Give me a few minutes,' he says. 'Then we'll go.'

Tammy starts to feel sleepy, like after a big meal. She lies down beside George, leaning in to put her cheek against his. 'This is how I thought it would be.'

His lips barely move against the side of her face. 'What?'

'The end of the world.' She kisses him. 'Sooner than later.'

She reaches down and switches on the flashlight, which is still hanging from her neck.

'Are you cold?' she asks, putting her arm around him.

George moves his head from side to side. She closes her eyes. At some point, the flashlight must go out.